AS YOU ARE

CLAIRE CAIN

Book Cover Design and Photography by Rainbeau Decker.

Formatting by Jeff Senter, Indie Formatting

ISBN-13: 978-1-7327718-2-6

*To Ma and Da, for always cheering me
on and never letting me settle.*

CHAPTER ONE

"LADIES AND GENTLEMAN, please remain calm. As you can tell, we're experiencing some turbulence."

The speakers crackled like something out of a 1980s disaster film, and I made a point of staring straight ahead at the tray table latch, pushing a breath slowly out my nose. The plane rumbled and rattled around me, and I willed myself to calm down.

I'd been on the flight for an hour now. I left DC after my first harrowing flight from Philadelphia, but it was a quick hop, more up and down than anything. That might sound easy, except the upping and downing was a prime feature of my overall dread of flying. And now here I was, halfway through what was quickly turning out to be the worst flight of my life.

The plane took a huge dip, so much so my body strained against the seatbelt as gravity forced what was up to go down, and nearly everyone in the plane let out gasps and a few shrieks. *Perfect.* I was going to die at the ripe age of twenty-seven, having done almost nothing but read and write papers and have two crappy boyfriends.

The plane shuddered and bumped along, and I pulled on my seatbelt one more time like it could have loosened in the thirty seconds since I'd last done it. I tried to return to my book. I gripped the small brick of bound pages and begged my mind to turn its attention to the green cover and the soldier piled high with the weights of the world and his vocation. I read the title: *Grunt. The Curious Science of Humans at War* by Mary Roach. *This woman. What a brain.*

I was approximately twenty-eight pages in. I'd purchased about twenty books on a variety of military-themed subject matters to get started on my research and so I didn't look like a total idiot when I started my new job. And now I was unable to even crack the book back to the page I'd dog-eared during boarding. (Some would say blasphemy, but I say, what else is the point of a paperback book? Should I baby and preserve it, or should I devour it? I say the latter.)

I smoothed my hand over the cover and then gripped the book, wishing the familiarity of a book in hand, a daily ritual, an elemental thing, would sooth me.

No dice.

The plane dipped again and my body pressed back in the seat as I shut my eyes against the horrible gush of terror that burst in my belly. I breathed in through my nose and kept my eyes closed, repeating to myself what I was doing and why I was on this plane.

I'm moving to a new job that matters. I'm moving so I can have time to write. I'm moving so I can help people. I'm more than halfway through this flight. I'm more likely to die in a car crash on the way to my new apartment than on this plane. Air travel is perfectly safe. Turbulence is perfectly norm—

The plane dipped. No, it didn't dip, it flat out dropped, and my belly, that one swimming with terror, dropped too, like we were on a roller coaster on the biggest thriller dip, except we weren't on a track. We were thousands and thousands of feet in the air surrounded by some sham of a metal like aluminum and all that kept us there was, I suspected, the sheer will of God and the pilots, who were probably drunk or busy sexting their girlfriends.

Ok, that was going a little far. But I hated flying, and my ability to assume every flight would end with my fiery death was a real skill. I'd coddled it and developed it into a full-grown boy of paranoia.

But back to my imminent death.

The plane finally caught the bottom of the air pocket, or whatever the hell it was that made turbulence happen, and leveled out. I kept my eyes closed tight, not daring to open them, my body still tense and fully expecting the horror show to continue any second. *Eleven minutes of this crap* I thought as I eyed my watch. Eleven minutes of straight up gut-wrenching awfulness in the skies. *Twenty-nine minutes until touchdown, if my watch hasn't betrayed me and the drunk pilots can still tell time.*

"Ma'am?"

My body had overheated in my panic, and my glasses were smudged. My jeans felt too tight around my belly, and my V-neck shirt was damp under my arms and at my back. My hair felt too tight piled on top of my head in a bun.

"Ma'am."

I took a deep breath and talked myself down. *It's fine. Turbulence is normal. Plane travel is perfectly normal and safe. You're more likely to die—*

"Ma'am?" The insistent voice came from right next to me and cut through my thoughts, and I realized this person was talking to me. I opened my eyes hopefully, like this stranger had the ability to control whether we'd hit another air pocket or a flock of birds and go plummeting to our deaths.

"Uh, yes?" My voice was rough and I wasn't sure whether I'd made any noises. I wasn't a screamer, so probably not, but my vocal chords felt surprised by my effort to speak.

"You... ok?" The voice spoke again, tentatively. It was deep, and a little gravelly, like it hadn't been used lately. I took another breath and breathed it out and summoned a polite smile as I turned to look at him.

"Yes, I'm ok." I smiled and took in the stranger, my seat companion in 11B to my A.

Oh.

Bright brown eyes in their own shade of milk chocolate looked back at me, hovering over a dark brown beard tinged with deep red. His lips pulled into a closed-mouth, slight smile. I felt the familiar discomfort with my peer whizz through my already agitated belly as I registered this partner-in-row-eleven was just a few years older than me. Max ten. Yep, a peer.

"Good. Good." He nodded his head a little, but his brow furrowed.

"Are you?" I asked, taking in his large build, his big arms, and his... *oh*. His hand. That I was holding. In a death grip. I released it as I said, "Oh my goodness, I'm so sorry. I don't even remember grabbing your hand. I'm so sorry!" I brought my hands to my face to press them over my mouth and shook my head at myself. If I hadn't already been red-faced from bracing against my impending doom, I might have blushed in awkwardness.

The man chuckled quietly. "Don't worry about it. This is pretty bad turbulence."

I pulled my hand away and adjusted my glasses that had slid down my nose. "It is, isn't it? I definitely hate flying, but this seems particularly—" And again. The plane dropped and then rumbled, and I rammed my back against the seat, taking short, shallow breaths. I felt a hand cover my right hand, the one currently death-gripping the arm rest between the seats.

"What's your name ma'am?" I heard that rough voice say. Sometime later I knew I'd spend time thinking about why this man was calling me ma'am when he was definitely close to my age. He couldn't be younger than me, could he? Had the turbulence of flight 707 prematurely aged me that significantly? But in the moment, I answered.

"Elizabeth."

"Good. Nice to meet you, Elizabeth." His voice was steady despite the plane's cruel jolting.

I couldn't respond. I had to stay braced against the seat with my eyes closed or I'd end up... I didn't know. The plane would crash, or at the very least, my body would disintegrate from terror. So I focused on bracing myself, every muscle in my body tense, barely hearing his voice.

"I'm Jake. We're going to be fine." His voice was still calm, but it had an edge of command in it, like his decision that we'd be fine mattered in the context of Delta flight 707. Strangely, I believed him. I let my eyes slowly open, one at a time, and tried to relax my shoulders.

"I'm so sorry you're next to me. I hate flying." My voice was shaky, my skin no doubt even more pale than usual.

"Where are you going?"

"Nashville. I'm moving there. I've never been there before, but I'm moving, so I'm flying, or at least I'm hoping we'll keep flying and not end up crashing before I ever do actually end up there." I babbled this nonsense and he stayed focused on me, his serious but patient face watching me, still covering my right hand with his left on the arm rest.

"That sounds exciting," he offered, and if I'd been in my right mind, I might have laughed at how serious and unexcited his voice was. He was focused.

"Yep." I said it in a gulp as I breathed through another series of rumbles. I kept focused on the tray table, kept focused on breathing normal breaths instead of shallow ones, and slowly let myself release the tension as the plane stayed steady.

"Should be the end of the turbulence folks, sorry about that. Pretty rough air there, but we should have a smooth flight now—'bout twenty-five minutes to Nashville." The captain's voice spoke life back into my brain, and I looked over at my apparently fearless seat companion.

"Again, so sorry," I said as I lifted my hand, and he quickly pulled his away. He was watching me, maybe waiting for me to freak out again or maybe curious about what kind of crazy person I was. I pushed my glasses back up the bridge of my nose and pulled my seatbelt tight, tighter.

"You going to make it?" he asked, just the smallest corner of his mouth turning up. His brown eyes studied me, and my addled brain took that moment to think *he has great eyebrows* like that was pertinent to the situation. Like eyebrows had bearing on me surviving this flight. *Ugh.*

"Yes," I said and then turned away because I realized we were locked in some pretty intense eye contact considering I had no clue who this person was other than he'd been willing to hold my hand so I hadn't evaporated into the abyss of fear a few minutes ago. "Where are you coming from?"

"DC area. Heading home now," he said. He leaned back in his seat but kept looking at me. I half expected him to shove in his ear buds and tune me out.

"DC is a great city. I like it," I said, trying not to roll my eyes at how incapable I was of small talk. "What were you doing there?" Before the words were out of my mouth, I thought it was too personal of a question. But that was something people asked a fellow passenger, right?

He shifted in his seat, and that serious, bearded face frowned a little. "Funeral." Just the one word, but it was enough.

"I'm so sorry," I said and watched a pained look cross his face.

"It was my father's. We weren't close." He said the words slowly, his voice still graveled, and I felt a pang of guilt for making him speak.

"I'm sorry. Losing a parent seems like a very difficult thing." I felt the impulse to pat his hand, or something, to show him my regret for his loss. We'd already crossed the physical boundary of handholding thanks to my complete inability to maintain sanity in the face of a turbulent flight, but I didn't want to seem aggressive, so I looked him in the eye, hoping to convey my sorrow for his loss, even if a distant one, with my eyes and face. He nodded.

"Your wife? Kids? Were they with you?" I asked, for some reason compelled not to leave our conversation there.

He shook his head. "No wife or kids. Not in the cards for me." His eyes flickered to mine, then back to looking ahead of him, past the curtain into first class and past the nose of the plane. Based on his intensity, he could see beyond the horizon.

"Oh, ok." I had no idea what else to say. I'd assumed he would have a family the way I assumed most people in their thirties did. That wasn't the case, but I'd realized that outside of New York, people usually did get married and start their families younger. The fact that he said it "wasn't in the cards" was so peculiar, I desperately wanted to ask him why he said that. But the situation didn't allow for that. It wouldn't help his grief to have me prying into why he thought he'd be a perpetual bachelor.

I turned my book over in my hands, then over again. I

fanned the pages and pictured my heart, which was still beating quickly, and imagined it slowing down. Sometimes I felt like if I thought hard enough about something, I could will it into submission. I could *make* myself calm down.

"And you? Is your husband moving with you?" His question startled me.

"My husband? Oh, no. No husband. No boyfriend. Just me. Not even a cat, though I should probably get one to satisfy the stereotype. Hopefully someday I'll have a... well. Yeah. So. Nope. Just me." I caught myself before I launched into telling this unsuspecting stranger about my very real desire to have a husband and children. That desire felt all the more real in the wake of my near-death experience there on flight 707.

Then, we sat there. We just sat and didn't speak anymore, which I felt like might be his natural state of being. I couldn't read him without turning to look at him and that would have been too obvious since we were smashed together in our seats, so I took out my book and read the same few paragraphs over and over again until we landed, layering a prayer for survival in my mind over the words of the book.

I HADN'T SEEN Alex much since I'd arrived two weeks ago other than our initial download during my move in about her engagement and my leaving New York, so she insisted I be her date to a work family party for her new fiancé, Luke.

It was supposedly a barbeque, even though it was late January and freezing outside. I had nothing better to do and wanted to see my friend, plus she suggested I might be able to talk to the battalion commander and command sergeant major, the men in charge, and get their support for my project. That seemed like a good way to multitask on a Saturday afternoon, and since I was more than ready to make progress on my project, there I was.

I pulled up to a nice house on Fort Campbell Army base, which sat right on the state line of Kentucky and Tennessee. The base was an hour's drive from the Nashville airport and slightly less from Alex's downtown Nashville apartment—happily for me, since I lived in Clarksville, the town right outside the base, it was a quick five-minute drive from my apartment to gate three. Since I was working with the education center and had funding for my research project and approval from the base commander to conduct research there, I'd been given access, which made getting on and off base a smooth process.

Alex saw me and waved as I stepped out of my car. I gave her a hug, and my mind eased a little bit at being able to hug her and touch her—a beloved friend and something familiar in an unfamiliar place.

"I'm so glad you came. We don't have to stay long, but I think you'll like meeting some of the people in the battalion."

"Remind me. Brigade is the biggest, then a bunch of battalions are in a brigade, and then several companies are in a battalion, right?" I was still learning the structure of military units on an Army post. I was quick to memorize ranks and other facts in general, but I wanted to make sure I had a handle on all of it as I began speaking with the leadership and soldiers. The idea of sounding like an ignorant civilian made me cringe.

"You don't need reminding, my little overachiever. But yes, you're right. Our battalion is the 1-401, the Rambler Battalion, and has five companies. Alpha, bravo, charlie, delta, and echo. Those are the NATO phonetic alphabet for the letters, and those are nicknames for the companies themselves, and then they all have their own little mascot." She patted my shoulder as we walked. She'd learned so much over the last eight months since she entered this world by way of dating her childhood best friend-turned-boyfriend-turned fiancé, Luke, one of the officers in the battalion.

"Got it. I'm good." I was nervous but felt foolish telling her that. This group of people, or at least several of the wives, had become her group of friends. Luke and Alex were engaged, and it was a matter of time until they were married because their togetherness had been barreling down the path of inevitability since they were five or something crazy. I'd been rooting for them since I met Alex our freshman year of college, a solid decade ago now.

I was happy for them. I expected to feel that drop-out of happiness that twists into self-pity once one of your dearest friends pairs up with the person they'll be life partners with, but I didn't feel that way about Alex and Luke. I was delighted for them. If anything, it made me more interested in creating a life where I was open to possibilities to find some-one. I was satisfied with my accomplishments in terms of my education, but I had some pretty serious professional goals and a lot of questions about my future. I wanted to be a mother, I wanted to publish a book, I wanted to run a marathon, and I wanted to find my partner, the one who'd be with me. I wanted the great love, the decades and decades together piling up memories and grandchildren and great-grandchildren.

But I was also a pragmatist.

I knew love was a fickle, slithering thing. It was hard to grasp, it was hard to hold on to, and my first two boyfriends had taught me it was not a guarantee. They'd loved me, and I think I'd loved them in a way, but not in the way I wanted. Not like the great loves in books, the romances I could devour in a sitting. And I knew that wasn't all real, but seeing Luke and Alex, and to some degree even my perfectly practical but entirely devoted parents, made me sure it existed, at least for some.

I wasn't jealous or sad, but I felt... ready. Like I was standing at the start of a race, waiting for the gun to go off and let me run.

Alex rang the doorbell and a woman answered the door. Her carrot-colored hair was curled to just under her chin, red lipstick bright on her lips. "Welcome, y'all!" She said and immediately pulled Alex into a hug.

"Mrs. Jenny Wilson, this is Dr. Elizabeth Kent. Ellie's my best friend, and she just moved here from New York." Alex patted my shoulder again, and I extended my hand to shake the woman's.

"I'm Jenny. So nice to meet you Elizabeth. Are you settling in ok?" Her hands were soft and warm and her whole demeanor was friendly and open. It was a relief, for some reason, to find this first new woman to be so easy going. I'd heard only good things about Army wives from Alex, but I wasn't sure if her exposure was tinted by who Luke was or her determination to see the best in people because she was planning to join their ranks in the near future.

"Thank you, I am. Just finding my way around but I like my apartment, and I'm looking forward to getting to work next week and getting my project started." We talked for another minute or two as she escorted us into the living room.

"I thought I heard my Italian stallion! Come here!" a voice said from the couch, and then a little ball of blonde-haired energy barreled toward us. She hugged Alex, her perfectly wavy shoulder-length hair glinting under the living room's track lighting. "You must be Ellie. Alex has raved about you. I'm Megan."

I took her outstretched hand. "So nice to meet you. I've heard a lot about you as well."

"You are the prettiest doctor I've ever seen. I know that's un-PC and I should be ashamed of myself, but can I say that I know you're a genius so the fact that you look like *this*" she gestured up and down my body, "is almost offensive. But I already like you and know you're good people, so... welcome to Fort Campbell." She gave me a perfectly white-toothed smile, a pat on the shoulder, and then sauntered off in her high-heels. I stood looking after, not sure what to say and looked to Alex.

Alex had spotted Luke through the sliding glass doors leading outside, and even though it was a chilly January afternoon, we went out to greet him since we hadn't taken our jackets off. Before we reached them, Alex whispered, "Don't be freaked by Megan. She's like that. She has no filter, is borderline offensive, and I'm pretty sure she just adopted you, so go with it."

Megan was being generous. I was pretty—I could admit that. But I was squarely in the realm of normal—not someone who'd cause such an outburst. I had medium brown hair (though it was very long), medium brown eyes, pale skin, medium height for a woman, athletic but an eater... it was all very medium of me. At least outwardly. I could admit that my brain was exceptional, as was my taste in friends, but Megan couldn't know about that yet since we'd only just met.

I laughed nervously as we stepped up to Luke, just outside a small circle of men talking.

"I wanna get you doing more for us, Harrison. I wanna see some of the younger soldiers certifying and moving up in skill level so we have a good rep by the end of this next year. They need something to focus on," a grizzled looking man with a slash through one cheek and bushy eyebrows said in a sand-paper voice.

"Roger, Sergeant Major," I heard a voice mumble.

"I think Benson would be a killer if he had more training," someone added as Luke turned to us. He hugged Alex and kissed her cheek and then smiled at me and held out his arm for a side-hug. His bright blue eyes blazed with heat as he looked at her and I couldn't help the smile on my face as I watched them. I hugged him back and smiled at him to let him know I was happy to be there (well, happy and incredibly uncomfortable, but who was counting?).

"Guys, let me introduce you. You all know Alex, and this is her friend Elizabeth. She just moved to Clarksville and will be working here on base. Ellie, this is Sergeant Major Trask, Sergeant Jake Harrison, Captain James Ashley, First Sergeant Grant Jones, and Lieutenant Ben Holder." The six men around the circle nodded at Alex and me, and I opened my hand wide, my arm bent at the elbow, in an ineloquent wave.

"Don't let us interrupt, we just wanted to say hi." Alex smiled at them and moved to walk away.

"Don't you think we need to train Luke here to be a combatives expert? You saw what Harrison did to him in the ring." A man with midnight skin and a glimmer of mischief in his eye smiled at Alex and pointed to Luke.

"James, are you trying to get him killed? If he gets more training, that just means he'll last ninety seconds instead of sixty." Everyone but the man standing directly across from me laughed a bit. I wondered why this guy, who looked so serious from the set of his jaw and the glint of his sunglasses, wasn't laughing too.

"What's combatives?" I asked the group, hearing my voice squeak as I spoke up. It was cold enough that my lips felt a little numb, and I was shifting my weight from one foot to the other trying to keep my blood flowing.

"It's what they call the Army's hand to hand combat. Soldiers train for it a little in basic training, and then occasionally we get a chance to get more instruction so we can progress in skill level. Most bigger Army posts have competitions at least once a year so people can watch and the soldiers can practice," Luke answered.

"I guess that doesn't sound as barbaric as I was imagining." I smirked at the man Alex had called James, and who I knew was married to Megan. I knew James was a captain who'd been in about a decade like Luke, from what I was learning. The other men smiled at my assertion, but the man across from me was staring at me, and I felt the weight of his stare like a wet blanket.

I felt the stare and heard the grunt, or something like a grunt, in the wake of my statement. I looked up, and my eyes met a pair of sunglasses. I couldn't see the eyes behind them, but the face behind them was angular, hard, and the brow furrowed. It might have been an attractive face—I couldn't tell you—because it was smirking at me, but not a friendly kind of smirk.

"Well." I cleared my throat and gave my mind a moment to formulate the right thought. "It seems a little on the barbaric side to pit people against each other for no purpose and have spectators cheer on the violence... right? But if it's for training purposes, I get that you guys need to be ready when you deploy," I offered cautiously. I could very well be stepping in it. I'd been in town all of two weeks, and this was my first social event.

"Training and being prepared is violent? It's barbaric?" the hard voice asked, one dark eyebrow raised in disbelief above the rim of his opaque sunglasses. The sun was bright behind him, so I still couldn't make out his face, but his posture was perfect and his shoulders and torso cast shadows at my knees.

"I don't think training and being prepared is violent. I think parading around a wrestling ring, or whatever you call it, and pummeling fellow soldiers to the cheers of crowds, seems like glorifying violence." I leveled the speaker with a polite smile. I was used to ruffling feathers in a professional context—I could debate with anyone. But this wasn't my area of expertise, I didn't know these people yet, and yet I found myself unable to stop engaging with this person.

The man in front of me, a more intense physical presence than I first realized, widened his stance and crossed his arms. His big, strong arms fitted only with a short-sleeved t-shirt. No jacket. So, he was crazy, too. I saw he was an inch or two taller than everyone in the circle, except maybe Luke, who was now standing next to me and Alex. The man in front of me pressed his lips together, and I could see the muscles in his jaw flex as he clenched, even with the glare of the sun behind him. Ok... I'd struck a nerve.

"It's hardly barbaric. No one gets hurt," he said. If I was writing a scene and needed a word to describe this guy's voice, it'd be implacable. It had incredible authority and self-assurance, and all it made me want to do was leave, but I'd just arrived. I felt a spike of annoyance in my chest as I continued moving side to side like an underachiever at a step class.

"People do get hurt, though. Harrison, you're crazy if you think no one gets hurt. Just because you don't, doesn't mean others don't," the youngest man, who I was fairly sure was Lieutenant Holder, commented, his blond hair, blue eyes, and baby face making him look painfully young compared to his nearest companion, Sergeant Major Trask. The way he spoke to this defensive brute was in a tone of adoration.

I cleared my throat again, hoping my discomfort wasn't as blazingly obvious to everyone else as I felt it might be. "Whether anyone gets hurt isn't the issue. It's a... um, it's a matter of anticipating violence, injury, or blood." I let my eyes sweep over the group, then spoke to friendlier faces. "It's the excitement over who'll submit and who won't. It encourages us to wish for violence, to wish for submission of one to the other, to wish for harm to come to someone else. I think it does something nasty in the hearts of spectators to want that kind of show. It's the same bloody impulse that has people watching beheadings online or why the colosseum fights with gladiators were ever a thing. It's a thirst for blood, and when fed, it becomes monstrous. It has real-world implications I'm certainly not comfortable with." I finished my diatribe and felt the silence roll around me. I felt the disgusted stare of the man in front of me and practically saw the irritation rolling off of his hunched shoulders and crossed arms. I couldn't see his eyes, but I could imagine they were something fearsome.

"It's not a bad point, Ellie. But I think if you ever saw it in person, you'd see it's pretty different. Different even than Olympic boxing and certainly WWF or televised wrestling. I don't think it brings people down. It's usually pretty fun and triumphant for people." Luke patted my shoulder lightly and looked at Alex while the other people murmured their comments in agreement with Luke's, all seeming to give me the benefit of the doubt that I misunderstood the whole concept of their tournaments.

And fine. I didn't like to be wrong, but it was *possible* I may not have had a complete view of the military experience just yet. It was possible. I was willing to hold out final judgment until I saw some evidence. I thought most people in the group understood that—my naivety—especially after Alex mentioned I'd just arrived and I was working as a civilian, but the man who'd been so irritated by me, the dude wearing only a short-sleeved t-shirt to a winter barbeque, who couldn't be bothered to wear a coat because he was apparently too cool—that guy? That guy did not get the new kid on the block memo.

So, yeah, that guy I judged. He had the look of some hard-edged, rough-and-tumble jock-turned-soldier, and if he was going to get his pretty pretty princess panties in a twist over a few comments from me? Well, good luck buddy, and I had no idea how he'd made it in the Army this long.

Maybe I'd gone a little over the top. The rest of the time at the barbeque was pleasant, but I had a hard time shaking my frustration and that edgy feeling I got when I butted heads with someone without resolution. I loved nothing more than a hearty debate, but when someone got defensive, it was annoying. It was especially problematic when it wasn't a professional discussion where the general approach was that sure, we'll disagree, but then we'll move on.

I thought soldiers would be up for a healthy debate over stuff like that, and the times I'd argued with Luke, he'd been all about it. Maybe Luke was unique, or more likely, Sergeant Serious was just narrow-minded. That was fine. I'd never see him again.

"Hello, I'm Dr. Elizabeth Kent, and I'm so happy to be with you today. Thank you for giving me a few minutes of your time." I was presenting to a room full of the 101st Airborne Division's leadership—basically anyone in a leadership role from the company level on up. This was my big moment to get them on board so that if they had soldiers who wanted to participate in my project, they would allow them to take the time to attend the meetings.

"I'm leading the grant-funded *Train, Educate, Succeed for Soldiers*, which is focused on accumulating data about when and how soldiers take college classes, whether or not they complete the course or a degree, and what their experience with the process has been. It was funded by a few small grants and one large one from an amazing organization called Operation Achieve. This organization funds projects that have to do with improving education opportunities for service members, and that's exactly what my project, TESS, is attempting to help do. I'll be located here on Fort Campbell at the Education Center for about six months of research." I took a breath. I was talking too fast and reminded myself to slow down.

"What I'm hoping to partner with you all on is to allow the time commitment required of the soldiers who will participate. Participants will need approximately two hours, probably less, over the course of the next two months. When the data collection and review is complete, they'll each receive a copy of the published study if they request one. But they will need time to come meet with me, to request transcripts from anywhere they've attended, and then to interview if they do meet the requirements of the study. I urge you to consider sharing the opportunity with your soldiers and allowing them time to participate. I'll hang around after this briefing in case anyone has questions. Thank you for your time."

I smiled and stepped back from the podium, then found my seat a few rows up the aisle, feeling my heart thumping away in my chest as it always did during public speaking. I wasn't particularly scared of it, but this room was full of people I hadn't met and who had no reason to respect me or even listen to me, but their participation, their buy-in on my project, was essential to its success.

After my presentation, one or two others followed since this was a large briefing for the leadership while they were all together. It dawned on me that I was lucky to get a spot in this meeting, and I silently thanked the director of the education center, Emily Wender. I knew she was behind getting me on the agenda—she'd been thrilled to hear about the project and generous enough to find me an office (which was again, pure luck, since normally there wasn't any space available in their education center).

When the meeting ended, I shook hands with a few familiar faces I'd met at the barbeque, including Lieutenant Colonel Wilson. He'd introduced me to Major Flint, the Battalion XO. I thanked God I'd made Luke and Alex give me a lesson in some of the most common acronyms and abbreviations. XO—executive officer: the second in command for a given group—company, battalion, and so on.

I then saw Captain Jackson, who I'd heard about from Alex.

"Dr. Kent, I'm Rae Jackson. I'm not sure if you're interested in officers, but I've got a master's degree I earned while active."

"That's definitely of interest. I'd love for you to consider participating." A new thrill of energy filled me at the thought of my first participant—every person mattered in a study that would be fairly small.

"I thought Alex told me you were a literature professor. How did you end up here?" she asked, and I was surprised to hear she and Alex had discussed me, though I felt an immediate warmth flush through me at the thought that Alex had been chatting with Rae about my project. Alex was easily my biggest champion.

"In a roundabout way. I was interested in adult learners acquiring their college degrees and interned at a community college in Brooklyn during my master's degree program years ago. During my Lit PhD, which was focused in composition and rhetoric, I focused much of my dissertation research on acquisition of writing patterns, particularly in non-traditional students. I've always been intrigued by people learning, and by extension, earning their bachelor's degree in a different way and time than I did."

"So after your PhD you somehow found the military angle?" Rae asked, her face open and interested. Her blonde hair was pulled neatly into a low bun at the back of her head, her uniform orderly and flattering despite the fact it wasn't fitted or any different from everyone else's in the room. I was surprised she asked me a follow up question since most people weren't even remotely interested in the finer details of my career or why I was doing the study.

"That was roundabout too. The original project was called TES, *Train, Educate, Succeed: Equipping non-traditional students and their instructors for success.* I looked at how adult learners were acquiring their writing ability, and I wanted to link with other researchers to find out how the participants in that project had fared in the long term in regard to graduation rates, job placement within their field of major, etc. Unfortunately, I didn't have the chance because the obligations to my department and the faculty senate became overwhelming on top of my teaching and other publication obligations."

"That's a shame," Rae said.

"It was disappointing. But happily, my interest shifted toward the military when Alex moved to Nashville and told me about Luke and his soldiers. I learned about how officers got their degrees before joining the Army, or at West Point, or in conjunction with an ROTC program, but that many enlisted soldiers join with little or no college. They then face the monumental task of taking classes in conjunction with their more-than-full-time jobs or waiting until they get out."

"It's a unique issue," Rae said.

"It is. Having even part of a degree completed, as long as it transfers to the ultimate school of choice, allows a soldier to get to work at a better-paying job upon leaving the Army much faster. It allows them to pursue their next phase without a four-year lag time. That's a scenario I'd like to see happen more often." I clasped my hands in front of me, never sure of what to do with them when I wasn't holding a book.

"It is problematic. I can say from my time as a company commander that I'm amazed at how soldiers manage their jobs, families, and still pursue their education. I tried to give as many as I could the time and leeway to get into classes at the Ed Center. My soldiers ended up with pretty good track records, although while we were deployed that's a very different situation. I'll definitely reach out to them and mention your study to the ones who haven't moved away." Rae smiled at me, and for a moment, I was entranced. Her face was free of makeup, clean and fresh, and her smile was practically paralyzing in its beauty.

"Thank you. That'd be a huge help." I'd liked her the minute I shook her firm, dry hand—well, long before that.

"So you're saying that everyone should get a college degree?" A gruff voice chopped at the air around me, and I turned to see a man I'd seen at the barbeque.

"Command Sergeant Major, good to see you," Rae said and nodded to the grizzled man with the slash in his cheek.

"Captain Jackson, good to see you, ma'am." He nodded back, and she excused herself with a light touch to my shoulder and another smile at me as she stepped away.

"Hello, Command Sergeant Major Trask." I extended my hand, and he shook it in his rough one with one sharp shake before I continued. "I certainly do *not* believe that everyone should or can get a college degree—they aren't right for everyone. But for men and women who've given up time, energy, and sometimes physical and mental health, if they *want* to pursue a degree, I want to figure out a way to make it more doable."

He looked at me a moment, squinting back at me through lash-less eyelids. The guy was intense. If the Grim Reaper was made flesh, he'd look suspiciously like Command Sergeant Major Trask.

"Well that's an excellent answer, ma'am. I'll make sure we get the soldiers to your meetings. It's a worthwhile endeavor, don't you think, Harrison?" Trask shifted his attention over my shoulder.

I turned around and saw a chest with a nametape identifying the soldier as "Harrison" about a foot away from me. I scanned up a sturdy chest and strong, corded neck to an angular jaw and finally up over other pleasing features to meet his eyes.

My mind stuttered.

It stopped.

All computation halted.

It was him.

Of course, it was him. There I was feeling pretty confident and proud of myself for not only a damn good presentation but also managing the painful task of small talk and meeting new people who were at times using a language I barely spoke, and there he was.

But the problem was, it wasn't just the *him* who I'd disagreed with at the barbeque.

It was *him*, him.

It was chocolate eyes from the airplane of death.

It was sexy red-and-brown bearded, eyebrows-of-perfection seatmate.

It was the guy who held my hand and calmed me down while I crawled out of my skin during the flight.

It was the guy who'd just buried his father.

It was the guy from the plane, beardless and whaddaya-know, a soldier.

He didn't say a word. My mouth hung open a bit, ready to say sorry, but he turned, and off he went. It was like he was fleeing the scene of a crime. He obviously knew who I was if he was standing in the room for my presentation. Now, or more likely when I saw the guy again, I'd have to apologize for *two* things, and the thought made my skin crawl. And then I felt a strange burn of shame streak through me, like I'd done something wrong by knowing him out of the context of his uniform.

I shook my head a bit as he disappeared down a hall, and Trask pulled my attention back to him.

"Do you know Harrison? He'll be an excellent candidate for your study," the rocky voice stated.

"Good. I'll... look forward to that," I said, still not quite able to breathe normally.

CHAPTER TWO

I TAPPED AWAY at my computer, quickly entering my notes in the spreadsheet I was using to track some of the results of the study. It was eleven in the morning, and I'd met with fifteen soldiers so far. Today's meetings were about explaining the study, getting a consent form signed, and explaining the next steps if they did want to sign the consent form and participate. So far twelve of the fifteen had agreed, and three were thinking about it. This was my last meeting until after lunch, and I was eager to wrap it up—I was hungry and getting twitchy because of it.

I heard a knock on the door and a throat clear as I saved the spreadsheet and said, "Come in," before standing up and reaching to extend my hand over my small desk to the soldier coming in the door. I pushed my glasses back on the bridge of my nose since they'd crept forward while I worked. I looked up and met the soldier's eyes just as our hands clasped to shake and immediately recognized the face. It was the grouch from the battalion barbeque, but sans sunglasses, and in uniform. Worse, it was my flight-from-hell buddy, whom I recognized but wasn't sure if he recognized me. He might not have seen my face—most of the time I had my back pressed against my seatback and my eyes closed.

His presence in my office was significant. It felt weighty, and my mouth filled with cotton at the thought of stumbling my way through an apology with this not-actually-a-stranger. *I'd held his hand and then basically called him a barbarian weeks after his father died!*

I tried not to let my embarrassment reach my cheeks before I said, "I owe you an apology, Sergeant Harrison."

We were still clasping hands, maybe because I was squeezing his in an effort to convey my contrition, and then he gently pulled his hand away and said, "No need," in his gravelly, low voice. When I heard it, now that I knew, it matched the voice that had talked me down from my midflight panic attack. I hadn't made the connection when we'd talked at the barbeque because I couldn't see him, and it wasn't a context where I expected to see him. He'd had a beard and been friendly on the plane. In that chilly backyard, he'd been clean-shaven, edgy, and kind of rude.

But I had been, too.

"Actually, there is. I called you a barbarian, and I didn't mean that. I was judging something I know very little about. I'm against violence—"

"You've chosen an interesting place to conduct your study if you're against violence, considering the Army's business is war," he interrupted me. I was making a heartfelt apology, and this tight-lipped camo-man was interrupting me to criticize my study—one he was evidently coming to participate in.

"Well that's precisely why I'm here. I want to make sure soldiers get an education while they're serving so when they get out, they have options that have nothing to do with their ability to shoot a rifle or perform in combat." I set my jaw and looked at him, resisting the strong urge to cross my arms and jut out my hip to accentuate my annoyance.

He stood there, arms by his side. He was unaffected by my rant, except one little muscle, there just under his ear, which I could see flexing as he gritted his teeth. *That's right fella, I know exactly what I'm doing here.*

He still didn't speak, so I did. "Do you want to proceed?" I tried not to sound as irritable as I felt. I'd met this guy exactly twice, bumped into him once, and here I was all riled up again after being in the same room for under a minute. Maybe it was my now-audibly rumbling stomach's fault. I should have had a snack midmorning.

"Yes, ma'am." And he sat down in the chair opposite me, across the desk. *Ok Sergeant Chatty, don't get too excited.* I sat down at my computer and grabbed the packet of information.

"This is the explanation of the study. The second page is the consent form. I suggest you review this as it explains what information we're collecting, what information we're sharing and with whom, and from there, what might happen with the results if everything goes well. The next page you see is a list of things I need from you before our next meeting, which will ideally take place in two weeks' time if you choose to participate." I stopped there to let him absorb the information. His eyes flitted over the pages and he looked back up at me. Ok. Apparently, that was my signal to continue.

"Once you decide whether or not to sign the consent form, you'll return that if you decide to participate, and then we'll schedule the next meeting. That's where I do most of the interview, which, along with your transcripts, is the bulk of the study. I'll ask that you stay available for questions and a final interview in a few months once I've got the data organized. Do you have any questions?"

He didn't move his head from where it was slightly bent

to look at the pages but looked up and said, "You've requested all transcripts. Do you want high school transcripts as well?"

"Yes. High school, and any college you have, obviously," I said.

"What about graduate work?" He was looking back down at the page, so he missed the flair of my eyes when I heard him. It wasn't that I'd never heard of an NCO—a non-commissioned officer—having a graduate degree. Typically, it was officers who went that route. NCOs rarely had time to complete college, let alone a graduate degree, while they were on active duty. A rush of excitement hit at the thought of the information this guy could provide in terms of how he fit in the studying and course work, and how he funded it. This would be a fascinating addition to the data.

"Not typically an issue, but absolutely. Yes, please." I clapped my hands together and watched him, but he was still looking down, and my smile faded a touch as I realized this guy wasn't going to be a forthcoming well of information based on the last few minutes. It felt a little like I was speaking to a giant ice cube.

My inability to handle someone misunderstanding my banter and debating for rudeness kicked back in. "Listen, just to clarify, I do not think you're a barbarian, nor do I believe any soldier is simply because he or she is a well-trained soldier. I said the wrong thing, which is not at all unheard of, and I apologize. I didn't mean to offend you or your professional... expertise, or interests, or training. Whatever you call it. I'm sorry." I let out a breath and watched as he raised his head.

He looked at me, his eyes narrowing for a moment, and then he looked down and signed the consent form with a flick of his wrist. He handed the packet to me wordlessly, and I took it.

I felt a tingle of something unnamed, a kind of awareness shimmering at the edge of my mind. Of course, my mind wasn't flat, or round, but an amorphous thing, but that was the best way I could describe it. I pulled out the staple from the pages, took the signed form, and then re-stapled the packet and handed it back to him as I stood.

"Thank you. How about let's keep the same appointment time and meet two weeks from now. Will that work?"

He was studying me, though his eyes didn't leave mine. *Does he recognize me as the woman from the plane? Should I say something?*

He nodded yes. I swallowed, finding myself shrinking under the intensity of his silent review.

"Ok, well then, see you in two weeks," I said and watched as he nodded, turned, and left my office.

I dropped back into my chair, leaned back, and stared at my computer screen where the lines of the spreadsheet blurred. I didn't mention the flight, didn't check to see if he remembered me. What if he didn't? I couldn't tell whether that would be better, or worse.

MY PARENTS and I had a standing call every Sunday night. That was when I called them and gave my latest news, which had always been pretty minimal since I carefully meted out what information I chose to share with the Drs. Kent. Their critical eye, even imagined over the phone, could wither me. Being an only child meant I was very close to my parents as I grew up, and that also meant they were determined to be fully engaged in my adult life.

The problem with this, if it was a problem, was that my values had diverged from theirs at an early age. I'd maintained all the things I thought they wanted me to while growing up, but I felt a shift in our interactions when I'd left the university a month ago (fairly suddenly, to be fair).

They were both doctors, my mother a brain surgeon and my father a family practice doctor. They weren't unfeeling, but they were ultimately pragmatic. They valued things that were concrete and that had direct application to "real life," as they were fond of calling it.

In high school, I felt a strong calling to the arts. I wanted to write and sing and even try out some drama, but they felt that debate, math olympiad, and model U.N. were more important because they would aid me in the future. They enrolled me in a science and math specialty charter school, and it certainly did put the heavy focus on math and science. I had no time to explore my other interests, though blessedly the school did have advanced English and writing courses, and I took them all.

When I went to college, I decided to break with their expectations but still found myself enrolled as a pre-med student my first semester. I inched away from that by my senior year and managed to major in biology and minor in psychology and writing because I knew I had no interest in becoming a medical doctor, and I convinced them that writing well would aid my ability to apply for grants and other things in my professional life.

They were approving of my Master's in Behavioral Psychology only because they believed it would help me parlay my education into something more, a PhD. I think they finally accepted I didn't want a medical degree, though I knew they always believed I'd go for a PhD in psych. But I didn't. Because all along, I was reading, and writing, and wishing I was in an MFA program for creative writing. I was accepted to a literature PhD program and the guilt I felt upon accepting my spot in the program was insane. I felt like I'd betrayed my parents, and it was ridiculous. I knew it wasn't a normal way to feel—I was an independent person who made her own choices, right?

My parents were proud of me, I knew they were, and they were even happy for me. But instead of pursing a PhD in creative writing and abandoning all sense of the left brain (as though they were entirely separate), I did choose composition and rhetoric. As I'd told Rae, my dissertation focused on acquisition of writing skills for non-traditional students, my TES project, and this was only because my program made a kind of allowance for me to incorporate in-person research from my courses and internships. It was a meet-in-the-middle option for my PhD, and it was fascinating, even if it wasn't my heart's true passion.

I think they accepted all of this because I told them I was going to teach, and teaching, to them, was an acceptable vocation on the scale from slovenly writer to life-saving doctor. When I told them I was leaving my teaching job, which I had not loved and they knew it, I knew they were worried. I knew they doubted my ability to make money and to sustain what I was doing.

That doubt wasn't altogether misplaced—I had doubt too. But what they didn't realize was that it was all a tool to get me to writing professionally, full time. And not just writing, but, gasp... writing *fiction*. I had to suppress a small whoosh of shame when I admitted this, even to myself, since years of carefully cultivated valuation of the sciences had generated in me a fear of admitting *stories* were of utmost value to me.

"Hi Mom," I said into the phone, steeling myself for the reprimands that were inevitably to come since I hadn't called them the week before. I'd finished settling into the apartment and was so tired I'd forgotten it was Sunday.

"It's good to hear your voice Elizabeth. We missed hearing from you last week," she said in her soft, calm voice.

"I know, I'm sorry. Everything is fine, but it has been busy."

"Of course," came my dad's voice, likely pressed up against my mom as she held her phone out on speaker. Even though they were endlessly pragmatic, they'd always been nauseating in their love for one another. There was never much space between them when they were in the same room. They used to say it was because of the years when they were both in school and then in their residencies—they'd been apart too much, so when they were together, they were glued at the hip.

"Well, I'm just letting you know everything is going well. I've got a good pool of participants for my project and met most of the soldiers this week. The leadership here seems supportive, so that will help the process. And the apartment is huge and almost feels like home already. I've even found a little time to write on the weekends so far..." I said before I realized it and trailed off.

"Oh. Well... good," my mom said.

I could hear the tightness in her voice. It was not that they were opposed to my writing, but I knew that when I left my job, they were worried it was so I could write. It simply wasn't practical—I knew that was what they thought without them verbalizing it. I reassured them the project was the reason and my focus, and it was, but that was probably because I wasn't ready to admit to anyone, even myself, that I was moving toward a big change. What I wanted was, in fact, to write full time, and this TESS project was my excuse to do something different so I had time to write and didn't have the competitive stressors of a tenure track to manage.

"How are you two doing?" I asked, ready to move on from

the ever-tense subject of me doing something unfathomably creative and insubstantial like writing fiction.

"All good here, darling. We're plugging along. Enjoying the blueberries from Costco, despite it being midwinter!" My dad was perpetually delighted by the ability to get ripe, bulk blueberries in winter.

"Well... good." I felt my frustration rising at the fact we couldn't talk about the things that mattered to me anymore, separated as we were by the fundamental belief that some things mattered and some things didn't, but which ones were in a given category was at issue. It was no longer a given that I believed the things they raised me to believe, and I was afraid that had started wedging us apart when I left for college.

"Glad you're settling in well."

"Thanks. Listen, I better jump off and get ready for bed. Busy week ahead!" I was sure they could hear the shortness in my voice.

Another Sunday night call done, another disappointingly surface-level interaction. I wished we could bust through this awkwardness that had snuck in over the last few years, but I wasn't up to being the one to pioneer that trail just yet.

To SAY the morning had gotten off to a rough start would be a gross understatement if there ever was one.

Typically, I wore glasses. I liked wearing glasses because I was used to them, and I found my eyes didn't get as tired when I wore them, especially if I was facing long hours staring at a computer screen. But I did like to have contacts, and I did like to make sure my eyes weren't inching closer to the inevitable blindness I knew I'd face as I aged (thank you grandmothers on both sides, who stared unseeing at large-print books under magnifying glasses, never surrendering their autonomy to read despite their ocular revolt, for being the harbingers of my future).

What this meant was I went to my eye appointments religiously. Every year and a day, I was there. And of course, my appointment came up just weeks after I moved, but a person can't squeeze in more than one eye appointment within a year, or she's going to pay out of pocket and that was not on my list of expenses to deal with. I found a local place one of Alex's friends recommended, and I scheduled an early appointment. It just so happened it was the morning before I began my interviews and transcript reviews for the project, but since the appointment was early, I knew I'd feel good having it out of the way before the rest of a very busy week.

I didn't plan for dilation. I didn't. And I knew I should have because eye docs liked to look in the back of your eye and glare at your optic nerve, or whatever it was they were doing when they dilated eyes, but I hadn't had to do that in years. I had the bright light-flashy thing instead, and I much preferred it, despite the mild sense of trauma I felt afterward as I blinked and the glare and shape of the light took minutes to disappear. I made the mistake of telling this doctor as much, and in his effort to be thorough, he ended up insisting, despite my many and varied protests, that I must have the full work up.

What I should also explain is that I hated the eye doctor with the fiery passion of a thousand suns. I started having the pleasure of glasses at seven. *Seven.* I was legally blind in one eye by *eleven.* When people told me to order from those precious online shops where you could get two pairs of ultra-hipster frames for $35, I wanted to yell at them and punch them and tell them to take their toddler glasses and shove them up their nostrils. Or now that I was in the South, I'd just say, "Bless your heart." Because one did not simply order adorable, cheap glasses when one's lenses would be an inch thick without the very expensive compression technology the fancier, in-person retail stores offered.

I didn't mind my glasses, nor did I mind my contacts. What I minded was going to the ophthalmologist and finding out I was one step closer to being unable to see. I was one half point on the vision Richter scale from being uncorrectable. I hated the eye doctor like people with a grill full of cavities and a history of root canals-gone-wrong hated the dentist.

In the end, all of my efforts to persuade this man, Dr. Randall Johnson, to simply refract my eyes without dilation and send me on my merry way with an updated glasses and contacts prescription, failed. Utterly. And I walked out of the office with murder in my eyes.

Or rather, I walked out and looked like a serial killer, only identifiable as something else by general lack of composure. (Of course serial killers are composed—their bloodlust steadies their hand.)

I arrived to work that morning with a sweat-stained green blouse, my winter jacket strewn over my shoulder since even the twenty-minute commute to the office on base hadn't given me enough time to cool down my nervous sweating, and my hair a frizzy, maniacal mess despite my attempts to tame the fly-aways sprouting from all directions around my once-demure bun.

Oh, and murder eyes.

Somehow, I made it through my meetings all morning, and I said a prayer of gentle blessings on the Ellie of a week prior who'd tucked a spare white t-shirt under her desk *just in case*. It wasn't a blouse, but it was better than the disaster area that was my upper half in the wake of my nervous eye-dilation breakdown. So now my cute and functional black pencil skirt was paired with a plain white crew-neck t-shirt, and I can't lie to you, I pulled it off. My necklace replaced, the white t-shirt looked like I wasn't trying so hard and wasn't *quite* as put together. But no sweat-riddled proof of my emotional instability when it came to all things eye-exams, so it was hard to complain. This was a small mercy.

Because of the amazingly poor timing of my dilated eyes, I couldn't even type notes. Having typed my too-many-pages-long dissertation during my PhD program and about a million other pages between writing assignments, proposals, grant applications, and my personal writing, I could type fairly well without looking at the screen. I tried to take a few notes, taking a painstaking moment or two every so often to make sure my fingers were in fact hitting the right keys, and thanked the good Lord I remembered my recorder for the day.

The fact that I'd have to follow up with every soldier I'd spoken with once I could read close up without making my eyes feel like magnets polarized against any computer screen only fueled the simmering rage and sense of injustice I felt low in my belly. It was in my guts, seeping into my bloodstream, and I knew the day wouldn't get better.

I could tell I'd end it in one of those crying jags that made you feel even more stupid and annoyed with yourself because what you were was mad, not sad or in the mood to cry at all, but you didn't happen to be a kickboxer who could just beat up a punching bag. Nor was I someone who was particularly disposed to punch-dancing out her rage. So, crying, and probably stress-eating something made with butter, was in my future.

By the time Sergeant Harrison walked in, I was hungry, emotionally exhausted thanks to my internal pity party, and physically frustrated with my inability to perform basic tasks.

Oh, and I felt naked. I don't know about you, but having

someone stare at my optic nerve hours before left me feeling a little bit like I was walking around topless.

"Ma'am," he said in his gruff voice from just outside my door frame.

"Hello, Sergeant Harrison. Thank you for coming." *Keep it professional. Get through this one, and you can cry a little bit while you eat some sub-par Burger King since yeah, of course you forgot to pack a lunch today.*

"Everything all right?" Harrison asked, still standing and inspecting me. For him to comment on this, he whose words were used with great effort, must have meant I wasn't pulling off my *I can do this despite the terror of ophthalmological invasion* look as well as I thought.

I looked at him through the dark rims of my glasses, his face ringed in a halo of light and his posture ruler-straight as I'd come to expect from him already. I didn't want to interact with this man more than I had to, knowing as I did that his curt replies and quite possibly, his general dislike of me, would be the overriding sensation of the morning.

And yet, he'd asked. And I didn't have much left in the way of coping strategies or filters.

"All right? Oh, yes. Sure. Everything is *perfect*. I forgot my lunch, so I'm going to be sentenced to eating Burger King *again,* and I have a headache and you probably think I'm on drugs because I'm standing here looking at you with shark eyes, but in fact, I just had an eye exam, so you don't need to be worried."

I shoved my glasses back on my face and squinted so I could make out his face in the bright office. He was smiling. Well no, he wasn't smiling. More of a smirk, really. He was smirking at me, but it was the most expression I'd seen on his face to date that wasn't accompanied by dislike.

"Did you say, 'shark eyes'?"

"Yes. Look at me." I opened my eyes wide despite the discomfort it caused and pointed to my eyes. "I look like a serial killer with shark eyes about to commit murder." I let out a frustrated breath. "Anyway, sorry about that entirely unprofessional outburst. Please, have a seat and let's get on with it." I gestured to the chair across from me and then sat in my desk chair.

"Mind if I turn off your light, ma'am? It's bright enough coming through the window, and I feel a headache coming on." He flipped the office light off before I answered, then took his seat. The change in lighting was such a relief I sighed audibly and wanted to sink down into my chair, but instead I sat up straight and crossed my legs.

"Thank you. I should have done that earlier." *Really.* Why hadn't I?

"Transcripts," he said, and he handed me a dark green file folder with neatly stacked papers inside. High school transcript, college transcript, and graduate transcript all included.

"Yes, this is exactly right. I apologize but I can't review them in detail today." I took a deep breath and worked to quell the ever-growing rage tantrum I could feel. "But I'll take a look as soon as I can and if I have questions, I'll email you. For now, if you don't mind, I'd like to record the interview portion." I placed my finger over the record button and looked at him hopefully.

He nodded.

"Ok, first if you could simply state your full name, rank, time in service, and then when and where you acquired your college and graduate degrees."

"My name is Sergeant First Class William Jacob Harrison. I've been in for fifteen years. I earned my Bachelor of Science degree from Austin Peay State University while here at Fort Campbell my first time seven years ago, and I earned my graduate degree from New Hampshire University online over the course of two years, culminating in my degree completion last May."

"Good. Now can you tell me what led you to pursue higher education during your time in service?" And so it went. I asked a question, he answered it with appropriate but never generous detail. His answers were similar to many of the others I'd heard: *I wanted to use tuition assistance while it was available. I wanted to ensure I had a degree so that upon leaving the Army I could begin working.* One of my favorites from the morning with several younger soldiers was *I was bored, and it seemed like a good idea.*

But the graduate degree, that was different. "Can you tell me about your experience getting your master's degree?"

"Yes ma'am," he said and looked at me with those eyes, and no, I hadn't mentioned I thought he was the man from the plane. Maybe he didn't recognize me, and that would be embarrassing, plus *hello*, off topic.

I waited for him to continue. "Please, go ahead. What made you pursue a master's?"

"There are two answers to that question, but the one best serving your purposes is I felt I had the opportunity at the time, I found a program that suited me and even worked with me during a relatively unexpected deployment, and I wanted to have a leg up when I got out and started the job search. I know simply being a vet isn't going to do me much good."

"I'm afraid you're right about that, despite Veteran's Preference programs. Can I ask what the second answer is?" He'd piqued my interest with his comment.

"Yes, ma'am, you can ask me. But no, I won't tell you," he said from his seat, back ram-rod straight with perfect posture. As I took him in, sitting there, radiating self-assurance but now sensing it wasn't misplaced or blustering like I'd thought at the barbeque weeks ago, I was surprised. I hadn't expected him to tell me no.

"Uh... ok. Fair enough. I think you've given me all of the basics, and now it's a matter of organizing the data. If I have more questions, I'll be sure to contact you via email." I stood and offered him my hand, and he stood and took it. We shook hands and I gave him a small, professional smile. He gave me a slight nod in acknowledgment and then was gone.

I watched him leave and then sat back down, my mind sifting through the information he'd given me. He had some helpful insights. He was a pretty peculiar guy. Who offered up two answers but wouldn't share them both? He clearly didn't understand what kind of catnip that was to someone like me who wanted all the answers all of the time.

I didn't want to admit it because it was a dangerous thing to think, but this guy had a completely intriguing drive and a compelling brain. Who completed a master's degree *while deployed?* Soldiers, that was who, but it wasn't like it was even a job requirement. He was one of those people, like me, who liked to learn. Whatever the second reason, I would bet the unspoken one was that he liked to learn.

I bet he liked to read too. I wondered what he read. All Vietnam histories and the autobiographies of generals. Maybe he read something surprising, like female comedian autobiographies, although it was nearly impossible to imagine his stoic demeanor cracking up over the pages of *Bossy Pants.* Maybe he—

Whoa there, shark eyes.

I'd launched into full-on inappropriate-land with this guy. It wasn't like I was thinking about his body—*Oh please do not think about his very tall, broad-shouldered body*—but thinking about someone's private reading list?

That was personal. And I wasn't thinking about anyone

else's reading list. He was a unique case—the first time I met him after the plane incident I'd called him a violent Neanderthal, but so far he'd proven himself to be a high-achieving, professional, compulsively courteous special case—I couldn't be thinking about his bookshelf.

The thing about a bookshelf was that it said a lot about a person. If I went into someone's house and their shelves were riddled with fantasy and mystery, I knew a thing or two about what they liked. Maybe they'd have piles of contemporary romance lying around. Maybe they'd have self-help books, or cookbooks, or civil war histories. These things gave a person hints, and when that shelf was in a person's home, it was personal.

Enough with the bookcase.

If I was right, and I was 97.5% sure I was (2.5% margin of error, of course), then I had met him before. He'd been calm, capable, reassuring, thoughtful, and coming home from his father's funeral. That paired with this perfectly-postured, highly educated, professionally successful Army persona was... dangerous.

CHAPTER THREE

Finally, the weekend. Somehow the week had felt much longer than five days, and I still blamed the eye exam fiasco of Tuesday for propelling me into a week of slow progress, lack of focus, and general frustration, despite my excitement over all of the data I'd gathered. As I pulled the two cloth bags full of groceries out of my trunk and slung one over each shoulder, I knew the schedule my evening would take.

1. Change into sweatpants
2. Pour a glass of wine
3. Turn on the oven for the store-bought pizza I had been dreaming of all day
4. Sit on the couch and watch some horribly insipid romantic comedy

I found solace in the impractical and impossible. And sure, part of me hoped I'd find myself in my own version of a marriage of convenience-turned-true love story, but I also liked that I was guaranteed a happy ending. With all of the frustration and uncertainty, I could sit down and shove my face full of calorie-packed pizza while watching the women and men onscreen deal with completely surmountable problems—and I knew they would win out because I'd seen them all before. If I hadn't, as long as I wasn't sitting down to an indie film, I was guaranteed it would fulfill the implicit contract that comes with a Romantic Comedy or Romance—the happily ever after.

I smiled to myself and let my mind wander to the book I was working on. I'd spend some time tomorrow writing after a run. I'd been pecking away at my first book, and I was finally feeling good about it. I felt like it had potential, and it was about ready to send out to agents. Better, I'd found an agent I thought was a perfect match for me and the book, and I couldn't wait to be at the point of querying her and seeing whether she'd think so too.

I did my best not to think about it and get anxious because it was something I was even keeping quiet from myself. Like maybe my parents, the Drs. Kent, wouldn't criticize the impracticality of writing a novel if they never knew how much I wanted to be a writer, and if I never admitted to myself it was happening and holding all of my hopes in it. In the end, I wanted it—in a very real way, and that was what brought me here.

I shook off that heavy train of thought and rounded the corner of the pathway between buildings in the apartment complex. It was a nice place that kept the grass trimmed and had paved walking paths between the buildings and around the perimeter. Sometimes, if I had absolutely no other option due to time, I ran four loops around and got two miles in. It was better than nothing.

But not tonight. Tonight, I would allow myself a full night off—from exercise, from writing, from research review, from caring about what the pizza would do to my arteries or my mile time.

And then I saw him.

The apartment on the ground floor of the building to my left, on the end, he was standing there on his patio in a t-shirt and jeans with his back to me, sipping a beer and talking to Luke, who was still in uniform. I ignored the fact I could tell it was him from behind, which made no sense. Other than the seconds-long retreat he'd made after I bumped into him at my briefing nearly a month ago now, I'd never seen him from behind. I couldn't see more than two feet away the last time we met in my office, so he was nothing but a moving greenish blur as he left that day. When we'd deplaned off our flight, he'd slid out of his seat and stepped back so I could precede him out of the plane. I hadn't thought about the courtesy of that gesture at the time since I was so focused on exiting the aluminum coffin as quickly as I could.

Maybe it was his posture, or that medium brown color of his hair.

"Ellie! Hey!" Luke flagged me down and sauntered over as I stepped off the paved path to walk the twenty feet toward him in the brown, wet grass.

"How are you, Luke? Feels like forever since I've seen you. Alex was telling me you guys are going to the movies tonight, right?"

"Yes, we are. We haven't seen each other much lately either. But hey, come meet Harrison," he said as he waved me toward him and walked the distance to the open back patio of what must have been Sergeant Harrison's apartment.

I followed him and tried to steel myself for this interaction. I could talk with people in a professional capacity all day long, but when it came to casual conversation, I was an F student. It was one of few things I was truly self-conscious about, and something I loathed. It was the reason why, when I clicked with someone, I didn't let them go. I'd experienced that with Alex as a freshman in college and had enjoyed the residual waves of comfort, love, and joy from that relationship for years.

I could handle Luke, too. I got over the hump of the initial awkwardness quickly because I felt like I knew him, and by the time he met me, he felt like he knew me, from all Alex had told us each of the other. He was my friend now, too, and I was glad for that.

But Sergeant William Jacob Harrison? We'd only butted heads, except during the interview, at which point he was purely professional, no small talk, no friendliness, except the very kind gesture of turning off the light to spare my dilated eyes the glare of fluorescence.

Let's not spend too much time analyzing why I remember his full name, shall we? I encountered it during the project, obviously, and now it's wedged in my brain, sturdy and immovable... not that I've tried to remove it.

My palms got a little itchy, and I shoved my glasses up my nose in preparation for a small battle, even if it was one-sided.

"Hello," I said, waved doofily, and kind of bent at my waist to accentuate the wave. The contents of the grocery bag over my shoulder shifted as I bent, and I felt the sharp point of a milk carton jab me between the ribs on my other side.

"Ma'am." He turned and looked up at me briefly, his brown eyes lighter with the blue sky above us reflecting in them and then looked back down at the grill where he stood, most of his back to me and Luke.

Yep. That was all he said. My eyes fluttered for a beat, absorbing the extent of his greeting. Clearly, I was not the only one who struggled with small talk.

"You can call me Elizabeth," I said, sort of laughing and nodding emphatically, all a bit much.

"You know each other?" Luke asked, looking between us, and then recognition crossed his face. "Oh, that's right, you met at the barbeque in January, right? The great combatives debate—I'd forgotten." He smiled and raised his eyebrows at me teasingly. Luke had given me hell about my tirade that day. Of course he'd bring it up now.

The jerk.

"I'm participating in Dr. Kent's—"

"—Elizabeth, please—" yes, I interrupted him.

He cleared his throat and looked at me through squinted eyes, likely from the sun, but maybe in annoyance—hard to say. "Elizabeth's study," he said, then turned his attention back to the grill.

"Of course. That's perfect. Jake's our overachiever in the battalion." Luke smiled congenially and comfortably, and I envied his sense of confidence. He was one of those people who seemed at ease in almost any circumstance.

"Yes, he's an impressive man," I said, nodding to myself. I stilled, quickly adding, "He's a great addition to the study." I thanked God my cheeks were already rosy from the cold.

"Now you know you're neighbors, too," Luke said. He looked between us again. "Well, you guys have a good night. I've gotta get going." And off he walked along the grass to his apartment, which I knew was at the far end of the same building where Harrison lived. Alex had suggested the apartment complex based on Luke's place, and they'd even given me a tour over the phone since I couldn't visit before the move.

But now, Luke was gone.

He'd abandoned me. Us, really, since Sergeant Harrison

clearly didn't have any desire to be talking to me any more than I did him.

I couldn't think of anything to say.

I literally couldn't think of a single. Thing. To. Say.

I stood there, my cloth grocery bags biting into my shoulders, even through my puffy winter coat, and my mind was as blank as a piece of virgin printer paper as I watched Luke clomp through the grass away from us.

"How are you liking it here?" The low voice came and shook me from the void of my thoughts. Startling back to Earth, I turned my eyes to him and saw he was standing next to the closed grill, a beer in hand, arms folded. He was studying me, that all-encompassing way he had that I'd experienced in my office weeks ago, and I felt the same urge to fold myself up into a small origami box and pin myself to a bulletin board.

Nothing to see here.

"Uh, good. It's good. I like it. Close to work. Alex is here every so often to see Luke, so that works out. She's my best friend, so, you know, that's good. The apartment's about three times larger than the studio I had in New York, so... all in all, it's good." I tried to cross my own arms but couldn't do it comfortably. Instead I stood there, hands on the straps of the bags, hoping I could find an exit ramp on this highway of discomfort.

"Good." And he lifted the lid to his grill, flipped a monstrous slab of meat over, then closed the grill and took a sip of his beer.

I watched the column of his throat move, his Adam's apple sliding up and then down as he swallowed. I was straight up staring at his throat, practically ogling the strong neck, the shadow under his chin. I noticed his t-shirt, yet again, and before I could blush or say something even more awkward, I asked, "Why are you always wearing t-shirts in the middle of winter?"

The corner of his mouth quirked a bit, and his eyes were steady on mine. I was standing a solid ten feet away, but I felt too close to him.

"Habit, I guess. I spent most of my childhood in cold places. Alaska. Upstate New York. It was cold as hell there in the winters, and I always waited as long as I could before I started layering." Other than the official interview questions, that was absolutely the most words I'd ever heard him string together.

"Ah, makes sense. Didn't like being all bundled up?"

"It delayed the feeling of never being able to get warm."

Something about that—something about the look or his voice or the way he took another swig from his beer like he had to after he said that—made me know what he'd said was important to him. I swallowed down my questions and made myself smile instead of dive in to my curiosity and risk overwhelming him.

"Well, enjoy your steak, Sergeant Harrison. Have a good evening." I turned to walk back to the path.

"Jake," I heard him say, and stopped, mid-stride. I turned. "If you're going to make me call you Elizabeth, then you should call me Jake," he said, fixing me with a somber stare, like asking me to call him by his first name pained him.

I gave him a small nod, and then kept going. I didn't want him to see my broad smile. His asking me to call him by his first, or, well, his middle name—that made it seem like we'd almost gotten over the awkwardness. I doubted it'd ever be comfortable but knowing I now had one friend in the apartment complex—Luke—and one semi-awkward and upsettingly good-looking acquaintance, was nice. Maybe someday it'd be two friends.

~

I was Saturday afternoon at four o'clock when I heard my phone buzzing from across the living room and realized I'd been writing for five hours straight. I sat at my small, teal writer's desk in the corner of the living room, my coffee mug and its contents cold and forgotten sometime hours ago.

I smiled at my mug. It was plain white but handmade by a student I'd had in a creative writing class one of my first semesters teaching as a graduate student. (I'd lucked out that semester and the professor slotted for the course took an unplanned leave of absence—I talked my way into teaching the class since I had a lighter teaching load than the other grad students in my year.) The mug said, "Blow Me, I'm Hot" etched into it in a scrawling cursive script surrounded by a swirling floral motif. The student and I had had many discussions on sexism in academia and the world in general, and it was a funny addition to my collection. She noticed I used different mugs all the time and the gift was so thoughtful and hilarious, I almost cried when she gave it to me.

My notes and papers littered the desk around my computer. I had timelines and outlines and character notes and little paragraphs I'd handwritten on notepads stuck in different places. I groaned as I hopped up to get my phone. I'd placed it across the living room on the kitchen counter, just through the doorway.

My knees ached and my right foot, the one that had been tucked up under my left knee for at least half an hour, was dead asleep. I felt the pins and needles start as I hobbled on my left foot the last few yards to my phone.

"Hello?"

"El. I heard Luke left you with Harrison after he threw

you under the bus. I've already officially reprimanded him," Alex said, though I could hear the smile in her voice.

"Ah yes, that was so kind of him. As though I'm not awkward enough, he brings up my best social faux-pas of the year so far. Granted, it's not even quite March, but still." I cringed inwardly just thinking about my barbarian comment. Though I wasn't entirely sure I was wrong, I knew I hadn't been right.

"What happened when my dear sweet and clueless manfriend left you and Sergeant Courtesy alone?"

"Sergeant Courtesy? That is a perfect nickname for him. He is maddeningly courteous. I don't think I've ever been ma'amed so much in my entire *life*. Not even the younger soldiers say it that much!" He really was courteous, almost to a fault. I wouldn't be surprised if we ended up at a barbeque together someday a few years down the line and he was still calling me ma'am or Dr. Kent.

(Ok, sure. Maybe it was weird that I was thinking of being with this guy, or even really knowing him, years from now. Don't worry about it.)

"I know. Luke told me he thinks that if Harrison ever gets married, he'll end up calling his wife ma'am as his term of endearment." Alex cracked up as she said this, and something about hearing her laughing hysterically along with the idea of a man calling his wife ma'am instead of honey or babe or darling or whatever married people called each other, was truly hilarious.

"Like, 'ma'am, you sure did make a nice dinner tonight' or 'hey ma'am, do you want to go to the movies Saturday?'" Alex was laughing so hard her voice had raised an octave. My own laughter had fallen silent, but only because I was laughing so hard I couldn't make sound.

"Or like, 'ma'am, I want you, so let's go do it after the kids are in bed.'" She cracked herself up again, and I heard her cackling even as I came back to Earth.

"Wait, wait. In your future marriage, you plan on saying 'Luke, I want you, so let's go do it after the kids are in bed'? That's the way you're going to seduce your husband?" Her comment was off the cuff, but it made me smile and feel a little flutter of excitement for Alex and Luke. By the end of the coming summer, they'd be married.

Crazy.

Finally.

"You'll never know, Elizabeth Carter Kent, you'll never know. Now tell me. What happened when my beloved left you hanging with Sergeant Silence is Golden?" I heard her let out a breath as she recovered from her laughing fit.

"He asked me how I liked it here at the apartments, and I asked him why he always wears t-shirts in the middle of the freaking winter, and he told me to call him Jake, and then I left," I said in one breath and then felt a wave of nervousness wash over me. Why did telling her that make me anxious?

"He did? He asked you questions? And wait, you asked him about his t-shirt? Who are you and what have you done with my best friend?"

"What do you mean? It was classically socially awkward me. It just so happened he was equally awkward, so that worked out." I felt a little drop in my stomach at the thought my comment about his t-shirt had been inappropriate. Had it really?

"No, it's fine. I never would have expected you to even *notice* a thing like someone wearing a t-shirt. You're not exactly about the physical appearance most of the time," she explained. And she was right.

I could go weeks without noticing her new haircut or new clothes. It wasn't that I didn't care about them, but that I was amazingly unobservant about that kind of thing. She used to keep track of how long it took me to figure out she'd gotten her hair cut or colored. One time our sophomore year she'd cut about a foot of hair off to donate. It took seven months and a second cut and color for me to notice, and even then, it was probably only because she prompted me.

"True, I don't. It stuck out at me at the barbeque and then again the other day because looking at his bare arms made me feel even colder than I already was. Or maybe because I've been surprised at how cold I've been here, so I'm mindful of how layered up I am? I don't know." I felt a little defensive, and she could probably hear that. She knew me too well.

"Nothing's wrong with that, especially if he didn't seem bothered by it. Or, even if he did, who cares?"

"He didn't seem bothered, but he's pretty hard to read. He's so serious." I could count the two times I'd ever seen him get close to something like a smile—once when I'd referred to my dilated eyes as shark eyes and again when I'd asked him about his t-shirt wearing habit.

(No, it's not weird that I can remember the number of times he has almost-smiled at me. He was that serious. Move along...)

"Ok, well, whatever. I have a chance for you to educate yourself *and* be entertained. Are you intrigued?" she asked.

"Of course. *Dimmi*," I said, using her favorite Italian command. She used to say this when she wanted details right away, like saying "Tell me" was any less efficient than "*dimmi*," but she liked the command. It had worked its way into my vernacular over the years.

"In two weeks, there's a regional combatives tournament at Fort Knox. It's about a three-hour drive, and Luke and I are going to drive up. There's a small handful of people from the battalion who'll be competing, and I think you should come.

It's so much fun, and you'll be able to get a feel for how non-violent and un-barbaric the whole thing is." She sounded smug saying this.

"You think you're cute, don't you?"

"I am cute, and you know it. Now. Say you're coming." Good grief she was bossy.

"It's a Saturday? Would we just go for the day?" I thought about how much I loved having Saturdays free, and then I thought about how rarely I did anything out of my routine, especially here.

"Yes, it'll be a long day, but the weather should be fine. I've heard March is usually pretty tame. Worst-case scenario we'll hit up a hotel, but I think we can make it back that evening. Plus, you'll get to see Harrison in action." She said that last part like it was a dangling carrot.

"You know I have nothing else going on. I'll make Sunday my writing day, and I'll go see the modern evolution of the gladiator at work."

"Oh my dear, sweet pacifist friend. I can't wait!"

THE NEXT WEEK was plodding along well as I sifted through interviews and typed up responses and added information into the fairly complex spreadsheets I'd created. It was humming along nicely until it wasn't, and I needed to get a breath of air and talk to a human. When I was working on the spreadsheets, I tended to keep my door either closed, or slightly ajar, in an effort to keep the sound from the hallways out. There was a fair amount of traffic at the education center, and I was easily distracted by snippets of conversations. In school I'd always envied people who could study or write papers *and* listen to music. My brain could most certainly not multitask, but I couldn't begrudge it much because I was quite good at studying and writing papers *without* music.

I stood and stretched, readjusting my skirt and blazer, then pushed my glasses back on my face. I tucked a few stray pieces of hair around my ears and smoothed down my pony-tail. I opened my door and found the admin, Erin, and two of the Army education counselors, Rebecca—Bec—and Lacy, chatting in the area between offices just inside the building's entrance.

"How's it going Elizabeth?" Erin asked in her delicate voice. Today she was wearing a Kelly green cardigan that made her green eyes look absolutely, unmissably vibrant. Not something I'd normally notice, but the combination was startling.

"Pretty good, thanks. But I think I lapsed into a mild coma from spreadsheets, so I needed a break. What are you guys up to?" I wandered over and stopped in the space they'd opened up for me in the circle.

"Well, Lacy here was telling us she had to take her daughter to the ER this weekend," Bec said.

"Oh no. Is everything ok? It's... Sarah, right?" I asked, trying to remember her other kids' names.

"Yes, Sarah. And she's fine. We thought she broke her ankle though because there was a lot of swelling. But that's not why we were talking about it. The nurse who helped us was one of the most beautiful people I've ever seen. Oh, my goodness. So now I need one of you three to go hunt him down and date him so I can live knowing I helped one of you find that beautiful man."

I shifted side to side, bending my knees and stretching my back a little as I chuckled. "So he really made an impression on you."

"Seriously. He's Latino—Puerto Rican, maybe? Gorgeous

brown skin, dark hair that's a little longer than most soldiers, probably because he's a medical guy. Oh. Mmm, mmm." She looked wistfully up at the ceiling.

"What would Jared say about these thoughts, Lace?" Bec asked.

"Oh, he knows. I told him. Even Sarah said something like, 'Dad, I think I fell in love with the nurse at the ER.' He was curious, so I filled him in. That Lieutenant Marquez is flat out gorgeous," she said with a smile.

Just then the doors opened behind me and footsteps of boots coming through the entrance up to the reception desk echoed in the small tiled-floor space.

"Oh, that's me. Catch you later ladies," Erin said with a smile and then sprinted back into the room where she sat behind her desk separated from the sign-in desk by a little partition for the welcome area. I heard her say something, though her voice was soft and muffled by the wall she was now behind.

"She's adorable," Bec said and smiled in her direction.

"She is. She's so nice. It's refreshing," I added.

"Well, at the risk of sounding like an overgrown horndog, *speaking* of gorgeous men who work on this post. Have you seen this one, ladies? I think he's going down to visit the schools, but seriously, take a look as he goes by," Lacy said in a hushed, low voice and then nodded behind me.

I made a point of investigating something on my shoes, bending over lightly to rub out a scuff mark, and then stood up, rotated to the entrance. My eyes immediately locked on none other than Sergeant Harrison, and just behind him stood another soldier whose nametape said, "Smith."

"Oh, hi there," I said and inwardly rolled my eyes at how breathless I sounded. It wasn't that he looked so severely handsome when I met his eyes that I felt like the wind had been knocked out of me.

No, it wasn't that.

It was just the shock—the surprise of finding him there when I wasn't expecting it. This man didn't strike me as one who did much without a thorough process of premeditation, so I knew nothing about his visit was a surprise.

"Hello Dr. Kent. This is Specialist Eli Smith." Harrison gestured to the young man next to him. The man seemed mostly like a boy to me with his boyish features and shaved head.

"Nice to meet you, Specialist Smith. Are you here to see me, gentlemen?" After shaking Smith's hand, I turned back to Lacy and Bec who both had pleased grins on their faces. I gave them a tightlipped, embarrassed smile and flared my eyes at them. They both smiled even wider at my embarrassment.

"Yes, ma'am, if you're available," Harrison said. I tried not to feel the resonance of his deep voice in my chest, but I could admit it... I did. That was a normal thing, right? To feel like someone's voice has taken up space in your body?

Normal?

"Yes," I kind of croaked and cleared my throat. "Yes, I am. Let's go to my office," I said and stepped aside with a hand gesturing in that direction. After the soldiers were in front of me, I gave Bec and Lacy a hard look. Lacy mouthed "later" and Bec nodded enthusiastically. *Oh boy.*

I followed Sergeant Harrison and Specialist Smith down the hall, and they stopped to the side of my door just before entering my office. I opened the door wide and moved around my desk. I gestured to the chairs but they chose to stand.

"How can I help you?"

"Well, ma'am, I know I'm late, but I was hoping I could

still participate in your project, or study, or whatever it is. Sergeant Harrison told me about it, and I thought it was pretty cool, so..." he trailed off as he watched me, waiting for a clue.

"Of course! Yes, I'd love to have you. Why don't I ask you a few initial questions, and then I can get you the paperwork and we'll set up the interview for a week or two so you have time to get your transcripts and such. That sound good?" I shuffled through a pile on my desk and found an untouched intake form with the consent form on top.

I explained the project, the consent, and what signing it meant and then asked him a few questions about his experiences with higher ed.

"I failed my first class—a writing class. It was online, and I didn't keep up with it. But I retook it here in person and it was great. After that I took another general credit every semester. I think I'm up to four now, though I... I had to withdraw from my History 1010 class this semester." He sounded genuinely regretful at this.

"I'm sorry to hear that. During the interview, and only if you're comfortable, I'd like to know why, but don't worry about that now. Review these and let me know if you have questions." I talked to him about setting up another interview and we set a tentative date for the following week.

"Ma'am, is there a restroom in the building?" Smith asked.

"Yes, down the hall to the left, you'll see it," I said and waved my hand in that direction.

All the while, Harrison had been a statue in the corner. If I hadn't been so totally aware of his presence in my office, I might have forgotten he was there. I was certain I'd felt his eyes on me at one time or another but had given Specialist Smith my full attention quite purposefully.

As Smith moved to leave the office, he looked at Harrison. "Five minutes," Harrison said, and Smith nodded as he left the room. I wondered why Harrison needed to give him a time, but I was still learning the many dynamics at play in Army systems.

I felt a little pulse of nerves burst in my chest and tried to focus on the calendar I'd pulled up on my computer. I tapped in the appointment and a few notes about Specialist Smith.

"Big Atwood fan." Harrison's voice startled me. He was standing in front of one of the bookshelves I'd filled, his hands behind his back, one of them gripping his patrol cap. His legs were spread wide in a relaxed pose as he studied my collection.

"Yes. Very much so. Are you?"

"Everything I've read has been excellent. I should read more of hers," he said casually.

I was surprised. I'd fully expected him to say he hadn't read her, or heard of her, or if he had, that he'd watched the television version of *The Handmaid's Tale*.

"Really? What's your favorite?" I cringed a little at the incredulity in my voice. At some point, I'd have to stop under-estimating this guy.

He turned toward me, his hand still behind his back. "Probably *The Handmaid's Tale*, but *The Blind Assassin* was brilliant."

I tried not to let his words affect me. I tried not to let myself zero in on his mouth, notice how his lips curved around the words and sent them out to me like a letter. Like an invitation. Like he was speaking a language only I knew.

Hadn't I said this guy was dangerous? I had.

I'd said it.

A while back.

I swallowed and said, "Oh, yes, that is a good one. Do you like Greek mythology? If you do, you might like *The*

Penelopiad—it's brilliant and, well... it's Atwood. If you like her, you'll like it."

"I remember reading her poem about the sirens when I was in high school..."

"'Siren Song,' such a good one," I added enthusiastically, but I couldn't help it. I never got to talk about this stuff with my coworkers anymore. There wasn't opportunity. And really, I hadn't much at the university either since we were all running around trying to build our dossiers and clinch tenure.

He looked like he wanted to say something else, even opened his mouth, but then shut it abruptly. I felt the loss of whatever it was he might have said, and I wanted to know... desperately.

"What else do you... uh, well, what else do you read?" I now sounded like a stuttering school girl talking to her high school crush, but there it was. I wanted to know, wanted to see if any of the books on my shelf matched his, if any of the books I'd imagined on his shelf were there.

He looked like he might answer me for a moment, but then I saw his guard come up, and the openness that had snuck over him was gone. He pursed his lips and said, "Excuse me, ma'am," and then stepped out into the hall to look toward the bathrooms.

I resisted the feeling of being smashed like a little transparent house spider just starting to build her web. I was small and fragile and didn't play well with his particular size of combat boots. Because I did feel it—I did feel smashed and totally shut down and out. I was surprised how disappointed I felt most of all. I wanted to keep talking and couldn't tell why he'd shut me out that way.

His words were polite, but his actions were rude and loud. My cheeks reddened as I felt the embarrassment settling over me like a shawl I'd walk around with the rest of the day.

In another moment he walked back by my office with Smith, and his eyes darted in and to me, and he gave me the most minimal nod of all nods in the history of man. His nod was a reluctant one, and I was glad he'd left the building so he couldn't feel the waves of embarrassment and confusion rolling off of me.

Why did this man shake me up so much? He was deeply attractive, yes. But that wasn't usually a problem. More likely it was the reality he wasn't just a physical thing of beauty, but that each interaction I had with him left me wanting more of his mind. I kept underestimating him, and he kept proving my preconceptions woefully wrong. It wasn't that I thought I was particularly brilliant, but we had far more to talk about than I would have thought, and when he allowed himself, it seemed to come easily between us. Not that I knew that to be true, but I'd gotten a small taste of it then, and he'd hooked me.

"He was here to see *you*! You know him?" Lacy and Bec snuck into my office and shut the door behind them.

"Don't you two need to... I don't know, do your jobs?" I shifted my weight in my chair, searching for a comfortable position. I felt unsettled and didn't want to talk about how I knew Jake Harrison and how gorgeous they thought he was.

"No. We need to know how you know him," Bec said and crossed her arms.

"He's a participant in the TESS project. I've talked with him a time or two," I said and busied myself with checking email on my computer instead of looking back at their over-eager faces.

"More than once. You've been in your office with that man more than once, and you came out alive? You weren't burned up on the spot by his asteroid-like beauty?" Lacy guffawed.

"Wow. That was almost eloquent and absolutely the most hyperbolic thing I've ever heard," I said.

"It's heavy and intense and hard to look at but hard to look away. Seriously." Lacy fanned herself. She really was an overgrown horndog.

"Listen, he's a soldier who's in my study, so I shouldn't be talking about him like this with you guys. Unprofessional," I said, my voice stern. They both smiled back at me, devious little grins.

"Mmm, yeah. I think you have a thing for Sergeant Stone-face," Bec said, and then she stood and walked toward the door.

Lacy gave me a pointed look and then opened the door. They left me, and I blew out a frustrated, heavy breath. I didn't want anyone else to be thinking about Jake's *asteroid-like* beauty. I didn't want *me* to be thinking about it most of all.

And I didn't want to spend the rest of my day thinking about Jake Harrison and his taste in books and his knowledge of poetry and his rose-colored lips. I didn't want to.

CHAPTER FOUR

I SUCCESSFULLY AVOIDED TALKING about Sergeant William Jacob Harrison for the full three-hour drive to Fort Knox. The fact that I was going to spend all day watching him fight was not going to help my efforts to ignore my brain's obsession with this man, but I avoided asking Luke the million questions I had. I resisted asking Alex, too, even though I knew she would tell me everything she knew about him.

Pulling into the gate, Luke collected our IDs and handed them to the guard. He waved us through, and Luke found his way to the building where the tournament was taking place.

"I did a little research, but I want you to explain things to me as they're happening too, if you can," I said to Luke. I'd done quite a bit of research on Army combatives when Alex invited me. This, as research often did, made me feel much better about attending the event once I read the clearly stated objectives: battle readiness, team building, confidence building, esprit de corps, etc. However, I also felt so much worse about my outburst. I'd already prepared another apology for Jake Harrison if we saw him up close and got to talk.

Whether we'd see him, I didn't know. But I got a little

jittery thinking about it. I didn't like being wrong, and I hated my not-infrequent habit of putting my foot in my mouth when it came to strong opinions. I wasn't going to grovel, but I felt a real, inescapable sense of embarrassment when I thought of this particular foot-in-mouth moment, so I was determined to address it again and then move on once and for all.

Luke smiled at me through the rearview mirror as he stopped the car. "It's pretty straightforward. At this level, you'll see the better fighters. At the smaller competitions they start out at the very bottom and the lowest capability, so there are the most restrictions on what movements are allowed— only open-hand strikes to the body and head, stuff like that. As you move up and the skill level grows, so does what's allowed, but the general idea is that injuring your opponent means injuring a fellow soldier which is bad for everyone, so you don't want to *hurt* your opponent. But you'll see these guys bleed, potentially. They can punch, kick below the head, stuff like that. It's usually pretty intense after the first few rounds."

I swallowed. I was a competitive person, but my parents had always been pacifists. They took their doctors' oaths to do no harm very seriously and carried that out to the furthest extension of interpretation—don't perpetrate harm and don't even be witness to it. We didn't watch football growing up— too violent. We didn't see movies that depicted violence because, well, the violence. What I had definitely *never* done was watch anything like this in person. I didn't even play soccer, and I always wondered if even that was too much for them. The cross-country team was it for me, and that was about as docile as they came in terms of contact.

I was genuinely nervous.

"Ok, great. That's good. Great," I babbled.

"You'll be fine Ellie, and you can hold my hand if you get

scared," Alex said and smiled sweetly at me. She was teasing, but I knew she meant it. It was not that I would be scared, but things like this could deeply affect me. When I saw the movie 300 I found myself so enraged and disturbed I didn't speak for the rest of the day. Both the violence and the insane objectification incensed me. Alex knew to be gentle with me, and I appreciated that. I wasn't a delicate flower, but my level of exposure was limited. I hadn't become inured to violence.

"I'll be fine. So, who all is competing that you guys know?"

"Harrison, of course. He'll win the whole thing. Benson, Wilks, and Kilbourne, as well. James will compete too—the only officer who made it. Not sure how they'll do, but it'll be fun to see how it goes," Luke said.

"That seems like a lot of guys from our battalion, right?" Alex asked. I smiled at the way she said *our battalion*. She was fully invested in Luke's life and ready to be Mrs. Waterford.

"Yeah, it is. It's pretty unusual for one post to send this many guys from the same unit. But that's because of Harrison. He's the best, and he trained these guys, so... there you have it," Luke explained.

"Wait, Sergeant Harrison trains other people too?" I asked. The idea of this guy as a teacher was intriguing.

"Yeah, he's level four certified, which is the highest cert. That's pretty rare to have in a unit, so Sergeant Major Trask has him do combatives courses as often as he can justify it. It can't happen all that often because there's not time, but Harrison's the best at instructing as well as the fighting itself. You'll see what I mean—even without knowing anything about this, you're going to see for yourself," Luke said and waved us in the door to the large building ahead of him.

"I think I see Megan, and that's Kilbourne's wife and some of her friends over there. Let's try to sit with them," Alex said and pointed to a group of women, one of whom was sitting with a baby carrier strapped to her chest. As we got closer I saw the baby was fast asleep, mouth slack and face totally relaxed. The woman's face—well, technically woman but she looked *so* young—was lit with excitement.

She and Alex greeted each other, and Alex introduced me, then she introduced us to the others. We chatted a few moments and then Megan beamed at me. "Hello there, Doc. I've decided I'm going to call you *Doc* because I've always wanted to have a friend nicknamed Doc, and here you are." She winked at me.

"That's fine by me, as long as you know I'm not a medical doctor."

"I know that. I don't care—I'm calling you Doc. More importantly, I hear you're a tournament virgin?" she asked with one perfectly arched brow raised.

"Yes. I am. Should I be nervous?" I stuttered a bit as she grinned at me. The woman had no problem speaking her mind, and I liked that about her.

"Not at all. Unless you get nervous around loads of testosterone and bulging biceps. Then yes." She waived at herself. "Personally, I'll be cheering for James, and I can't say I mind at all that he'll be all frustrated and energized when he loses to Sergeant Harrison or whoever else." She raised her eyebrows suggestively and I laughed. Alex didn't hold back her chuckle either.

"I told you, she's hilarious. And I hope I'm making lewd comments about Luke after a decade of marriage." Alex patted Megan on the back.

Megan's smile never wavered, but her eyes seemed serious. "Let me tell you, it has not come without some blood, sweat, and tears. But if there is something hotter than a man who has seen you at your worst, your darkest moments, and then still loves you, I just cannot imagine what that is."

The announcer stopped Alex and me from commenting as he began the tournament. Four soldiers marched in the colors—the American flag—and then a young sergeant sang an amazing version of the National Anthem. The soldiers around the huge hall stood at attention, and I loved how strict and straight they all looked, snapped up with full focus on their banner, their guide. I felt tingly with nerves and a strange feeling of thrill coursing through me as my hand rested on my heart and I tried to keep my knees from wiggling.

I couldn't tell what kind of building this was, but it looked like a huge gym. There were four mats laid out around the large space and a slightly raised boxing ring in the middle.

"The rounds will start around the room. The final fights will take place in the ring. They'll work through by weight class, so it ends up taking quite a while, even at this level," Luke explained.

"Kelly's a lightweight. He's on the low end so he's going to be struggling," Kilbourne's wife, Jenny, said.

"Yeah, you never want to be at the bottom of a weight class. You want to be at the top but not tip over. One time when Harrison was cross-fitting like a beast he tipped up to heavyweight," Luke said.

"Did I hear 'Harrison'?" a guy said and slid down the bleachers a bit. He was by himself and had a green hat pulled low over his eyes, his hair curling under the edges in all directions, clearly indicating his non-military status.

"Yeah, you know him?" Luke asked.

"If you mean Will Harrison, then yes, he's my brother," the guy said, extending his hand.

"You must be Henry. He's mentioned you." Luke took his hand and shook it. "I thought you were still in college?"

"Yeah, spring break. About to graduate so I didn't want to blow a bunch of money on a big trip. So here I am supporting the big bro in the wilds of Kentucky," he explained to Luke, then looked past Luke to me and Alex. "And you ladies are?" This kid was a lady killer, anyone could tell. He had a bright smile, a dimple in one cheek, and dark brown eyes. He was absolutely adorable. I could see just a touch of resemblance between him and his older brother, but his smile and the radiance that came from his face made him look like a totally different species next to the image of his stern brother.

Alex introduced herself and then it was my turn. "I'm Elizabeth. Ellie."

"Pleased to meet you Ellie. Mind if I move over to sit by you?" This kid. He was all charm. He was busting his move, and I couldn't help but laugh at his very direct approach.

"Sure, come on over. You can tell me what I should be looking for," I said with a friendly smile.

"I'll do my best. It's been a while since I've gotten to watch Will fight," he said. It sunk in that he was calling him Will, not Jake, which I wanted to ask about but didn't even know the kid. Or his big brother. I also realized he wasn't a kid —he was probably twenty-one or two, but I felt old next to him. He still had that ruddy hopefulness that came from life before graduating and realizing college was a safe, easy place if you let it be. At least, it had been for me.

"So, what happened when Harrison fought in the heavy-weight?" Alex asked, and I felt grateful she did so I didn't have to.

"Oh, he destroyed everyone. No contest. But still. You don't want to class up if you can help it. He had more bruises than usual after that one. You want to be the biggest guy in your class, not the smallest."

Just then we heard the first bell, and I turned my attention to the space in front of us. We were on a big set of bleachers that sat in front of two mats that made up two different rings. The big, raised boxing ring was in front, and then two other mats were on the far side of the room. I could see pairs of soldiers dressed only in their camouflage pants and green t-shirts stepping up to each other in each of the four mats. Each ring had its own judge's table with score cards, timers, and a few people scattered around the edges of the designated spaces talking to the people about to fight—their coaches, based on the way they were focused in on the fighters with intensity, their lips mumbling orders we spectators couldn't hear.

"There's Will," Henry said, pointing to the ring to the right, just in front of us. I hoped my slow inhale wasn't obvious. Another rush of nervousness and some unidentifiable feeling filled me. Dread? Excitement? I couldn't tell.

Harrison put his mouth guard in and met his opponent in the middle of the ring. A bell dinged, and off they went. They grappled for a few seconds, Jake dropped to the mat and used momentum to pull his opponent down, wrapped his legs around the soldier's waist, arms locked around his neck, and then they broke apart.

And then it was over. "Wait, what just happened?"

"Danes tapped out. So, Harrison won that one," Luke explained. I'd heard someone yell "sweep the leg, Danes!" before they went to the mat, so Danes must have been the opponent.

"But that was so fast!" I said, unable to keep the disbelief from my voice.

"Yeah, that's Harrison for you. Until he gets to the later rounds, they'll all be like this. He's insanely good." I heard Luke say this as I watched Harrison pat Danes on the back, his head nodding a bit as he said something to the man. They met again in the middle. The same lightning-fast series of events played out, faster than I could track to see what exactly Harrison was doing to make Danes tap out, and then the bout was done.

Harrison looked around the bleachers as he walked to his bag left on the sideline and his eye caught on Henry, who waved at him. His eyes shifted to mine, and I felt a jolt fly through me when our eyes met. I raised my eyebrows at him, resisted the urge to wave and smile, and then looked away to find Alex before I started blushing or doing something stupid. My heart was racing, and I couldn't figure out what to look at because Alex, like a traitor, wasn't there to catch my attention.

What just happened?

"So how do you know HRH?" Henry said, turning to me, and I prayed he couldn't tell I was flustered.

"HRH?" I said, trying to make sense of his words.

"William. I used to call him Prince William or HRH—His Royal Highness—when we were growing up, just to piss him off." Henry smiled a dazzling smile at me and I laughed. Then I realized the joke.

"Oh, and you're Henry! Is your mom a big fan of the royals?"

"You know, I don't think she was all that much. Funny enough, her name was Diana. We are William and Henry, sons of Diana." He smirked, but I could see he kind of liked this little fact. I noticed how he spoke of her past tense and tucked that away to think about later.

"Don't tell me your father was Charles."

"No, he was also William Jacob Harrison—the first, of course, which I suspect is why Will now introduces himself as Jake." He looked at me with a small frown on his face.

"I was wondering why you called him Will. He did introduce himself to me as Jake. I guess that makes sense," I said.

We sat watching the matches play out in front of us for a few moments before Henry spoke again.

"How did you know?" he asked quietly as another round began in front of us. I looked out at the fights happening in the four corners and my eyes scanned for Harrison. He was standing at the far end watching a fight from the sideline, occasionally yelling something I couldn't hear to one of the fighters.

"Know what?" I asked.

"That our father's dead?" he asked, his voice still low, silently telling me this wasn't common knowledge.

"Oh. Well. He told me once. Your brother did," I said in a halting, near-whisper. I hadn't ever confirmed that Harrison was the man from the plane, but I *knew* he was. Now I was sure of it. But it felt weird to acknowledge that to his brother when I hadn't even told Jake I knew it was him. Maybe it didn't matter, but I felt like it did. It was a strange experience, and I wanted to revisit it only with Jake.

"I'm surprised. He doesn't tell people much about family," Henry said, and I saw his eyes flit around my face, inspecting me. With his face serious and his brows knit together while he assessed me, I saw the similarity. The same strong chin and nose, darker eyes but the same shape. Angular cheek bones. His face was younger, of course, and less weathered, but the relation was clear.

Before I could say anything, another round started. The day went on like that, round after round. Just before two, the last preliminary round ended. Jake had won every round he fought, and it seemed easy for him. He certainly made it look easy. There was an hour break before the final fights began and about two hours until Jake would fight again. James had been eliminated in his third bout, and since they'd hired a sitter for the day, Megan said they were heading home early to relieve her. We decided to go get some lunch, and I invited Henry to drive with us to the PX food court to see what was available.

"Can you wait a minute? I told Will I'd wait for him to find me before I grab lunch so I can see if he wants something."

Just then, up walked Jake Harrison.

And see, here was the thing. Like Alex said, I wasn't all that tuned in to the physical—certainly not at first. This was also true of my interactions and relationships with men. Sure, I occasionally noticed certain things about them—striking or strange or interesting physical attributes. But usually, that wasn't what caught my attention. I wasn't drawn to bulging biceps or exceptional glutes, even though I could admire them. The two boyfriends I'd had were on the skinny, nerd-physique side of the spectrum, which was fine. Much like a zombie, for me it was always the brains.

But sitting on uncomfortable metal bleachers all day watching Jake Harrison physically dominate every opponent he encountered had a confusing effect on me. What I saw wasn't violence or barbarism but control, skill, and confidence. It was methodical, calculated, focused.

And *damn*, it was appealing.

So as that same Jake Harrison, endlessly serious and unsmiling and evidently deadly in a fight, approached his brother and greeted him with a genuine smile and open arms, a small part of my brain malfunctioned. Some new synapse attempting to form just stopped, short-circuited, unable to make sense of the utter beauty in front of me. It was like someone painted a Byzantine celestial halo around his head—he was glowing, and I couldn't look away.

If a serious Jake Harrison was appealing, a smiling, warm, loving-big-brother Jake Harrison was lethal to any attempt I might have had at avoiding thinking this man was attractive.

He came to a halt and hauled his brother to him, giving him a big hug, and I heard his low voice say, "Glad you made it, Harry." He released Henry and then stepped back and knocked the brim of the bright green hat on Henry's head up so the hat flipped backwards off his head.

"Glad I could make it, too, Wills," Henry said with one of his own thousand-watt smiles. He seemed to be genuinely delighted by seeing his big brother and was absolutely buzzing with energy now that Jake was there. It was adorable and completely endearing.

"You met Dr. Kent," Jake said, since I was standing right next to Henry. Henry looked at me, and back at Jake, then back to me again.

"Wait, *you* are Dr. Kent?" he asked with all the disbelief one voice could hold.

"Yes. Elizabeth Kent. That's me," I said awkwardly, waving my hands like jazz hands before I found the will to drop them down again. I caught Alex giving me a *why are you being so weird* look before I looked back at Henry.

I couldn't figure out what had happened, but there was a definite beat where no one said anything, and the two Harrison brothers looked at each other meaningfully. What *that* meant, I had no idea.

"Uh, is that bad? Did your brother tell you I've been torturing him with interviews and endless paperwork?" I asked, chuckling nervously now, twisting my fingers together in front of me to avoid any other Fosse-inspired gestures.

Henry crossed his arms and looked at me again. "No, no, nothing like that. I recognized your name, that's all. He told me about the project," he said, still switching his attention back and forth between me and his brother.

"Oh, well... good," I said and swallowed loud enough I could hear the gulp.

Henry looked back at Jake for another moment, then tossed an arm around my shoulder and gave me one of those sunrise smiles—dimples, oozing charm, and all. "Don't you worry there Ellie," and he punctuated the "Ellie" with a flick of his eyes to his brother, then back to me, "he'll be fine."

Jake shifted his weight from side to side and inched his duffel bag up higher over his shoulder. He was looking at me, and I couldn't for the life of me read his expression. On the surface, it was neutral—almost bored, for that matter. But his eyes kept flickering between mine, then down to my shoulder where Henry's hand rested, then back to my face.

"I'm sure he will," I said, still trying to decipher what was going on.

"I'm going to grab a shower and then if you can get me something to eat, Harry, I'll eat it when you're back. That work?" His attention was fully on Henry now, and I felt the muddling sensation of relief and disappointment.

"Yes, your highness. I know you need to keep your strength up. Ellie and I'll find you something good," he said and raised his eyebrows.

Jake nodded once, turned on his heel, and walked in the opposite direction. I looked from side to side, waiting for... something. I didn't know.

"He's not totally socially inept, but he doesn't get out much. If he's not at work, he's home. Don't feel bad he didn't even have the human decency to say goodbye to you." Henry chuckled and then steered us to the door, dropping his hand from my shoulder.

"Why is he alone if he's not at work?" Why I asked this, I couldn't say.

Well, that was a lie. I *could* say. I wanted Henry to fill in the gaps. Did this man not date? Was he really refusing the female population of the world his magnificence?

Ok, whoa, again, we were getting too carried away here. But honestly, being subjected to his physical power was like watching the very survival of man. If I were looking for an attractive mate on the most basic level, I'd want myself a Jake Harrison. He was supremely intelligent, radiantly attractive, and physically powerful. If we were in the woods of prehistory, I'd be choosing *that guy* to mate with because I'd know he'd protect me, find me food, and make me some real cute babies.

(So... the day had taken its toll.)

"I live in Florida, and my grandma does too. Our parents are gone. My dad was an only child and my mom's family was never part of the picture. So, it's just us." Henry's words shook me from my Paleolithic musings.

I was about to say something, something more than, "Ellie like Jake, want make babies," when Henry added, "And he doesn't date. Ever." He looked me right in the eye when he said it. Was he warning me off? Had I said anything about wanting to procreate with his brother out loud?

"Oh... that's..." What could I say? *Unfortunate? Sad for women everywhere? A waste?*

"Yeah, he's an idiot," Henry said, and that was the last of it. We arrived at the food court and it was time to get serious about sustenance. Maybe food could shake me out of my haze of cavewoman's desire.

CHAPTER FIVE

HOURS LATER, we arrived back to Clarksville around midnight, and I was exhausted. The fights had been completely amazing. The day was long, but those final fights were worth it. The rounds were far more intense, and Jake was crazy good. Totally exciting, amazingly good. He put on a little more flair for that last round, took a little more time to take out his opponent. I wasn't sure if it was for show, or because it actually took him longer, but somehow, I doubted that.

In the second round of the final match he got punched in the cheek *really* hard. I thought for sure he'd go all the way down, but he didn't, nor did anyone stop the fight or call a fowl or whatever happened in that situation. He would have a black eye, I was sure. I expected to see a burst of rage from him, but instead he shook his head, rolled his shoulders back, and in a matter of seconds, wrapped up the round by pinning the guy bodily before his opponent knew what hit him.

We didn't end up talking to Jake again. He'd arranged to meet Henry on the opposite side of the building from where we were parked, and we were all exhausted and ready to get on the road, so we left. I felt bad about not seeing him and telling him congratulations, but a part of me was glad.

I had spent a total of nine hours that day watching him fight, coach, or stand around and wait. What this meant was I had absolutely nothing else to distract me from appreciating what was in front of me. Sure, there were hundreds of other soldiers and people, my best friend sitting next to me, a good friend next to her, a new acquaintance to my other side, fights going on in four corners of the room, and all manner of generalized hubbub. But wherever he was, my eyes were on Jake Harrison. I couldn't help it.

Something in his posture demanded I look at him. Somehow, he'd used that gruff voice to bend my unconscious to his will and require my eyes to constantly seek him out. I tried *not* to see how powerful his body was, but that was absolutely unavoidable in this context. I tried *not* to notice the flat stomach, the way his t-shirt fit him perfectly and outlined muscles, front and back, that I'd like to get to know.

(In other news, who was I? Since when did I think about someone's back muscles?)

I tried not to notice how his cheeks reddened with exertion and how his chest expanded after he'd release a particular hold when an opponent tapped out. I tried not to notice the absolute focus on his face, the coiled energy as he waited for a round to start, the quick footwork he'd only had to use once in the final round.

I failed in those valiant efforts.

And the whole smiling, hugging brother thing. *Come on.* Couldn't he stay the stern, inflexible grump I thought he was thus far?

Thankfully, I was tired enough that instead of lying awake thinking about the aforementioned muscles (ugggghhh, just saying that made me cringe, but it was true) or the smile or the brother stuff, I passed out. I woke up ten hours later feeling miraculously rested and just in time to make it to Nashville to meet Alex for yoga.

~

I PARKED my car and stared out the window for a moment, summoning the will to exit the car and walk to my apartment. It was a gorgeous day and yoga had felt energizing and relaxing and good, but the hour-long drive back home drained me. I felt sluggish and still overheated. It was mid-March, but a warm, bluebird day, and the sun made the sixty-five degrees feel remarkably warm.

Finally, I hauled open my door and stretched tall after getting out of the car. The used Subaru Forrester I'd bought a few days after I moved to Clarksville was proving a trusty steed thus far, despite the fact I was a reluctant car owner. My New York life was carless—I missed public transportation and being able to read while I went from place to place. I was still making peace with having to pay attention while I traveled. So far, that was one of the biggest things I missed about New York.

Pulling my fitted tank top down, I adjusted the waistband on my yoga pants and locked the car door. I walked slowly and felt the sun warming my shoulders. Closing my eyes, I stood for a minute in the grass. Then I felt a thwack to my belly and doubled over before I opened my eyes. A white Frisbee lay at my feet, and I picked it up in one hand as I ran a hand across the point of impact.

"Oh man, I totally didn't mean to throw it that hard! I'm sorry!" I heard a familiar voice say. He was backlit by the afternoon sun, walking toward me. Henry.

"I'll admit it wasn't particularly pleasant to have my

peaceful moment sliced open by a Frisbee, but I should probably be thankful it didn't hit me in the face," I said and tossed the Frisbee. It floated over to him delicately and his eyebrows rose.

"I'm impressed. Are you a closet Frisbee enthusiast, Dr. Kent?"

"Absolutely not. Unless it's for typing or inserting food into my mouth, my eye-hand coordination is crap," I said as I walked over and met him in the grass just off the pathway.

"HRH and I just finished a game of Frisbee and were going to have a beer. Join us," he said as he walked with a hand around my shoulders to the little patio I knew was Jake's.

"I don't want to intrude on your family time," I said, slowing my steps and looking toward my own apartment in the other direction. I wasn't sure I wanted to see Jake again so soon. I'd had a *whole* lot of Jake yesterday and didn't trust myself not to be awkward. Plus, every interaction I'd ever had with him had been pretty painful in one way or another.

"Nonsense. There's no one else I'd rather talk with. Stay put, I'll grab you a beer," he said and pointed to a chair on the patio. I sat on the edge of the seat, not leaning back or looking too comfortable. Henry left the sliding glass door into the house open but closed the screen. I looked inside but the brightness outside and darkness inside made it impossible for me to make out much more than a few dark, bulky shapes—couches or other furniture. Then I heard them talking, and though I'd like to say I either got up and left or just willed myself not to listen, that was neither possible nor likely. I listened, unabashed.

"The very fine Dr. Kent is awaiting a beer on the back patio," came Henry's hushed voice.

"Don't say 'fine.' It makes you sound like a douchebag,"

answered Jake's voice. I stifled a laugh—good grief, he was crusty.

"Look at her, and tell me she's not," Henry said, and then continued, "you cannot tell me you aren't interested."

"I don't date." That was all Jake said in response, and I slumped back in my chair. Ouch.

But what was I expecting? And would I even *want* to date him?

Fine. Yes. I probably would. At this point, there was no denying my interest, despite his taciturn demeanor.

"You're an idiot. You're the dumbest person I've ever met," I heard Henry say.

"I don't date." Jake's voice came again, low and edged with annoyance.

"Idiot," I heard again, and then the screen door was sliding open. My cheeks were red, but hopefully they looked that way from the sun and not from overhearing a very stark rejection.

"Here you are, lovely Ellie," Henry said and presented me with a Sam Adams. I took it and thanked him, studying the beer for a moment when I heard Jake coming out of the sliding door behind him.

I needed to tell him how great he was yesterday. I needed to not be awkward. Both seemed impossible.

"Hello," Jake's voice came, and I looked up and met his chocolate-honey eyes.

(I think this is how you know you've taken a step past the casual observation of someone being good-looking. You start thinking of their body parts in terms of food, something to be savored or devoured. *Lord help me.*)

I smiled back at him, but my voice wouldn't budge, so I raised my beer a little, like that was an appropriate response.

"Ellie, I have a confession to make," Henry said and

looked at me from beneath his brow with a contrite expression. *Oh boy.*

"What is it?"

"I looked you up on ratemyprof.com."

I nearly spit out the sip of beer I'd taken. "Why?"

"I had to know. *Had* to know what the kids were saying about you, Dr. Kent." He turned to Jake and said, "It's a website where you can rate professors." Then he turned back to me. "And just as I suspected, you had high ratings and a consistent 5-alarm average." He smiled at me, his little dimple flashing a moment in his right cheek, and I rolled my eyes and shook my head in response.

"I haven't been on there since I started teaching. I can only imagine what students have to say." They could be complimentary or cruel, and that usually directly correlated to the grade they'd earned. I'd stopped looking after my first semester teaching as a grad assistant in my master's program because all it did was infuriate me that the kids who'd failed had any say since ninety percent of the time they'd failed for not showing up, not turning anything in, or cheating.

"They say you're brilliant, engaging, demanding, and you have high expectations. And that you're hot, obviously," he said, his smile growing wide as he undoubtedly watched my chest, neck, and entire face turn beet red in embarrassment.

Instead of speaking, I took another sip of beer and avoided looking at Jake who, apparently unlike my student reviewers, did not think me so hot.

Good grief, why did I think that?

"What I want to know is, did you ever hook up with a student?" Henry had a gleam in his eye—this kid was trouble.

"Absolutely not," I replied without a moment's hesitation.

"Why not?" Henry pulled his chair toward mine and sat

down in it. Jake was standing just outside the door, leaning back against the unopened portion, observing.

"Aside from it being unethical, I don't typically find myself attracted to my students. If I did, I certainly wouldn't date while I was in a position of authority—"

"—ohhh position of authority, *yes*. I like the sound of that —" Henry interrupted.

"—Stop being an idiot, Harry." Jake's voice ended Henry's outburst and was punctuated by Jake lunging toward Henry and knocking his baseball hat off his head.

I laughed a little as Henry reached for his hat and nearly fell off the chair. When I looked up, Jake was watching me. "Sorry. He's an idiot, as you can see," Jake said.

"Don't worry about it," I said, trying not to show how embarrassed I was by the comments. It wasn't really Henry, rather it was the persisting sting I felt in the wake of Jake's clear lack of interest in me after I'd spent a very long day yesterday coming to terms with my very real attraction to him (even if it was mostly a primal thing).

"I'm not an idiot. I'm just trying to figure out what my chances would be if Dr. Kent was *my* professor. I can guarantee you I'd be—"

"Stop what you're saying before you embarrass yourself or Elizabeth." Jake's voice cut Henry off once again, and this time he held that commanding tone I'd heard before.

"Well do you have a boyfriend, then?" Henry asked me, that glimmer of mischief in his eye still sparkling.

"Uh... No." Why did I say *uh*? It wasn't like there was a boyfriend or even a potential for one. I had barely dated, and I hadn't had a boyfriend in years. I was also not embarrassed by that or ashamed of it. It had, for the most part, been a choice, or at the very least, a lack of motivation and desire. Despite all of that very mature thinking, I felt my cheeks burning with a blush.

"Dating anyone?"

"I haven't had time to meet anyone," I said, using every bit of willpower I had not to look at Jake.

"You haven't met anyone you'd be interested in dating since you got here?" Henry asked, nudging my knee with his. What was he wanting me to say? *Yes, your brother is attractive to me on almost every possible level.*

I cleared my throat. "Irrelevant. No time for it." More than ready to move away from talking about me, I looked at Jake. "I wanted to tell you that you were great yesterday. I'm sure you already know that, considering you won and so did almost everyone you coached, but still. You were great." I could hear the nervousness in my voice, feel the tightness in my chest as I paid him this compliment. I couldn't quite tell why it made me so nervous—I was simply relaying something true, something I really did think. There was no good reason for me to feel that twisty feeling in my guts when I spoke to him, but I did.

He nodded, accepting my words without a word of his own. I shifted my eyes away from him and looked out along the path, eying where it curved toward my back patio, just out of sight around the corner at the end of an adjacent building.

"Did it convince you that we're not barbarians?" When I heard him, I looked back at him, his face unchanged except his eyes, which held the same mischievous glint Henry's had moments ago.

I couldn't stifle my laugh—both because I was surprised at his comment, which seemed free and less restrained than he usually was with me, and because it was all I could do to give myself a moment to recover. "Definitely. It was far from barbaric. It wasn't even violent. It was..." I stopped myself, searching for the right word. I was rarely at a loss for words, but it had been happening more often lately. I needed more rest.

"It rendered her speechless, Wills. Looks like you were so bad, she can't even think of a way to describe it," Henry joked, and Jake shook his head slightly, one side of his mouth tilting up into a hint of a smile.

"You guys are such *brothers*. No, it was great. It was interesting, and it seemed purposeful. Technical. Smart. Which, I am sorry to admit, I wasn't expecting." I gave Jake a contrite look.

"Have you really never seen wrestling or anything?" Henry asked.

"My parents are hardcore pacifists to a level that is ridiculous, so we didn't watch *anything* akin to fighting growing up. Tennis was as exciting as it got. I went to a charter high school that only had a small sports program, and wrestling wasn't one of the options. We didn't even watch football. And as I got older, I didn't have opportunity. I've been locked away reading and writing papers for what feels like a decade, so educating myself about hand to hand combat methods in the US Armed Forces hasn't *quite* made it to the top of my list. But, now I know. I get it, and I see the appeal." I took another sip of my beer and set it down on the small table next to me.

"I'm glad you came and saw for yourself, then," Jake said.

"Me, too," I said with a small smile, not daring to look him in the eye.

I stood up then, feeling like I'd run out of things to say and was more than ready to get going. I didn't recognize the shy feeling I had, didn't like my inability to verbalize my thoughts. It was time to leave. "I'm going to head home. You guys have a nice evening. Thanks for the beer—I'll owe you one."

"You have a good one Ellie," Henry said with a wave.

Jake gave me a nod, and I headed home, trying to ignore the obnoxious thudding in my chest as I walked.

It had been two weeks since I'd seen Jake, or Alex, for that matter. Well, that wasn't true. I saw him as I was walking to my car. He was unlocking his front door, and I gave him a tight-lipped courtesy smile and wave, and he gave me a nod and stepped into his house.

A gripping interaction, to be sure.

If it had been a movie, I'd have shouted something charming at him or maybe even stumbled and made a joke about my clumsiness. As it was, the interaction was over so fast all I could feel was like I'd dropped a silver dollar and couldn't find it.

The fact I hadn't seen or talked to him didn't stop me from thinking about him now and then. But I wasn't prone to pining, and I didn't even know if I liked the guy. He was obviously a physically attractive person—sure. He was also extremely smart. Very capable. Well-spoken when he chose to speak. He was interesting enough—that unwillingness to offer more than the necessary details did absolutely stoke a fire in me to know more about him.

So, totally unappealing. Not at all interesting, or someone I'd want to get to know better. At all. *Done.*

I'd heard him clearly when he told Henry he didn't date in *direct* response to Henry suggesting he might be interested in me. That was a pretty clear indicator *he didn't want to date me.* So, I could admit I felt ragingly frustrated when he popped up in my mind. I'd filed him under "Not Happening" in my little alphabetized mental card catalogue of potential friends, colleagues, and relationships. Just to the right of that category existed "In Your Dreams" where lived several celebrities and fictional characters including, but not limited to, Mr. Darcy of Austen fame, Mark Darcy of *Bridget Jones's Diary* fame, and George Orwell.

(*1984* was the first book I loved with a mind that was mature. It was the first of many I read early in high school that cracked open my world, a bit with fear, a bit with wonder at the whole universe Orwell had created. What can I say but a brain that thinks in such a challenging way had me at "It was a bright cold day in April, and the clocks were striking thirteen.")

And then, there was what Jake had said in that curiously stark tone on the plane when I asked if he was traveling with family. *No wife or kids. Not in the cards for me.* If he wasn't the marrying kind, then I was better off not getting involved in the first place because I *did* want a husband, and kids, and the whole package.

So again. Not an option.

The good thing was, my TESS project, and my writing, were keeping me plenty busy. I was friendly with the other people in the education center, but we were all busy with our own work, and rarely socialized for more than a minute here or there—even Bec, Erin, Lacy, and I.

I'd settled into my little office well, moved in the one last box, and now had the few bookshelves brimming with books. I had a photo of my parents' house tucked away behind the door so I saw it when I closed the door. It was one I took when I left for college. I wasn't sure if it was to remind me of where I came from, or to remind myself why I didn't want to go back, but there it was. On the wall behind me were my degrees—undergrad, master's, PhD. I liked seeing those three little ducks in a row on the wall, waving the flag of my over-education. I'd come to think of them that way over the last year and a half as I realized with a sinking weight in the pit of my stomach that I *didn't* want to be a part of academia. I'd thought I did, but my first full year of full time, post-grad faculty work had been eye-opening.

The competition wasn't the fun kind between colleagues and peers. It wasn't inspiring and compelling. The gossip was wearying and demoralizing. I knew it wasn't that way everywhere, but it my department, it was.

The strange entitlement of many students, even at a school like that where only the best were admitted, was baffling. And the cheating. *Dear Lord*, how I couldn't stand it. What more perfect antithesis to the whole point of college was there? Never mind the fact that cheating meant gobs of memorandums and paperwork for me and hand-wringing by students, some of whom very purposefully cheated and some only kind of accidentally did so.

By the time my first full post-grad year was done, I knew. I knew I didn't want to be there. I'd been teaching for more than five years as a part of assistantships and my degree funding, but I'd convinced myself that once I was a true-blue professor, like there *was* something in a name, I wouldn't care about the other stuff.

In fact, the pressures and the frustrations, felt more real. The time I thought I'd have to write fiction diminished as it became clear any free time I did have needed to be devoted to professional development, contributing to my department, or writing in my field—all to work toward obtaining that elusive golden carrot called tenure. And *that* was a thing I then knew with certainty I didn't want or need.

"Over-educated, under-satisfied, and searching"—that was what I'd told Alex I was in one of our recent conversations. But the thing was, I knew what I wanted if I let myself be honest, and my few short months at Fort Campbell had taught me it was ok, and I told her so.

"I love the work I'm doing now—the research on my own, pioneering a little bit, but still getting to interact with soldiers. I also love that when I leave work, I have no sense of guilt."

"I know you always felt like you *should* be working on publications or grant proposals or committee work when you weren't doing office hours." She knew because she'd been there during the long years of my PhD except for the two she was in Boston for her master's, and even then, we talked at least weekly.

"The timeline of my project matters, but there's no hard end date other than when my funding runs out, and I padded the calendar so I have plenty of extra time if need be. On weekends I can write, and I'm wrapped up in the book I've been writing and editing in the evenings now too." I'd been working in my writer's group online, and we gave each other deadlines and shared chapters of our work to get feedback and help—I felt deliriously happy to be doing the work I'd wanted to do since the beginning of high school.

"I can't wait to read the whole thing. I'm in suspense!"

"Not much longer, I hope," I said. I loved that even though we lived closer, we still called each other. We were both going in different directions, so we didn't see each other that often, even though Luke lived in the same apartment complex as I did. But sharing my sense of peace with her meant it was real—it wasn't just horded to myself, and it seemed to multiply the sensation.

Maybe it was being away from teaching, or maybe it was that I felt like I'd found my stride. Maybe it was being back near Alex, or maybe it was being out of New York City and back into a less urban setting like that of my roots in Kansas. Maybe it was finally taking real steps to write. I didn't know for sure, but I knew I was happy, and what a soul-expanding proposition that was. My deepest breaths a year ago were but gasps compared to now.

As I stretched back in my seat and pushed away from my computer, I felt excited by the prospect of the weekend just a day away. I had plans to go out with Alex in Nashville on Saturday, and though I dreaded the drive, I knew we'd have fun. I was coming to the final few chapters of my book too, so I'd finish that this weekend, easily. And the project was coming along. I'd sorted all the data and was finding I had some solid recommendations I could make based on the information I'd gotten from the soldiers. I had some real, actionable items that would, I hoped, make a difference to soldiers at some point. Operation Achieve was absolutely going to feel their grant had been well-used.

I heard a light knock on my door and looked up to see Alex standing in my doorway, her face red and streaked from tears, and the hairs on the back of my neck raised.

CHAPTER SIX

"WHAT HAPPENED?" I asked as I rushed toward her and grabbed her with both hands. I squeezed her shoulders, her biceps, her elbows, then clasped her hands in mine. I searched her face and waited, my breathing ragged as I waited for her words to eke out past new tears.

"Specialist Smith. Do you remember him?" she said, her voice small and shaky.

"Eli?"

"Yes," she said, and I watched as she swallowed hard.

"Of course. He's part of the study—he took two classes before his last deployment. I haven't seen him in a while though—he hasn't responded to my last email," I said, a splash of dread filling me up, up, up and over like a pitcher of water filled a cup too full.

I squeezed her hands, willing her to speak and tell me.

"He killed himself last night," she said in a sob, and then we were hugging, holding on to each other for dear life. We were both crying now, her sobbing, and my eyes shedding tears while I stared at the pale, tiled ground of the hallway. I pulled her into my office and shut the door, and we stood there crying, the only sound her weeping and my own breathing coming short and quick.

After what felt like an hour but was more a matter of minutes, she pulled back. "I'm so sorry to tell you at work, but I was afraid it might have made the rounds of the rumor mill and I didn't want you to hear it from someone else. It's just awful," she said, her face crumpling in tears again and she shook her head.

I couldn't speak. I wasn't sure what I felt or thought other than I kept thinking *He's too young* and wishing she was lying.

"Luke said they'd already sent him to in-patient care twice. They'd had him on suicide watch even after he came back and were debating trying to send him again." Her voice broke and she looked around my small office for something, then sat down in the chair next to her.

"He's so young." I stopped. Not anymore. "Wasn't he just twenty?" I asked.

She nodded in confirmation. "I don't know what to do. How to help Luke or anyone else. They're all in work mode over there, trying to figure out how to help his friends. He's in Bravo company, and that was Luke's company before he switched out. Luke said he was a good kid but just couldn't get a handle on things, whatever that means. They were doing everything they could. I know they were..." she trailed off and slumped into a chair.

I knew we needed to talk about this. Strangely, we'd been here before, in a way. Our sophomore year of college there'd been several student deaths in our class, all suicide. Overdoses, and one girl who jumped from a balcony. We hadn't known them, but the need to talk through the events was overwhelming.

"I don't think there's anything you can do but be there for him if and when he's ready to talk to you about it."

"I know," she said, sniffling. She had such a tender heart, and I loved her for it.

"Will they do a memorial for him? Some kind of service?" I asked. I didn't know how this worked, but there had to be a procedure. The sad fact of veteran suicide made that a must.

"I think they're still working all of that out. I'll let you know."

"Please do." I would be there. While the loss of this young soldier wasn't a deeply personal thing, it was to Luke, and it was, by extension, for Alex. It certainly felt personal to me now in a way it hadn't before I arrived at Fort Campbell.

"You know, Harrison was acting first sergeant for a bit while Luke was in command. His original first sergeant was injured toward the tail end of the deployment, so Harrison stepped in. He's the one who sent him to the evaluation and recommended they send him to in-patient the first time," she said.

I felt my heart sink lower, if it was possible. One more person in my very small network who would be shaken by this. I thought about when Jake had brought Smith to see me the first time. I remembered how he'd told Smith he had five minutes in the bathroom and realized he'd been on suicide watch then—that was the reason he didn't leave us alone while I talked with the younger soldier, and then why he was policing him like a child thereafter. My heart sank lower knowing Jake would undoubtedly be affected by this loss.

∾

THE REST of that day was a blur. Alex stayed with me another hour as we talked and cried a little more and finally agreed she would let me know what I could do for her or Luke or anyone else if there was anything. She called me that night to tell me they'd scheduled the remembrance ceremony for Friday afternoon.

They didn't want the whole battalion going into the weekend without some kind of official interaction. They'd planned it for 1pm and then would have a long safety briefing reminding the soldiers about their resources. They'd even have counselors available at the meeting, the MFLCs, the Military Family Life Counselors from the base who took confidential meetings and no notes or names, so the soldiers would know who they were and how things worked if they wanted to meet with them.

Friday felt like a day shrouded in dark gray tint on every level. Even the weather was gloomy and depressing with incessant drizzling rain and gray skies. The service was absolutely heartbreaking. I held Alex's hand far in the back. Soon enough Megan joined us and took Alex's free hand. We stood with a small handful of other friends and family members from the battalion who'd come to show their support. The soldiers gathered in the chapel. Even though it wasn't the official memorial service, they made sure it was separate from the work spaces and regular battle rhythm as they called it.

I was surprised by how many soldiers cried—even some of the older NCOs and officers had glistening eyes at one point or another. I saw Rae Jackson sitting off to the side with a few other soldiers from what I guessed was a different battalion. Sergeant Major Trask and Major Flint flanked Lieutenant Colonel Wilson, jaws clinched and shoulders bunched. James stood by Luke, his face serious. The young Lieutenant Holder who'd been so enamored of Jake at the party months ago was red-eyed and disheveled. I tried not to stare but found myself noticing Jake's stony face looking drawn and surprisingly expressive. He struck me as someone who'd put on his impassive face mask and let no one see his grief, but he looked obviously wrecked. He didn't cry, at least that I saw, but his demeanor was notably different than its usual stoic severity.

The battalion commander pleaded with his soldiers to remember Specialist Eli Smith and to remember that there was always a way out, always a resource, always someone who could help. He listed the suicide helpline, referred to the MFLCs, and tried to do whatever he could to assure the soldiers the stigma attached to seeking help wouldn't damage their careers. I didn't know if what he was saying was true, but I hoped it was. The chaplain's prayer was as good as it could have been in such a situation.

Alex and I parted ways with the other spouses and then each other. We canceled our plans for the weekend, knowing she'd want and need to focus her attention on Luke.

I kept wondering about Jake, wondering who would talk with him. Maybe he'd call Henry, though I doubted he would. I knew they were close since he told Henry about being in the project, but it didn't seem like he'd share this awful thing with his brother—it seemed like he'd keep it from him so it wouldn't worry him. I hoped I was wrong.

I couldn't think of going home to my empty apartment after the long day, even though being home usually felt like a haven. I drove around town until I decided to go to a movie. The dark theater, some popcorn and Coke, and the latest dumb comedy helped distract me from that swallowing pit in my chest. That quicksand feeling I'd felt before, something scary and hopeless and broken and inescapable. I couldn't imagine feeling there was no hope, and the reality that so many did, and so many who'd come to that point because of what they'd seen in life or at war, felt dangerously destructive and terrifyingly real in my life. It was easier to ignore when I wasn't associated with the military community.

I hid in the theater—from myself, from reality, from the gray, rainy weather. When I emerged two hours later I was full of popcorn and surprised to find the sun working its way down toward the horizon and the purple and pink sunset sky peppered with clouds. I took a deep breath of the cold air and smelled the clean scent of rain on asphalt. The clouds must have been holding warmth in because the crystal sky had given way to a chilly spring evening.

I drove home with a sense of sad stillness, my mind mostly blank and my heart calm, if still low. I locked my car and noticed Jake's Jeep was there, a few spaces down from where I usually parked. I wanted to go knock on his door and make sure he was ok, but I knew that wasn't my place. We weren't even really friends. I locked my car and watched the sun slip all the way out of sight, feeling relieved it was dark now because it was dusk instead of just gloomy. The moon was shining behind me and somehow that little reflection of light felt like the reminder I needed that it wouldn't stay dark forever. Tomorrow was a new day that followed this cold, darkening night.

I walked the path to my apartment, but I couldn't stop myself from glancing over my shoulder to look at Jake's patio. Maybe I could see him inside, sitting and talking on the phone, and I'd imagine it was Henry on the other end.

Instead, I was surprised to see a figure slumped down in a patio chair, a glass resting on his knee, his head resting in a hand. I changed course immediately.

I didn't know what I'd say, but I knew I couldn't go home

and not spend the rest of the night worrying about him. Everything in this one little moment spoke to me, grabbed me, and demanded I go to him.

"Jake?" I said, my voice rasping a little as I used it for the first time in hours.

He raised his head and let the hand it had been resting in drop to the glass that held, I could see now, brown liquid. On the small table next to him was a bottle of Jameson. He was silent, his eyes rimmed with red, his cheeks flushed but his face somehow still ashen.

I didn't know what to say. *Are you ok* seemed useless. *I'm so sorry* didn't help. What could I say?

"Can I have a sip?" I asked, gesturing to the glass resting on his wide thigh.

He handed it to me and I took a small sip, enjoying the heat and smoke of the whiskey burn down my throat and into my belly. I handed the glass back to him and sat down in the chair to his left.

We sat there a while, both staring out at the last streaks of color disappearing from the sky, the night now fully settled in around us. I wasn't sure how long I'd stay, but I knew I'd stay another few minutes, just to make sure he was ok. Not that he'd tell me, but it seemed like just being next to him was something I could offer.

"Did you know my mother died?" he said, his gruff voice breaking the silence of the little patio world where we lived.

"Henry said something about her, and he used past tense, so I thought she had, but I wasn't sure," I said, feeling like my voice was too loud even as I tried to quiet it.

"She killed herself when I was twelve," he said without looking at me, and the air whooshed from my lungs.

"Oh no. I'm so sorry," I said, my voice low and strained,

feeling like I wanted to double over, but that didn't make sense since I was sitting down.

"Henry was nine months old. Severe post-partum depression compounded by my absent, perpetually-deployed or disengaged father." His tone was edgy and his voice rough, but the fact that he was offering up these personal details told me this wasn't his first glass of whiskey.

"That's a nightmare. I'm sorry you had to go through that," I said, looking at him as he continued to stare out across the grassy field that made up the center of all of the apartment buildings in the complex.

"It was. It was a nightmare. I know a little of what the Smiths are feeling." He took a drink and then held the glass out to me without looking at me, and I took it. I took another drink and handed it back to him.

"I know the broken feeling that hollows you out. I know the confusion. The feeling of betrayal. The anger. Then back around to the weight of the sadness, like something heavy is sitting on your chest and you can't move from under it." He took another sip. I watched as he swallowed it down, his face not changing as he did it. He seemed more numb and calm now than he had earlier. I wondered how long he'd been here.

I didn't know what to say but could also tell I didn't need to say anything even though I wanted to. Listening was what I could give him tonight.

"At least he didn't have kids," he said, and his eyes shifted to mine. I was sure there was pity written on my face, but I hoped there was compassion too. I hoped somehow I was showing him how sorry I was for him, for the Smith family, that anything like this ever happened.

"Yes, that's one good thing," I said quietly.

We sat there in silence again for a while. He passed me

his glass another time or two, and just when I was starting to feel like I should go, he started talking again.

"I told them he wasn't straight yet. I told them, and they knew it too, but there's only so much you can do. And I know that. I know it's not anyone's fault, which is good, because sometimes it *is* someone's fault, but this time it wasn't. Everyone did what they could, and this kid was too damned lost." His voice broke a little at the end, and I looked up to see his eyes were glassy. His voice and body were relaxed from the drink, and he was stringing together sentences one after another more generously than he ever had in regular conversation.

"Is that why you brought him to my office?"

"I thought being involved in something might help. He wasn't my responsibility anymore, but I thought it'd get him looking at taking more classes, give him some direction—something." His eyes flickered up to me, then back down to the spot in front of him.

"It was a good idea. It was worth a try," I said, feeling completely incapable of consoling him, but wanting him to know I thought his efforts to help were better than ignoring the problem. He clearly hadn't done that, based on what Alex told me and what he'd filled in just now.

"I blamed myself for my mom for so long. I thought I should have been able to help her more or make her happy. I wondered if it was because I was a bad kid. I was pretty sure my dad blamed me, or even Harry, but my grandma finally convinced me that wasn't true. I hope it wasn't true. Sometimes I still wonder if there's something I could have done." He took another sip of his drink and then held it there in front of him and watched the amber liquid swirl around as he tilted it back and forth.

"Jake, there's nothing a twelve-year-old could have done,

no matter how thoughtful or loving. You were a child, and what happened with your mom was an awful thing, but it's not something you could have stopped, I don't think." I spoke before I even realized I was speaking, my whole consciousness focused on making sure this man knew he wasn't responsible for his mother's suicide. I didn't know all of the details, but I knew enough to know it wasn't his fault.

He nodded his head a few times slowly before he spoke again. "I know that. I know that. I do." He was quiet again and then said, "I mostly blame him." It was just above a whisper, but it was clear.

"You blame your father?"

"I know he might not have been able to help, but he was always gone. *Always.* And we weren't fighting two wars then. He opted out of our family life whenever he could—took TDYs and unaccompanied assignments where we couldn't go with him. He left her alone with me, and he left when Henry was three months old on an *optional* assignment." The bitterness in his voice was undeniable. "He might have been able to tell something was wrong, but every time I think that, I realize how unlikely that is. She might have hidden it, but even if she hadn't, he wouldn't have noticed her enough to see something was wrong."

"I'm sorry."

"So am I. I wish he hadn't been gone. I wish I didn't still blame him, even now that he's dead. He ruined her."

There was nothing I could say to that, so I took a small sip from his drink, the liquid creating a kind of mourner's comradery, and handed it back to him.

"But from him I learned a lot. How not to be. What not to do. Not to be weak and marry and have kids and then not be strong enough to stay with them, be with them."

"Is that why you're not married?" I asked.

"Yes. Not that I've ever been close. But that's why, yeah. I won't do that to someone else."

I could tell he must be feeling the whiskey in earnest now since his gestures were more overt, and I was sure he wouldn't be saying any of the things he was in any other circumstance. I felt torn—sure I should go and leave him alone and sure I should stay and keep him talking.

"So, it's just you and Henry now that your dad is gone too?" I asked.

He nodded again. "Yes, just us. And my grandmother, but she's getting older. She lives in Florida in a retirement community. That's why Henry goes to school down there."

"Oh, I didn't realize that's why."

"Yeah, he sees her every weekend, almost. He's a good kid. She raised us, even when we were stationed in Alaska and New York. She lived with us when my dad had to go TDY or whatever he had going on. She found me—saved me, I think." His voice was thick and I found myself holding back tears. Maybe it was the whiskey.

"Saved you?"

"If Grandma hadn't been there to keep loving us after Mom died, I think I would have stopped enjoying things and loving things. It's not natural to me, still, but I think she kept me from becoming angry for too long," he said. He took a drink of his now-refilled glass and eyed me over the rim.

"I'm glad she could be there for you. I'm glad Henry sees her a lot too. I bet that means a lot to her."

"It does. I should go visit her more often. I call her once a week, but I should go see her more."

"I'm sure she'd like that," I said and looked out at the sky, dark and glittering with stars and satellites.

"She'd like you," he said, and when I looked at him, he was studying me, his face serious but relaxed.

"Oh?" I asked, not sure what else to say.

"Yeah. She'd like you" he said and nodded in confirmation, agreeing with himself.

"Why do you think?" I asked and tried not to let the laugh I felt rising in my throat escape. It almost felt unfair, like I was cheating at some cosmic game, to let him keep talking. He should guzzle a gallon of water and pour himself in bed, not continue talking to me in a way I was sure he'd be embarrassed by in the morning. Although this man didn't strike me as someone who got embarrassed. It was hard to imagine he did anything he didn't want to do.

"She'd like your moxie," he said matter-of-factly, like *that* was a word anyone used.

"My moxie?" I asked, wondering if I'd misheard him, my smile slipping through my formerly stoic face.

"Yes, your moxie. You're determined and opinionated and stubborn as hell. I think she'd like you," he said, like it was obvious what he meant. I chuckled as my cheeks heated. I felt a little buzz of pleasure fly through me at his compliments. At least, I thought they were.

"Thank you?"

"Yes. It's a compliment. Deal with it," he said a little roughly like I was frustrating him, and I shook my head.

"Ok then. Thank you."

"Good. Now you need to go home," he said in that same rough, demanding voice.

"I'm sorry, I shouldn't have—"

"Don't apologize for being kind to me. It's late, and I should go to bed and so should you." He stopped and fixed me with a look to make sure I'd heard him and would comply. "Goodnight, Elizabeth," he said from his chair, not moving to go inside.

I stood up and stopped in front of him. "Goodnight, Jake,"

I said, my hand itching to reach out and run my fingers through his tousled short brown hair, to cup his cheek and bring my face close to his and tell him he was thoughtful and kind and that he'd be ok, but of course I didn't. He nodded, and I walked across the grass, a small smile on my lips, even though my heart was breaking for him, for the Smith family, for the whole Rambler Battalion.

CHAPTER SEVEN

I DIDN'T SEE Jake again for more than a week. A solid week. I won't lie and say I hadn't thought of him and replayed the conversation we had that night about a hundred times. He was so clear about how he was affected by his mother's death. He didn't say much about his father, but what he had said was startling.

He ruined her.

Did he think that was what happened in marriage? Maybe if that was the only example I'd seen, I'd feel the same way. Fortunately, I had my parents. As peculiar as they were, their love for each other and their determination to support each other was blinding. At times as a child, I'd been annoyed by it. I took a moment to admonish myself for that stupidity.

And I thought about when the conversation had lightened a little bit and moved to his grandma and how Henry saw her weekly and how he, Jake, called her every week. That was adorable, and one more thing I didn't need to know since it only made him more appealing and yet still just as unavailable. The conversation was the brightest spot to a dark, dark day, but I'd left feeling confused.

The fact that he said his grandmother would like me, and told me I was determined and stubborn, had given me no small amount of pleasure. It was a strange feeling in the midst of all of the sadness, and maybe that was why it felt so good. As much as I was drawn to Jake even more now that I knew a bit more about what made him *him*, and what made him that reserved, sometimes harsh man, I allowed myself to feel happy about taking another step toward friendship with him and refused to think about anything else. This guy needed a friend, and I was in the business of collecting good ones. That conversation certainly felt like a step in the right direction.

I was sitting out on my patio with my computer in my lap and my feet resting in a chair across from me on a warm Saturday afternoon. I'd moved outside because I was tired of my dark apartment when it was so gorgeous in the spring breeze. Even though I had to squint to see my monitor in the sun, it felt good to be sitting in the fresh air and to feel the sun warming my toes through my socks. I had my *You Can Make Anything by Writing* mug Alex had given me two years ago when I declared I wanted to write a novel sitting on the table next to me, full of inevitably cold coffee. Next to that, in my typical form of celebration, was a thin flute of bubbling Prosecco and a bowl of fresh strawberries I'd gotten at the Clarksville farmer's market downtown earlier that day.

I was tapping away when a shadow fell over me.

"Hi," he said, and I squinted up at him, the sky behind him framing him in blue.

"Hi!" I said and saved my work, set my computer down on the table. I willed the excitement at seeing him again to stay locked down so I didn't start prancing around like a puppy.

"I wanted to say thank you," he said from where he stood a few feet away, and I watched as his eyes moved over the table and its contents.

"Please sit down and tell me what you're thanking me for," I said as I pushed out the chair I had been resting my feet on. He moved around it and sat down. I crossed my legs in front of me, now aware of my shorts, coffee-stained t-shirt, and hair piled high on my head twisted into a bun held tight by my usual Bic medium blue pens. I tried not to be aware of his perfectly fitting dark green t-shirt and his relaxed jeans and tennis shoes. I tried not to notice he had a 5 o'clock shadow that was... more than a little attractive.

Shut it down, Elizabeth.

"For the other night. For sitting with me," he said, leveling me with a surprisingly intense look.

"You don't need to thank me for that," I said, pursing my lips together to keep myself from talking anymore, and then grabbing a strawberry from my bowl and taking a bite. Maybe if I could keep my mouth full or closed, I'd make it out of this conversation without betraying my interest in him.

I'd been doing pretty well with remembering he wasn't an option, and even felt secretly relieved by that since he was overwhelming and confusing and maddening all at once, but here in person, he was testing my resolution to forget about him as anything other than a friend.

I set the strawberry's stem and its tiny green leaves down in a little bowl I'd brought out for that purpose. I smiled at the sweet taste and realized he was watching me.

"Strawberry?" I held the bowl out to him.

"Sure." He took one off the top of the pile and his eyebrows rose up a little as he tasted the sweetness. "That's a good strawberry." He smiled at me, and I felt my belly flip a little at the sight of his white teeth and curving smile. Wow, it had been a while since I'd seen that, and never directed at me.

I loved the surprised look on his face, and that he'd forgotten to be serious long enough to let me see his real smile.

As much as I wanted to stay and bask in the glow of that, I thought it might be weird if I just stared at him.

Calmmmm.

"They're from the farmer's market. I will say there's very little I love more in life than early, farm-fresh strawberries." I beamed at him, happy to be sitting with him for a moment, eating the berries I'd forgotten about as I typed away in the fading afternoon light. I popped another berry in and noticed how he watched my mouth as I chewed, swallowed, and licked the strawberry juice from my lips.

After a moment, a beat or two as his eyes blinked at my mouth and I saw him staring, he cleared his throat and asked, "Are you celebrating something?"

"Yes, actually. I hit the halfway point of editing my book, and it's in better shape than I thought it was going to be. I decided I'd incentivize the process, which I tend to dread, by promising myself Prosecco and strawberries if I got to a certain chapter by noon today. I did, so—voila." I gestured to the berries and sparkling glass next to me. "Want a sip?" I asked as I held out the flute to him.

He took it from me, his fingers grazing mine as I handed him the thin stem of the glass, and I tried not to think about the fact that I hadn't touched him in months, not since we'd shaken hands in my office on the day we officially met. He raised the glass to me and said, "To your editing progress," and took a small drink.

He handed the glass back, and I took a sip too. "Thank you." I offered him another berry which he took, and we sat there eating berries quietly for a few moments. I was comfortable just sitting there, being quiet next to him. It was rare that I could sit without having something to occupy my mind and even more rare that I could sit quietly next to someone. My internal dialogue tended to seep out when I was near another person for too long, always ready to debate or discuss, or at the very least, embarrass myself with painfully awkward small talk. But with Jake, it wasn't uncomfortable, and even though I was happy to see him after our more serious conversation over a week ago, I was glad to just sit there with him.

Well, mostly glad. But I did need to clarify. "Jake, I hope you know you don't need to thank me." I eyed him, hoping he'd know I was talking about that night.

"I can see you believe I don't, but I do. It would have been much worse without you." He looked back at me, his usual intensity not faltering for a moment.

I didn't know how to respond, but I was glad he said it. As my mind leapt around trying to think of what to say next, he spoke again.

"I wanted to apologize too. I said a lot, and I hope I didn't make you uncomfortable." His eyes narrowed as though he was trying to peer inside my mind to see if I was upset by the conversation.

"Please don't apologize. You didn't make me uncomfortable, and I hope you know what you said is safe with me. I won't repeat it."

"I wasn't worried about that," he said before I stopped talking.

"Oh, ok. Good," I said, feeling a bloom of pleasure grow in my chest. In some small way, I knew that meant he trusted me. I knew, too, the list of people Jake Harrison trusted was short.

I could see his eyes dart around and felt sure he was about to leave, but I wanted him to keep talking. "Are you... doing ok?" I asked.

He looked at me for a moment, his eyes shifting back and forth between mine. He picked up another strawberry, and before he bit it, he said, "Yes. I'm all right. Are you?"

He was still looking at me, and something in his look made my whole body take notice. I felt my heart start beating faster, my chest rising and falling a bit more rapidly, and I swallowed down the rush of nervousness that appeared out of nowhere. It was like the air around us shifted, like it knew something I didn't, and yet my body certainly knew the secret. "Yes. I am."

He nodded slowly, his eyes like amber in the afternoon light, and I felt lightheaded. Maybe it was the Prosecco getting to me, though I'd had less than half a glass.

"Good," he finally said and sat there a beat, then stood. "I'll get out of your space and let you continue your editing. Have a good evening, Elizabeth."

"You too. Thanks for coming by." I tipped my Prosecco toward him and then took a sip, mentally berating myself for the *thanks for coming by* moment, obviously my smoothest move of all time.

I sat and watched him walk away toward his apartment, the pastel sky lit by the setting sun backdrop, and I felt the warmth of the bubbles in my belly. I felt a little glowy—yeah, glowy. I felt like I had an Iron-man-like light radiating from my chest. I'd accomplished a lot in the last few weeks, and my novel was in great shape. I'd been focused and productive on weekends. I had a bowl full of perfect, sweet strawberries for my enjoyment and still half a glass of Prosecco. And now, I thought, I had Jake Harrison's friendship. A fledgling thing, but I couldn't keep myself from a smug smile as I sat and enjoyed the sunset in a place that felt more and more like home.

And the view of Jake's retreat wasn't half bad either.

THE NEXT DAY WAS SUNDAY, and after a morning at church

and grocery shopping, I spent the bulk of the day editing. By early evening, my mind was mush and I knew I needed to take a break or risk feeling exhausted before the week ever started. So, without thinking too much about it, I grabbed two beers from my fridge and wandered over to see if Jake was home.

The mid-April evening was cool and quiet, aside from the sounds of kids playing on the playground across the parking lot from the apartments. Sure enough, Jake sat on the porch, his long legs stretched out in front of him, his cell phone to his ear, his head nodding up and down. When he saw me his eyebrows quirked up, and I held up the two beers. He nodded to the seat to his left, the seat I always seemed to end up sitting in, and I could hear him say, "I love you too, Grandma," as I sat down.

He hung up and put his phone on the table between us, then leveled me with a questioning look. "Hello, Elizabeth."

"Hello, Jake," I replied, a small grin on my face. "Thought you'd have a beer with me before I go cross-eyed from editing."

"Don't you take breaks?"

"Well, no. Not right now. I don't have that luxury since I'm juggling a few different balls in the air, and I need them all to stay there for now. I have to keep working until I can drop a few, and then I can work out a better schedule that lets me off a few days now and then. But for now, I write whenever I'm home."

"So, I should be honored you're here and not still pecking away at your keyboard?"

"Yes. Yes, you should," I joked and took a sip of my beer

"Well then, I'm honored you chose me to spend your very small and inadequate break with," he said and tipped his bottle to me. I met the neck of his bottle with mine and when they clinked together, I smiled at him.

"You weren't exactly first choice, but..." I trailed off and he laughed.

"I see how it is. I'm the default because I'm your neighbor."

"Yes. Your proximity is advantageous." I nodded enthusiastically, and he shook his head at me.

"Noted."

"What do you do on the weekends, Jake? Besides call your grandmother." I nodded to his phone on the table next to him.

"Every Sunday, I call Grandma. I also usually talk to Henry, but that's a little less reliable. I don't know what else..." He looked around for an answer. "I work out. I hunt, depending on the season. I read. Movies. Regular stuff." He seemed shy about his response, inspecting the bottle in his hands instead of looking back at me.

"Did you answer my 'what do you do for fun' question by saying 'I work out'?" I smirked at him and his head shot up to look at me. When he saw I was joking, he shook his head again.

"Well I do, just like I know you do. I'm a pretty boring guy." I decided not to comment on the fact that I found him to be anything but boring or enjoy the fact that he somehow knew I worked out. Whether this was simply from observing me in exercise clothes, or seeing me jog around the complex, or something else, I didn't know. But I was *not impressed* with myself that my reaction to this news released a little bevy of butterflies in my chest. My body was failing to listen to the logic my mind was all-too-frequently trying to smother it with —this man was not interested in me, and those butterflies might as well be moths in a cedar closet.

"You don't, like, go out with friends? Or anything?" It slipped out before I could stop it, and I felt the embarrassment trying to push forward into my face, but I willed it back. I hadn't outright asked him if he was dating someone, although I did want to know, despite the fact I knew better than to be asking or hopping down that rabbit trail with him mentally. He'd made clear he wasn't interested when Henry was in town, and that wasn't going to change just because we shared a drink or two.

"Not really. Most of my friends are married with kids at this point. I'm the old, single guy." He raised an eyebrow at me, as if asking what I thought, but then continued. "What about you? You don't go out with Alex?"

"I do. Sometimes. But she's busy with Luke, and she works some weekends in Nashville, so it's not all that often. I'm kind of a homebody at heart, so I don't mind being at home, doing what I want to do in my own space."

"I get that. After my first deployment all I wanted to do was go out and be with people and do whatever I wanted to when I wanted to because I hadn't been able to do that. After the second one and every other one since then, I've wanted to be home. The normal routines, the space, the quiet, the food— I like those predictable, familiar things."

"How many times have you deployed?" I was surprised I didn't know, but then, we hadn't talked about stuff like this in our meetings in my office or in any other conversation.

"Five times to the Middle East," he said, and I watched as his thumb scratched at the edge of the label on the bottle he held with his other hand.

"Five?" I asked, incredulity in my voice.

"Yep. Three full year deployments, one that got cut short to ten months, and one that was right about nine months." He said this nonchalantly, like it wasn't an insane amount of time to be gone.

"That's more than four and a half years, Jake. No wonder you like being at home." I felt the impulse to thank him, but I swallowed that down, knowing he wouldn't want my thanks. "That seems like too much."

He let out a long breath before he looked back at me. "It feels that way sometimes. But I'm almost done."

"You are? You're only, what, thirty-three?" I remembered his birthday from his paperwork, remembered he was almost exactly six and a half years older than me, our birthdays opposite each other—mine in December, his in June.

"I went to basic training when I was seventeen. I've been active duty since the day I turned eighteen. I'm almost to sixteen years—will be in a few months."

"That's mind-blowing. You've had an entire career, and in all that time I've been in school. Just school and more school, not doing *anything* with my time. I've been out of my grad program for less than two years. I feel like such a slacker." I swallowed down the real sense of panic that I hadn't done anything, hadn't started my working life in the way I wanted to, and watched as he peeled the last of the label off.

"You should. You should feel like a slacker, *Dr.* Elizabeth Kent," he said and gave me a pointed look.

I gave him a closed-mouth smile, one of those regretful, chagrined ones, in response. "My point is, it's amazing you'll have completed a twenty-year career before you turn forty. That's something to be proud of."

"Thanks."

We sat companionably for a moment and sipped our drinks. I heard him shift and set his bottle down on the table.

"Well, do you miss it?" he asked.

"Miss what?"

"New York. The City. The center of the universe, of course," he teased. This was a far more lighthearted Jake Harrison than I'd ever encountered. I felt a little flustered by his chattiness and wondered what he was so chipper about.

"Oh! Sure. Yeah, I do sometimes. Mostly when I'm driving because I don't like driving. But I like the space here. I *love* the space in my apartment. And I think I'm finally used to how quiet it is." I smiled to myself and looked out over the grass of his backyard and beyond.

"I like New York. It's overwhelming, but you can find these pockets of calm and wonder."

Something about the word "wonder" coming from his mouth made me feel like I was walking sideways. It set me off kilter enough so I couldn't tell what was up or down.

"That's it exactly!" I exclaimed, and it was an exclamation. I sort of shouted it, revealing my amazement at his perfect word choice. I lowered my voice and continued. "That's the perfect way to describe it, or... those parts of it. Those corners and neighborhoods and those silent moments alone with the Temple of Dendur or in the Masters' rooms at the Met. It's like you have the whole world, all of history to yourself sometimes."

I glanced at him and he was looking at me, studying my face. "How do you know that? Did you live there? It's hard to get that feel on a short visit," I asked.

"My dad did a year at West Point when I was in high school. I went into the city a lot, and at that point he didn't challenge me on much. He let me go, probably because he knew it could have been worse for him. I was straight-laced and studied hard, so he knew I wasn't going off to get drugs or whatever. Looking back it's a little insane he let me go by myself. But I'm glad he did." He gave me a small smile.

"Well listen, I don't want to be encroaching on your time at home any more than I have, even if you were my last resort pick for my break."

"Yeah, I was about to kick you out. I need to pack," he said and took the last swallow of his beer.

"Pack?"

"We're in the field this week for an FTX."

"FTX?"

"Field Training Exercise. War games, shooting ranges, stx lanes, all that good stuff. If we don't freeze overnight, it should be a good week," he explained.

"I hope you don't freeze, and I hope it goes well. Have a good week." I stood up and carried my bottle with me.

"You too, Elizabeth."

I FINISHED the last few notes for my first draft of the TESS project on Wednesday of that week. I emailed all of the participants a copy of the information and invited them to come in the following week for a meeting to explain the results. I was sure less than a third of them would come, but I liked to provide the opportunity for people who participated in a study to understand the outcomes and what their data meant to the project as a whole. This wasn't always possible, so I liked that I was in a position to do it now.

I felt relief. I'd given myself six months, and I finished the project, in solid first draft form anyway, in four and a half. That meant I had plenty of time for editing and revision before I submitted it to the organizations that would use the information. I'd submitted my request for an expansion of the project in March, and I was hopeful that would provide me enough funding to do so.

It would also help me justify not going back to a teaching job within the calendar year. It would let me keep writing and hopefully get to a place where, by the end of the year, I could support myself with my writing full time. That would take an incredibly aggressive writing schedule, but I was ready. I had to take a deep, bracing breath and let it out at that thought. It still scared me.

I'd finished my book, or at least had made peace with it enough, and had been sending query letters to agents. I'd sent a few in the weeks prior but hadn't wanted to pursue my top choices until the book was as polished as I could get it. Working weekends and nights had made me productive. I'd sent my latest draft to a girl in my writer's group who'd offered to copy edit the work if I'd return the favor down the line when she had her novel ready, so of course I said yes. Her feedback was helpful in the last round of edits, and now I was ready for a break, ready to let loose a little, and having things wrapped up would be perfect. I was meeting Alex for brunch on Sunday and planned to spend Saturday doing whatever I wanted. Probably a long run, a movie, and whatever else I felt like, because I *could*. Guilt free.

I wondered if I should call my parents and tell them. I could tell them about the project completion *and* the book— maybe that would soften the blow, or double excitement. That was far from likely, but it seemed like a good way to let them know the book and my writing were still happening. We'd been steadily avoiding any mention of my writing for weeks since it only brought out tension between us.

When Saturday rolled around, it was a rainy, dark morning. I'd decided to go to the gym for my run instead of braving the rain, knowing I wouldn't last. I couldn't stand having wet feet.

Hours later when I pulled into my spot, I saw Luke unloading something from his truck on the far side of the parking lot and then noticed Jake pull in a few spaces down from where I'd just parked. My stomach fluttered, and I rolled my eyes at myself. Even though I knew we were friends, I found myself thinking about when he might be back, whether

I'd see him that weekend, and how things had gone in the field.

I was sweaty and my long hair was pulled back into a now-disheveled knot. I'd run for a long time at the gym and was ready for a long, hot shower, clean clothes, and a good book.

And food. Definitely food.

I pulled on my rain shell over my tank top, ignoring the slightly nauseated feeling I had as I stood up out of the car. I knew my legs and feet would get wet, but I wanted to wave at Jake before I ran to my apartment. By the time I was out of my car, he was pulling bags and other items out of his trunk.

"Do you need help?" I half-yelled as I approached him because the rain had escalated to a downpour. Water was running down my rain jacket, down the bridge of my nose, down my legs, into my shoes, everywhere.

Jake turned around to face me, and my eyes widened at the sight of him. He was wearing his camouflage uniform, which was soaked. He had his patrol cap pulled low on his head, and his face was painted with dark streaks of olive green, brown, and black paint. He looked dirty and savage and rough. He looked wild.

He looked insanely, magnificently hot.

He set down the bag he was holding and took a step closer to me. Without thinking, I took a step back. His eyes ran from my neon pink running shoes up my bare legs to my shorts and then my open rain jacket and my soaked tank. My chest was rising and falling like I'd just stopped running, though it had been a half hour or more since I left the gym. His gaze was a palpable thing, like he was running his hands along my body, and I felt my chest, neck, and cheeks heat.

He stepped toward me again, water spattering off the bill of his hat, soaking into his uniform, running over his paint-darkened cheeks. He stood right in front of me, maybe twelve inches away. He took each side of my rain jacket in one of his hands and slowly snapped three of the buttons—one at my belly button, one at my chest, one at my sternum. He didn't actually touch me then either, just the jacket, but it felt like he had. I swear I could feel the snap of the buttons between his fingers on my skin. I could feel his eyes lingering on my chest, then my neck, then my lips.

Then he reached up and gently took my chin in his hand. His warm, rough thumb swept over my bottom lip, wet with rain, and he said, "Go home, Elizabeth." He held my eyes captive with his for another moment, my own incapable of looking away (not that I wanted to), and then stepped away.

As he was grabbing his bags again and slamming his trunk door, I shook myself out of the fog he'd created by standing next to me. I forced my feet to move in the direction of my apartment, rain squishing in my socks and between my toes, and I did not look back.

CHAPTER EIGHT

WHEN I CLOSED the door to my apartment, I leaned back against it and stared out into nothing for a few moments. I couldn't bring words to mind. I couldn't bring thoughts to mind either, except one thing.

All I could think of was his warm, rough hand on my chin, his thumb on my lip, and his eyes. They'd slipped over me like a silk sheet, liquid and smooth and suggestive.

What.

Just.

Happened.

I shook off the daze and looked around the room, wild-eyed, feeling frantic. My adrenaline was dropping, and I registered that I'd run nine miles and hadn't eaten anything since before the run hours ago, so first, sustenance. I grabbed a banana and shoved it in my mouth, chewing, swallowing with ravenous focus on one corner of my hallway carpet that curled up and I constantly tripped over.

I was soaking wet and still sweating from both my run and the subsequent encounter with now suddenly extremely sensual Jake Harrison, so I jumped in the shower. I thought very carefully about my mile times, the next time I'd run, the way my knees felt, how sore my hamstrings already were, and avoided any thought of Jake. It was far too soon for him to join me in the shower.

Oh good grief.

I thought of the slightly chalky feeling of my tongue after the banana, which was still mostly green. I thought of how much water I'd need to drink and that I should start my coffee maker.

When I got out and dried off, I found sweatpants, my phone, and the couch, pulling my long hair into another damp bun on my head. I wore my contacts that day to avoid running in glasses, which I realized when I reached up to shove them back on my face and found them missing. *Right.*

Alex picked up on the third ring.

"Alex," I said, my voice serious.

"What's wrong, El?" I could hear the concern in her voice.

"I don't know what's happening," I said. I needed my brain to calm the eff down because I knew I wasn't making sense.

"What do you mean? Start from the beginning or give me something so I know what you're talking about."

"Jake Harrison. I like him. He doesn't like me—I heard him tell his brother he had no desire to date me. So, like any sane woman I have continued to enjoy his physical attributes while doing my best to not think about him since he was so unequivocal about his lack of interest in me." Professional summarizer. That was me.

Alex choked a little and sputtered a cough. "You think he's not interested?"

"I know it. I heard him say it."

"Um, ok. Then, what's wrong?" she asked.

"I just... He just... I don't know. I saw him in the parking lot, and it was strange." *That's putting it mildly.*

"What did he say?"

"He said, 'Go home, Elizabeth.' That's not what was strange, though. It was the look he gave me," I said as I remembered the way he looked at me and felt myself sink farther into the couch.

"What look did he give you?" she asked, and I could hear her voice becoming pitched with frenetic energy.

"It was like... I don't know. I could swear it was like he... wanted me. You know... *Wanted* me." I felt my cheeks flush thinking about his eyes again, how intense and hungry they'd seemed. My heart was wild in my chest as I waited for her to laugh at me. It felt so stupid to say that out loud.

"*Oooh.* Oh that's a good look on him, I bet." I could hear the smile and excitement in her voice, and I shook my head.

"I'm probably wrong. I haven't dated in years. I have no idea what I'm talking about, really," I sputtered, trying to reason my way out. I jumped up and started pacing a path from my couch, to the front door, along the entryway, turning just before the kitchen and back around to the front of the couch.

"Give yourself more credit than that, El. You're not an idiot. It sounds like there was a moment. But, he didn't say anything else, or do anything else?"

"He said, 'Go home, Elizabeth,' and then he grabbed my chin and ran his thumb over my lip." I blushed again at the memory, my fingers running over my lips as I remembered the feeling of his on me.

"Oh. My. Shortcake. *Yeah*, he wants you. That *was* a moment. I can confirm. A man doesn't touch a woman's lips unless he wants to kiss them. I'm sorry, but no, that doesn't happen." She sounded giddy.

"But, I heard him. He said he wasn't interested. Plus, I happen to know he doesn't date nor does he want any kind of serious relationship. And he's never done anything like that. Any time we've been near each other, it's been totally platonic, not even any flirting. Definitely no touching."

"I don't know what to tell you El, but it sounds like Jake Harrison has the hots for you," she teased.

"Ugh, I am not mature enough for this," I said as I slumped back down on the couch, curled my knees up to my face, and rested my forehead on them.

"What do you mean? You're twenty-seven years old."

"I mean, like, what do I do now? What do I say when I see him again?" I felt anxious at the prospect already. I had no idea when I'd see him again, but my heart was hammering like he'd knocked on my door.

"I think you act *normal*, my dearest. Or... you act like yourself. I think you wait to see what he does next, but otherwise, you do whatever it is you've been doing. Onward." Her voice was reassuring and solid now, and I felt myself relax a little.

"Normal. I can do that. Onward. Yeah."

Because normal is a thing that people can be. Yeah.
Especially me. Especially around him.
Totally.

∾

On Tuesday morning, I received an email from Jake. It read:

Dr. Kent,

I apologize for my slow response. I have been in the field and did not receive your email until yesterday. I am interested in reviewing the summary of the TESS project data and learning about your associated conclusions and recommendations. Could we schedule a time to meet next week?

Very respectfully,

And signed with his Outlook email signature. I was used to this, and expected nothing less, though the formality floored me for a minute. Then I realized that, even if he did like me (just thinking that made me feel like I was in junior high), he wasn't going to convey that in an email. For this guy, it may have even been his way of showing me respect, a kind of scholarly, super serious flirting.

Sure. *Suuuuuure.*

SFC Harrison,

I'd be happy to meet with you. Are you available next Wednesday at 10:30? It shouldn't take more than thirty minutes of your time.

Very best,

And my signature block.

And there we had it. He replied, just as formally, and confirmed he'd be attending the meeting next week. I felt...

flummoxed. I wasn't sure how he'd act around me, but I suspected that in the professional context of my office, it might be just as standoffish and formal (that word again!) as it was the first few times we met here.

That would be good—that would guide me. If we met in my office, on my terms, and I knew what I would be discussing with him (the study), I wouldn't spend the entire time wondering if he'd touch me again or if I'd catch another glimpse of the heat with which he'd looked at me the weekend before. The fact that I felt irritable and restless at the thought that it'd be over a week until I'd see him in that context was more than a little annoying.

I had *no* business wanting him. Whatever that was in the rain—however appealing it was to be the recipient of his attention in *that* way, I couldn't hope for that to happen again. I *shouldn't* hope for it, and if it did happen again, if I were being a smart person, like I tended to think I was, I should shut it down.

Because he'd made his interest clear in the form of the overheard rejection when he spoke to Henry, and I knew he had no interest in a future based on more than one conversation with him. I had no interest in a fling with my extremely attractive and ever-present neighbor—I knew myself. First, *flinging* wasn't my thing. Second, the unfortunate reality that I felt much more for him than attraction made anything on my end the opposite of casual.

And that was the other problem. There was a slim chance I'd make it all the way until next week without seeing him again. Very slim. But I hated the idea of seeing him casually on his patio or as we both walked to our cars—I'd inevitably say something awkward, or betray my curiosity about what happened, or generally *be awkward* as I tried *not* to be awkward or mention what happened.

So, Jake... that thing when you touched my lip and I nearly liquefied just standing there. 'Member that? Yeah, me too...

If we could move forward without acknowledging what happened, maybe have another normal conversation, that'd work fine. So, it needed to be next week, and it needed to be in my office, and not any time before then.

∾

I'D MIRACULOUSLY MANAGED to avoid Jake, but that wasn't luck. I'd been *busy*. I ended up working through the weekend on a secondary grant proposal, hoping it would be a useful addition to the funding package I'd already applied for through Operation Achieve. This funding felt critical at this point, and even though I wasn't expecting to hear anything until the end of May, I started getting worried. I'd gotten a little niggling sense of doubt at some point, probably for no good reason, and now I was scrambling to look for backup funding just in case. But then, I wasn't great at *just in case* without worrying, so I was simultaneously working my butt off and trying not to think about anything at the same time.

This worked not at all.

The best news, though, was that after approximately twenty-seven *Thanks but no thanks* responses, *someone* had liked my book. Best—it was my top choice for an agent based on the authors she already represented. She'd apparently liked the book and had already given me feedback on the full manuscript only a week after she requested it. She indicated she was eager to read it after I reviewed her suggested changes to see how well our ideas worked together and that when she reviewed the changes I made, she'd contact me. I was bouncing off the walls at this news, and when I called Alex, she promised she'd take me out for a celebratory toast on

Saturday. She had about eight million other things going on during that day for her work and couldn't stay with me past six o'clock that night because she had to go to a formal event with Luke, but she insisted on meeting me in downtown Clarksville for a drink.

EVEN THOUGH I loved staying in and cozying up on weekends, I was incredibly excited to be going out to celebrate. I took some time on myself. Finally getting to the end of the official documentation for this other grant proposal and needing to give it a rest until Monday anyway, I stopped working around three that afternoon. I showered, curled my long brown hair into waves, and even did my makeup. I wore a fitted black cap sleeve dress that flared out around my waist and ended a few inches above the knee, and some peep-toe high heels. Seriously, this was not my average outing, but I knew Alex would be gussied up for the event with Luke, and I felt like being fancy.

I wasn't someone who reveled in makeup and making an effort, but I couldn't deny the power of the process. I wasn't usually particularly attentive to my appearance, but I enjoyed the results when I did pay attention. As I walked into the Black Buck Brewery, I was completely overdressed, and I didn't give a damn. Alex was already there, waiting for me at a high-top bistro table in the bar area, thankfully also wearing a too-fancy navy cocktail dress, with two glasses of beer in front of her.

"Here she comes, my fancy author friend!" She hopped down from the bar stool and hugged me.

"Thank you, thank you. So happy to be here," I said with a congenial wave to my non-existent audience.

We sat down at the high table and I shimmied in my seat, too full of pent-up energy to sit still.

"Ok, so *dimmi*. All the details. Go," she said, beaming at me. I took a moment to enjoy her delight—what a rare and lovely person who is so good at being happy for others. I said a silent prayer of thanks for this dear friend and then began telling her all of the details. I told her about the process of sending out the book, how many people I'd contacted with query letters and then all about the email I'd gotten days ago expressing interest after the agent had read the full copy of the novel she'd requested a week before.

"So, I already made the changes she suggested and sent it back today. I know it's not locked in, but she sounded so positive and excited. Her suggestions were mostly brilliant, too. I'm just... I'm amazed. I don't think I could have asked for it to go better than this. This is the agent I've had my eye on since I figured out how the process works, and I can't believe she wants to take me on—or is even considering it. And you know I don't care about money. It'd be amazing to make money at this so I don't have to do anything else, but with the TESS project going well, and hopefully funding for the expansion, that buys me time to keep writing and working and just..." I trailed off, feeling overwhelmed by the hope and excitement I felt.

"I love this. I just love it!" Alex raised her glass. "To you, amazing Ellie. May you continue your streak of awesomeness, and may you know how very loved you are, with or without it." She clinked her glass to mine and took a sip as I took a drink of my beer, swallowing down the lump of emotion that snuck up on me during her toast.

"Thank you, my friend. Thanks for cheering me on all this time."

"You know, I'm going to have to get you another coffee

mug in celebration. I've been looking but haven't found the right one yet."

"Oh, can't wait." I smiled at her, loving the feeling of being known so well. Alex understood me—my drive, the struggle I'd been on to even allow myself the time and space to write fiction, much less turn my world upside-down and do it half-way seriously, and now the elation that came with someone else thinking my writing wasn't half bad. She also understood my devoted love of punny coffee mugs.

"Well, hello there, Jake," Alex said, looking behind me, her eyes wide and smile full of delight. At that name, I felt a swirl of excitement and nerves course through me.

I swiveled in the chair to see him. Sure enough, there was Jake Harrison, looking like some kind of dreamy slow-motion fantasy out of context. He wore a black t-shirt with a logo I didn't recognize and jeans that had been washed a few hundred times. He looked incredibly attractive, but not like he was trying. This man was meticulous, but not about his looks. My eyes swept over him, up over his clean-shaven face, and met his eyes. I noticed he had that little glint in them, the one that told me he was smiling at me but wouldn't let me see.

Stingy.

"Alex. Elizabeth. Good to see you." His voice was smooth and familiar—I'd missed hearing it. I hadn't seen Jake since he told me to go home that afternoon in the rain. I'd managed to avoid him for nearly two weeks. Well, no, two weeks exactly. We'd emailed the week before and were supposed to meet to review the TESS information, but he'd had to cancel our meeting that was scheduled for the previous Wednesday due to a pop-up mandatory sexual harassment training for the whole division. I'd missed seeing him but was also thankful for the space. I still felt unsure about what to expect from him.

"What are you up to, Jake? I thought you were a home-body hermit-type?" Alex asked.

Jake stepped around my chair and stood next to me, then set his beer on the table next to mine. "Yes ma'am, I am that. But I got talked into coming out for a drink with some guys, so here I am," he answered her, then looked at me.

And then he kept looking at me. I looked right back at him and then took a drink of my beer because I could feel myself working up to some kind of awkward declaration. What I'd declare, I didn't know, but I could feel it welling up and needed something to wash it back down.

"This amazing woman is celebrating. You should toast her," Alex said, and I gave her a wide-eyed look that said, *What are you doing?*

"What are you celebrating, Elizabeth?" He shifted so his body was facing me, his full attention on me, and I swallowed hard and cleared my throat. He leaned closer—was he *too* close now? Was that a normal talking distance people used?

"Um, well, I got some good news," I said quietly, suddenly self-conscious and feeling mildly ridiculous. It wasn't like I'd been offered a contract with the agent. Statistically, it was unlikely to work out.

"She's going to be published, and it's a big deal," Alex said, her voice demanding.

"Really? Is it the book you've been editing the last little while?" Jake asked.

"I don't have a publisher yet, but I do maybe have an agent. An agent who's interested, I should say. And yes. Yeah, that's the one," I said. If nothing else, I'd heard from an interested party. Even if *nothing* came of it, I could be proud of carrying the book through to that point.

"Congratulations. Cheers to you for having the guts to write a book and then the follow through to edit it and even attempt to publish it. That's awesome," he said and raised his glass to me. I picked mine up and tipped it so it knocked against his and then smiled at him. A trill of excitement raced through me at the reality yet again and at having him there to know about it

"Why don't you join us, Jake?" Alex said and gestured to a table behind her that had an extra seat. "Pull up a chair."

"Sure," he said.

"Aren't you meeting people?" I asked, suddenly very aware of him and how incapable of conversation I felt.

"They'll understand if I sit here and talk with you for a few minutes." He held my attention without moving for a moment, waiting to see if I'd wave him away, then slid the other chair to our table.

Jake sat with me and Alex, and since Alex knew I was feeling tongue-tied, she regaled us with the tale of woe she'd experienced earlier in the day—a small event she organized for her event planning job in Nashville had gone awry in just about every possible way.

I made an effort to focus on her, and not on how Jake's knee pressed against mine under the small table, or how close our hands were where they rested on the table next to our drinks.

After about fifteen minutes, and a full twenty minutes earlier than she'd originally told me she'd have to leave to meet Luke, Alex stood up and grabbed her purse from the back of her chair.

"You can take care of my girl, right Jake? I've got to head out." She smiled at Jake expectantly and ignored my death-glare. What was she doing? Why was she leaving? Why did I feel only part murderous rage?

"Oh, no, that's fine—" I started, but Jake answered her before I could finish.

"Yes ma'am. I'd be happy to." He nodded and then looked at me. "That ok?"

I looked back at him, his brown eyes and perfect eyebrows and the brown hair he might have even styled a bit. I looked at his angular jaw and somehow *didn't* let my eyes linger on his very nice-looking lips. "Sure."

What else could I say? *No, I'm not sure what to say to you* wouldn't be very engaging. *You look too handsome and I am going to embarrass myself* was more accurate, but also not something I could or would actually verbalize.

Alex moved around to give me a hug and I hugged her back, a little dazed, and heard her whisper in my ear. "Call me later," she said, and when she pulled back I could see the devious look on her face. She raised her eyebrows meaningfully and I shook my head at her. She thought she was so cute.

Jake moved to Alex's chair across from me. Now his knees rested on either side of my own, the inside of his knees touching the outside of mine.

I let my eyes flit around the restaurant, watching an endless stream of people entering, waiting for seats, looking for friends.

"So, who are you meeting?" I asked him.

"Some guys from work, but they'll be fine. It was a whole group. They won't miss me," he said, his focus full on me. This man could focus like no one's business. He made me feel like an ant under a magnifying glass with even his most casual looks.

"I feel bad. I don't want to ruin your Saturday night," I said, feeling an intense wave of embarrassment heat my cheeks. I swallowed down the last of my beer, getting ready to leave when he said the word.

He laughed lightly, then said, "I wouldn't say you're

ruining it." He finished his own beer, and then asked, "What are you having? Do you want to get an appetizer?"

I watched as he flipped through a small menu on the table, his brow furrowing as he read the options. Was he staying with me because Alex had asked him? He was hard enough to read, and I was feeling like a charity case, and a little like a school girl.

I took a breath and rested both hands on the table, willing him to understand. "Listen, really. I finished my beer, and I knew Alex couldn't stay long. I don't want you to miss your time with your friends."

He looked at me for a beat, and then closed the menu. "I understand, Elizabeth. I won't be missing them if I'm sitting here with you, trust me." He cocked an eyebrow up, waiting for me to show I understood. I nodded in response to his silent question and refused to let myself blush and smile and maybe even fist-pump like I did in my imagination at that moment.

He pulled his phone out of his pocket, tapped out a message, and tucked it back in his pocket. "Now they know. So, nachos or buffalo wings?"

I smiled at him, feeling myself ease a little bit at the idea he was not feeling obligated, or at the very least, he was making the best of it. "Definitely nachos."

CHAPTER NINE

WOULD it be stupid to say I was surprised at how much I enjoyed talking with Jake? Because I did. We sipped another beer and destroyed the large plate of nachos. We talked more about my book, about how crazy his work had been lately, and then about trivial things. I couldn't get over how funny and interesting he was, and more so, how fun he was to be around.

I knew he was attractive and had a lot of depth to him, but I wasn't prepared for how much I liked chatting with him. It felt different to be sitting in a restaurant, eating food and talking—almost like a date. It was public, obviously, but lighter, somehow. I was able to step away from some of the nerves I tended to have when I was alone with him, and so far my mind was obeying my command not to think of our moment in the rain.

"What was your favorite subject in school when you were growing up?" he asked.

"Definitely reading. Then writing. I was always good at math, but I lived for my writing classes in middle school and high school."

"That isn't a big surprise. And now here you are, about to

publish your first novel." He gave me a warm smile and I felt that smile heat me.

"What about you?" I asked him.

"Definitely science when I was younger. I remember all of that stuff so well and nothing else. Learning about frogs and spiders and doing those papier-mâché volcanoes with baking soda and vinegar."

"Oh yes, that was fun."

"Yeah. My favorite. And then in eighth grade I took The Physics of Toys. It was taught by this teacher I thought was cool and it blew my mind. We played with toys and learned the physics behind how they worked—gyroscopes and kaleidoscopes and yoyos and even bowling. It was such a great way to learn, and it stuck with me." He was smiling again, or still, and I sucked in a breath as I looked at him, watched him take his last bite of nachos, watched the muscles in his jaw work as he chewed.

He was painfully good looking, sitting there across from me, oblivious to exactly how much his proximity was affecting me. I'd forgotten that for a while as we talked, but now the awareness was back in full force.

"We should probably pay and let someone else have our table, huh?" I said, realizing we were now surrounded by people waiting in the bar area and the line to get into the place ran out the door and wrapped around the side of the building. We'd been there over an hour already.

He nodded while he finished chewing and grabbed his wallet to pay. I unzipped my purse at the same time, and he narrowed his eyes at the hand fishing for my wallet, and then at me. "Not a chance," he said.

"This is clearly a situation in which I buy your beer and nachos since you were coerced into ditching your friends," I said and slapped my debit card down on the table.

"This is clearly a situation in which I buy *your* beer and nachos because you're celebrating." As he said this, he slid cash onto the little tray that held the bill and grabbed my card. He gave me a playful look, and then walked away, out the door, and out onto the street.

I hopped down and followed him out, weaving through the crowd and out the front door to find him a few yards away, looking at the sky in the opposite direction. I walked up next to him and put my hand high on his arm to let him know I was there. As soon as I touched him he turned, looking at my hand, and then at me. I took my hand away quickly, although I admit reluctantly, since I very much enjoyed the feeling of his shoulder, the curve and dip of the upper part of his triceps.

"Thank you," I said. He nodded in reply and handed me the card he'd swiped inside.

"Do you need a ride home?" he asked, and I swear I saw a little hope in his eyes. But that was crazy.

"No, thank you. Alex and I drove separately since she had to go to the thing with Luke. Thanks though," I said and wished I hadn't driven so I would have an excuse to stay with him.

Stop that nonsense, woman!

My mind had been betraying me all night with thoughts of how handsome and fun and funny and generally delightful this man was, but I couldn't ignore that I knew him—I knew he wasn't interested in anything with me, at least not anything like what I wanted.

I turned and slowly walked up the street to the lot where I'd parked, and he followed me. I started to speak, but before I could, I felt his hand slide over my hair from the back of my neck to where it ended mid-back, and then his hand come to rest on me there.

Something about that—the way he'd touched my hair so

gently—made my breath catch, and all of my senses focused in on the feeling of his warm hand on my back as we walked. I couldn't stop myself from looking over at him, searching for some kind of... *something*. I wasn't sure what I thought I'd see, but there was nothing. He walked next to me and looked ahead, his hand steady and secure on my back. He had his typical bearing, that determination that was rooted and locked into his spine, like no one could set him off course, even on this casual stroll.

This was another one of those moments. It was a mixed signal, wasn't it? Or was it? I supposed it wasn't unusual to walk with a friend this way. But it felt significant, this physical contact in an otherwise entirely physically sterile relationship. Other than the time he'd touched my face in the rain, which was charged and highly memorable, I'd had no physical contact with him other than a handshake and then just now, when I put my hand on his shoulder. Oh, and the touching knees.

So this? This very strong, large hand on my back, and the *hair thing!* Yeah, that made me all tingly and nervous.

He walked with me right up to the driver's side door of my car, and I saw his Jeep parked a few spaces down. He let his hand drop away from my back when we stopped.

"Thanks for letting me crash your evening," he said, his voice rich and a little rough from talking loudly in the restaurant.

"Oh. Uh, sure. Anytime. Thanks for the beer and nachos and... yeah. Thanks," I said, finding my keys in my purse and feeling ridiculously unnerved by his proximity and the tone of his voice and basically everything about him in that moment.

"I'll see you soon, Elizabeth," he said, and stepped back, and away toward his own car, but turned back and put his hand on the hood of my car. "Actually, are you going home? Why don't we have another drink?"

I was standing in my open door, and my pulse kicked up again. "Sure, sounds good." *See how casual and cool I am, since this is no big deal?* —I tried to convince myself. "But you bought here, so you have to come to me. I have Sam Adams, I think, or wine. I'll meet you on the patio."

"Perfect," he said with a nod and walked to his car.

I got in my car and shut the door. I wanted to sit there and stare at the pink and purple sunset and think about how close I'd been to grabbing his hand, how much I wanted him to kiss me, and how much I needed to shut all of those thoughts down, but I worried he might still be watching, or at least be aware of me, since he was only a few spots down in the row of cars.

I started the car and made my way home, relieved to find he wasn't right behind me so we wouldn't see each other again in the parking lot for what would be an even more charged version of a very date-like doorstep scene, even though having him in my space would probably make me crazy. It was a nice night, so we could sit on the patio—a safe zone.

As I drove, my parents called, and rather than having the guilt of avoiding their call on my conscience, I made the fatal error of answering.

"Ellie, good," my mom said, short and direct, as always.

"Hi Mom. I have some good news, so this is great timing. I have an agent interested in my book. She's reading my revised draft and should be contacting me in the next week or so about representing me," and with that, I felt my belly swirl and drop. Fortunately, I pulled into my parking spot—while I knew I'd be nervous sharing this news, my whole body was sending me the *flight* signal.

"Oh? Congratulations," my mom offered.

"Yes, well done," Dad chimed.

"So when will you be teaching again?" Without a beat, there it was.

"This was a one semester deal, right Ellie? I'm sure you're ready to be back in the city," Dad suggested.

"I don't plan to go back to New York—not any time soon. I'm focusing on writing and the TESS project for now." My voice was shaky, and I hated that I might sound unsure to them. I closed the front door and set down my keys, my purse.

"Well... ok. But what about your career? You don't want to be out of academia for too long. Gaps on your curriculum vitae will not be helpful for your tenure prospects." I could picture them sitting together, holding hands, worrying about my future.

"That's not my biggest concern right now," I said in a low, steady voice. I wasn't ready to lay it out, to explain that I wanted to be done teaching. I certainly wasn't ready to force them to be proud of my writing when it was such an afterthought.

"A school there in Tennessee, then? Maybe Vanderbilt?" Dad suggested.

"I don't think so..."

I could practically hear my mom smile sympathetically, like she thought I was a misguided child. "Well honey, you know we think what you're doing there is great, but—"

"You know what? I have someone coming over, so I better go. Thanks for calling, guys. Talk to you soon."

"You all right?" I heard the voice and blinked my eyes back into focus. After I hung up with my parents, I'd slumped into a chair there on my patio, staring off.

"Oh, yeah, of course," I said, sitting up from my slouched position as Jake approached. He sat down in the chair next to me. It had only been thirty or forty minutes since I'd seen him last, but I felt a little lurch at having him there, like I'd missed him.

"You don't look it," he said in a low, calm voice.

"I just got off the phone with my parents."

"And how'd that go?"

"I told them about the book." My voice sounded small and thin.

I could feel him watching me, waiting for me to say more as I picked at a small thread hanging from the hem of my dress resting just above my knee.

"It went about as well as I expected." My voice broke on the word *expected,* and I felt a familiar sense of shame rush through me. Why had I expected them to be excited for me? Why had I tricked myself into believing they'd understand me, finally?

He was quiet, still, maybe because he didn't know what to say, or maybe because he could tell I needed to talk it through. I cleared my throat, forcing the emotion back. "I told them I had an interested agent and was waiting on details. They asked me if I'd applied to any teaching jobs in the area or if I was going back to New York for fall semester. They said 'Congratulations' and launched right into what job prospects I had. I think they would have had a stronger reaction if I'd told them I got a great deal on avocados at the store yesterday."

"Do they know how much it means to you? Your writing?" he asked.

I kept my eyes on the line of trees bordering the apartment complex's property, now turning into a dark barrier against the twilight sky.

"I don't know how they couldn't."

"Have you told them?"

"Have I said outright 'I want to be a writer and I don't want to teach anymore'? No. No, I haven't. I don't think I can." I felt the frustration growing in me, a little seed had been watered that evening, and now here he was, fertilizing it, unsuspectingly prodding at the most sensitive parts of me.

"You can."

"You don't even know me Jake, you can't say that." I frowned.

"Maybe not, but—"

"There's no 'but' here—" I started.

"I know enough to know you're brave enough to tell your parents what matters to you."

"No, listen to me. You don't understand," I said, starting to feel genuinely frustrated. Some small part of me realized my frustration wasn't with him, but that didn't stop me. "They paid for my college. They supported me. I'm their *only* child. They put all their eggs in my basket, and I'm supposed to call them up and say, 'Hey guys, thanks for all the love and encouragement, not to mention your significant financial investment in my education, but I'd rather write stories'?" I clamped my mouth shut and squeezed my arms tight around my middle.

"Do you believe they'll only be happy if you're teaching?"

I took a deep breath and let it out slowly, trying to expel some of my rising tension. "I think part of me feels like they are never going to be happy because I am the wrong kind of doctor." I felt hollow after saying it—something I'd felt for years but never said out loud.

"The wrong kind?"

"Yeah, I'm Piled Higher and Deeper. I'm a PhD, not an MD. They're both medical doctors. And while I know they said they embraced the truth years ago when I made clear I *wasn't* going to go to med school, I can't help but feel like I'm this perpetual disappointment. And then I go and basically throw away that education in favor of trying to do this thing that doesn't even require all the years of ridiculous school I've had."

"Do you believe being a writer is the same as throwing away your education?" His questions kept coming. He wasn't letting me wallow, and I had been doing fine wallowing on my own without his prodding me to *think.*

"No! Well, part of me does, yes, but I also know it wasn't right for me. I felt dead last year, Jake. I hated going to work, I hated departmental meetings, I dreaded checking my email. What kind of life is that? I spent all of last year mourning the loss of the life I *thought* I wanted—I tried to talk myself into it. I spent the five years of my PhD program willing myself to want that life, and when it came time to live it, I was miserable. So even if it does mean throwing it away, I can't be upset about that because the alternative... I'm not cut out for it." There it was again, the shame. All the hours, sacrifice, and effort I'd given. All of the tears and late nights and missed opportunities for something else. All of the energy and the tamping down of the other parts of me, and here I was.

"That doesn't sound like you're throwing it away. It sounds like a hard, sort of crap lesson to have to learn, but it sounds like you did everything you could to make that life work." He leaned forward on his knees and looked up at me.

"I suspect my parents would disagree with you." I could hear the bitterness in my voice.

"Why?"

"Because. Writing is impractical. Yes, everyone has to write. But writing *fiction*? Something that's purely for pleasure? Writing something that doesn't necessarily educate or ameliorate a problem? That's worthless to them."

"It's hard to imagine that's true, but sometimes you have to part ways with what your parents wanted for you."

"Did you? Part ways?"

"You know my dad was a soldier. He was an officer. Very successful career. He expected me to go to West Point—The Academy, like he did, and then commission as an officer, just like he did." He was sitting facing me and looked down at my knee in front of him. He reached out his index finger and painted a circle on my kneecap, then looked back up at me. "It's why I enlisted."

This distracted me from my own frustrations for a minute —both his touch on my bare knee, which meant I had to remember to exhale now that he'd stopped touching me, and his admission. I cleared my throat so I wouldn't sound as breathless as I felt. "I've always wondered why you enlisted. With your degrees, why not... you know what I mean?"

"Yeah, I know."

"So you enlisted to stick it to the man, literally," I said.

He looked at me and gave me a small smile. "I did. I hated his absentee-father guts in high school but wanted to be in the Army. I always had, even though I hated what our lives were like in some ways, especially after my mom was gone. So, I enlisted, and then just to piss him off even more, I made a point to get my bachelor's and master's degrees so there was no disparity of education between us. I could have gotten a commission if I wanted, but I made a point *not* to."

"So that's the other reason for the master's. You mentioned two reasons in the intake interview. I've wondered about that." I leaned over and rested my elbows on my knees, which brought our faces close—inches apart.

His eyes flicked to my chest, then away and I realized he might have just gotten an eyeful if the V-neck of my dress was gaping. His brow wrinkled and he looked off at the horizon. "Well there you have it."

"Was he mad?"

"He was. But over the last... five years or so, we made peace. I needed it as much as he did. We weren't close, as you know," he looked at me for a moment, and then continued, "but we made peace. In the end, I know he respected what I did and respected my career. I'm good at what I do, I've been recognized for that, and that helped him recognize it."

"Hmm," I said quietly. There was so much there to comment on.

"You can follow your own path and still be a daughter your parents are proud of."

"I don't know." My voice was small again. I glanced at him and saw him watching me.

"I do," he said with certainty. Coming from him, it was an absolute. It was like my bravery was a prime number, or something elemental, when he said it that way.

I looked at him sitting next to me, his back straight in the patio chair now, looking at me with all the focus and intensity possible in a given square mile of humanity as if to impress that truth on me. I felt a few small pieces of my cracked little heart being patched back together at that thought.

"I'm not giving them very much credit, am I?" I asked.

"Probably not enough, if they're anything like their daughter."

"I don't think I've ever told them what I want. I've spent so much time trying to do what I *thought* they wanted me to do, to make them proud, and to be sure I was a daughter who carried on their legacy in some way, that I just... lost the ability to tell the truth about myself." I looked down at my knees, then pushed back so I was straight in my chair, and he wouldn't have to avoid looking in my direction. Each time he'd glanced at me since I leaned over, even once I'd placed a hand on my chest to flatten the dress to me, he'd been very deliberate about looking me in the eye. At another time, I might have felt a little thrill at how hard he seemed to be working to stay focused on me, but in that moment, I simply appreciated it.

Had I really been lying to my parents for decades? I hadn't meant to, but saying that out loud, I felt the truth of the words drop like an anchor. I felt the disappointment in myself, the sadness for the dishonesty in my relationship with two of the most important people in my life, well up and overflow. Tears slipped quietly down my face and I rested my left cheek on my hand, now propped up by the arm rest of the patio chair, so my face was toward him, then closed my eyes.

We sat there for a few moments, me with a few more tears sliding down, and him looking out at the sky. He pulled his chair so it was next to mine and we sat shoulder to shoulder. If I wasn't so sad, I wouldn't have been able to sit still.

"So what is the truth about you, Elizabeth?" His voice broke through my efforts to breathe deeply and calm my heart and mind. His question sounded simple enough, but I'd spent a lot of time rehearsing the answers.

"I want to write. I don't want to teach... at least not full time," I said, trying that on. "Honestly, I don't want to teach at all. I want to write. If I could write every day, I'd be living a dream." I closed my eyes again and let my own words settle over me. That was true. That was the truth about me.

"Tell them," he said, his voice gentle, but still sturdy. Strong.

"I don't know if I'm that brave," I whispered, the heat in my cheeks betraying me.

"You are," he responded immediately in that same gentle

voice, but his eyes were boring into me, willing me to believe him.

I looked up at him and studied his face from my seat. He was watching as I did, turned toward me as much as was comfortable, and apparently not fazed by my open assessment of him.

"Do you think it's silly? My caring so much what my parents think—at this age?"

"No. I don't think you should feel indebted to them. But I'd give anything to have my parents be a part of my life. Even my dad, which is of course messed up that I'm realizing now, months after he died." He ran a hand over his head and then held onto his neck with the same hand. "I don't think you need to apologize for caring about them or for how much you value what they think of you."

I nodded to myself, sure he was right. Whether I felt the same way or the confidence and surety of his words convinced me, I didn't know, but I knew he was right.

"But I think, if you're going to keep caring what they think, you have to let them know what *you* think, too." He shifted his chair a bit so he was facing me.

"I agree." My voice was quiet and small.

"I'm going to leave you alone now..." he trailed off and stood up. I felt a little spike of panic at him leaving and not just because I didn't want to be alone. I knew I didn't want him to leave because I liked him, and I loved talking to him and just sitting with him. He was calming, and challenging, and yes, often confusing, but I wanted him there. I let my legs slide out and stretch, and then stood up.

I grasped for something to say, but my brain was mush. I was spent on all levels, and yes, it was time for him to go, even if I didn't want him to. As I surveyed the trees, trying to think of one last thing or some way to say thank you besides those two words, I felt his hand on my shoulder.

I startled a little, and by the time I turned to face him, he was sliding that same hand to my back, and his other hand pulled me to him, and he was hugging me.

The Earth, in that moment, ceased spinning on its axis, stopped its rotation around the sun, and all sense of time and space evaporated. All that happened in the universe was Jake holding me to him, hugging me, bodily infusing me with his comfort.

My arms wrapped around his back of their own accord, not that I would have stopped them. I tucked my face into his chest like that was where it belonged and felt his chin rest on the top of my head. I breathed in deep, deeper, and then let out a shuddering, relieved breath. His body was warm and solid, and I could hear his heart beating fast in his chest under my cheek.

He pulled back from the hug and I reluctantly let my grip loosen, then looked up at him. He was still holding me with one hand on each of my shoulders. His focus was on my face now, studying me and looking for something.

He said, "You're an amazing woman." He drew me close again and his lips fell to my cheek and pressed there, then he pulled away completely.

I looked at him, my heart hammering in my ribcage and my mind scrambling for something to say, but my lips wouldn't part, wouldn't form a word, and my voice wouldn't speak. Then all I could come up with was, "I never got you a drink."

"Next time."

I nodded, feeling pleasure at his assumption we'd have a drink again—spend more time together.

"Goodnight, Elizabeth," he said, giving me one last look as

he shoved his hands in the pockets of his jeans, and off he walked.

I stood there watching him, feeling the riot of emotions crashing through me. There was so much to think about, to tease through, to understand. He was thoughtful and wise and empathetic. He was honest. He was comforting to me. He was insightful and a little maddening in the way he pushed, but it was productive pushing.

I said things to him I'd never said aloud. I still felt upset, but I felt clear about what I wanted and what I needed to say to my parents, at some point.

After hours of emotional upheaval—first in elation and celebration, and then in sadness and disappointment—I felt calm. I felt peaceful. It wasn't that he'd given me some new sense of self-worth or solved a big problem—no, it wasn't that.

It was that he held up a mirror, demanded I see my reflection aright, and then made that seem like the best and most obvious thing in the world.

He didn't shy away from asking me hard questions. He didn't wince or seem embarrassed when I cried. He didn't handle me like I was weak or frail for crying or being upset, but he didn't fail to empathize or share part of himself too.

Oh, dear.

CHAPTER TEN

On Wednesday of that week, I got an email from the grant officer for the non-profit, Operation Achieve, who'd provided the largest part of the funding for the project and who I'd submitted my application to more than a month ago. It wasn't exactly bad news, but it set off my alarm bells.

I called her immediately for clarification.

"Ms. Dunham, does this request for more information indicate an area of concern for the board?" I slowly blew out a breath and sat rigid in my chair.

"Absolutely not, Dr. Kent. We're sifting through everything now, still in the preliminary stages since we're not convening for another little while, and a few members had questions about the future of the project and the expansion you suggested. I thought I'd request more information so everyone can see what you have planned, and that way we have as much information as possible. Nothing to be concerned about." Her voice was soothing. I believed her, and it did make sense.

"I understand. Can I submit this to you by the end of the day?"

"Yes. No rush as we've got another week or so before we meet."

"Ok, thank you for your time." I hung up and got to work outlining in full detail the ways I would expand the project. I knew the results from the Fort Campbell study were fascinating, and there were more soldiers arriving every day, so I could easily expand within this post and grow the numbers. There were so many Army bases, I could easily expand the data beyond this one, and it would gain steam and attention, and maybe even help change policy or availability for higher education for active duty soldiers at a larger level. At the very least, it would get my little project more attention and hopefully lead to commanding officers encouraging soldiers to get into college courses now rather than later.

By Friday afternoon, I had written out a full, detailed proposal for the project expansion detailing how the funding would be allocated if granted and my anticipated results based on the first round I'd just completed. It was four in the afternoon and I was ready to leave. Most of the government employees got to leave at three on Fridays. I wasn't beholden to any specific office hours since I wasn't an hourly employee and my work was done, but I was having a hard time finding the will to move myself and go through the motions of getting home.

Once I shook off the lethargy and general malaise that came from sitting for an entire day even when it was gorgeous and springy outside and calling to me, I shut down my computer, gathered my purse and keys, and left. There were a few stragglers left in the building who'd lock up, including Erin, who didn't have the luxury of being a government employee and had to stay until closing. I stopped by her desk to say goodbye.

"Any big plans this weekend?" she asked, tossing her red

hair over her shoulder, beaming at me. This girl was always smiling—always. She seemed almost too sweet, except every interaction we'd had was completely genuine.

"No, not really. I'm ready to relax and... not be staring at a computer screen." I rubbed my temples for a second, willing away the headache that had crept in over the afternoon. "You?"

"Me? Oh... no. No... no plans. Just... hanging out," she said, and I noticed her pale cheeks were now a cherry red color. *Hmm.* Ok. So... she did have plans but wasn't going to tell me about them. She didn't owe me anything, and it was adorable that she showed her hand so easily.

"Well sometimes that's nice. Cheers to an uneventful weekend, then. Have a good one," I said as I gave her a wave and wandered to my car. As I tossed my purse in and took off my blazer, Jake's Jeep pulled up, and Henry hung out the driver's side window.

"Henry!" I said and walked up to the car.

"If it isn't Dr. Kent herself," he said and graced me with one of his mega-watt smiles. I ignored the little drop of disappointment in my stomach when I saw Jake wasn't with him.

"What are you doing here?"

"I'm a free bird! I graduated Tuesday, and here I am. Will drove me back with him after the ceremony and I'll fly home. I'm staying with him for a few days before I head back south and start an internship." He smiled again, clearly proud of these latest developments.

"Congratulations! I was thinking that was next week. I'm sorry I lost track of time or I would have sent you a message. And congrats on the internship."

"Thank you. Well listen, come to Jake's tonight. You don't have plans, do you?"

"Actually, I—"

"Just come. It's a little barbeque for me. Well, it's Cinco de Mayo but in my honor." He fluttered his lashes at me and then smiled *the smile* again.

"Oh, good grief. Of course I'll come. I wouldn't miss it."

"Good. Seven o'clock at Jake's. Bring yourself and a list of compliments and praises to throw at my feet upon seeing me." He winked and off he sped. I watched as he braked completely at the stop sign, then drove away. Even though he seemed wild, he was carefully obeying the signs and speed limits—clearly he was used to the strict rules of driving on a military base, just as I'd expect from a kid who grew up on military bases.

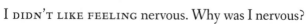

I DIDN'T LIKE FEELING nervous. Why was I nervous?

I told myself the party was a fun celebration of Henry, which it was. But I hadn't seen Jake since he comforted me after the call with my parents, and while that shouldn't make things awkward, in my mind, it did. Or it was because he'd caressed my lip in the rain and tenderly touched my hair.

Or, it was because I'd realized something.

I was a little bit maybe sort of falling for Jake Harrison. I wasn't sure to what degree because I hadn't ever had a relationship like this one. Or really, a non-relationship. Maybe friendship was a better title, sure. Whatever the case, I was hiking on an unmarked trail.

By the time I got home from work, went for a run, and got cleaned up, it was nearly seven. I put on jeans at first, but then felt like that was too casual. I couldn't tell what level of fance the occasion called for. So instead I found a ¾ sleeve striped t-shirt dress. The material was thick enough so it didn't cling to me. It was more fitted at the top but had straight lines so it hung comfortably by my hips instead of making me feel shrink-wrapped and on display. I didn't want to seem like I was trying too hard. This was a friend's dinner at his brother's house, who also happened to be my friend.

My thoughtful, intelligent, unnervingly appealing friend who, I'd discovered during our hug last weekend, smelled like clean laundry with a little twang of soap and mint, and it was also... well... appealing. And whose defined, strong arms and muscular chest happened to be, well let's be honest about it, appealing, too.

Did I mention we were just friends?

Since I'd washed my hair after my run, I left it down and curled at the bottom. I also wore a little make up. I had good skin, but a little something to smooth things out, some mascara to make my eyelashes bright behind my glasses since I couldn't face contacts after a long day at the computer, and some lip gloss, and voila. At 7:05 I walked to Jake's with my key in my pocket.

My body was racing with anticipation at seeing Jake. There was little I could do except keep walking toward his apartment, take calming breaths, and remind myself he was my friend. It felt like something had shifted, and he was more... friendly?

Ugh.

I could see a small group of people spilling off the patio and onto the grass at Jake's. I saw Henry throw his head back and laugh and then pat his friend repeatedly on the back. I caught his eye as I approached.

"So glad you could come," he said and pulled me in for a quick hug and a peck on the cheek. His cheeks were flushed and his eyes were dancing—this guy was fun in a bucket.

"So glad to be here to celebrate your amazing accomplishment. You are truly astounding, and we're all lucky to be here in your presence," I said in a robotic voice and then laughed at his delighted face. "Was that appropriate praise for you?"

"Perfect. But keep it coming. Jake stepped inside—I'm sure he could use your help," he said and then turned his attention to someone who called his name a few feet away.

I introduced myself to a few people on the way to the apartment. The sliding door was open about two feet and a screen door was shut to keep the spring bugs and gnats out. I slid open the screen, stepped in, and closed it behind me.

I could still hear the mariachi music behind me, but the atmosphere inside was totally different. The living room held a comfortable looking tan couch, a dark leather chair, a large TV, and a round, wood dining table and four chairs in the designated eating nook. His layout was exactly the same as mine, just switched around a little. I was surprised to note there wasn't a single bookshelf in the room. That was extremely disappointing because I'd thought I might get to check out his collection. No such luck.

I could see him through the kitchen doorway. He was piling up a platter, cutting board, tongs, and a few other things in one arm and held a case of Corona Extra in his other.

"Can I help you?" I asked and walked to him with arms outstretched, ready to take something from the pile in his hands.

"Hi, yeah, grab that," he said, nodding with his chin to a pitcher of what I assumed was margaritas.

I followed him back out the door and set the pitcher on the table next to the cups and the case of beer he put down. He set a bag of chips in a bowl and then carried the cutting board and tongs to the little area next to the grill. While he lifted the grill cover and pulled off a big slab of flank steak, then gave a grill basket full of vegetables a toss, I emptied the bag of chips into the bowl. He closed the grill's lid, left the tongs, and moved back to the door, then said, "Come with me," over his shoulder, and of course, I followed.

I slid the screen door shut and crossed over to stand in the doorway of the kitchen. He set the large wood cutting board down and grabbed a knife from the block next to his stove. Putting the knife down, he rinsed his hands and then turned his attention to me. He walked to me—so fast I jumped because he'd been so focused on his mission with the meat I didn't expect him to talk to me until he'd finished slicing it. But before I could step back, he wrapped his arms around me and squeezed me tight. He lowered his head so he curved around me and enveloped me, and I hugged him back. As he let go, his lips grazed my cheek lightly and my stomach fluttered as I felt his smooth cheek and jaw press against my own for a moment. He smelled like fresh laundry and smoky like the grill.

"Glad you came," he said, his lips turned up at the edges just a little.

"Me too," I said and smiled back at him.

He stood there with one hand on my upper arm, looking at me. Just as I was starting to get unnerved, he said, "Better carve this meat and get it out there." He walked back to the board and started slicing.

"How was your week?" I asked and then immediately felt awkward about it. We hadn't had much casual conversation lately—or ever. We always ended up diving right into the middle, into moments that had already started—never at the beginning.

"It was pretty good. Busy since we're prepping for NTC in a few months, but generally good," he said, glancing up at me here and there as he sliced. It felt good and normal and the clinched fist that was my insides relaxed a bit.

"Who is everyone out there? Your friends? Or Henry's?"

"Henry's. He has a few friends who drove up from Nashville and then one who's crashing on the couch tonight," he said, widening his eyes a little.

"Ah, good luck with that."

"Yeah, I'll take it," he said and then put the meat onto a large plate. He grabbed tortillas and a few small bowls and handed me several toppings and some cheese. "Ok, back out we go," he said and gestured to me with his free hand.

We set up the food and people immediately crowded around the table where the fajitas and tacos awaited them. The spread looked impressive, especially considering it was two bachelors hosting, but I supposed that was selling them short. I was learning there was very little Jake Harrison didn't do well.

He handed me a red solo cup with a margarita in it complete with a little lime garnish on the side and ushered me over to the edge of the patio just out of reach of the grill's smoke.

"I'm impressed," I said, taking a drink from the cup. Delicious.

"This is all Grandma. She bossed us around, even from Florida. She loves to entertain and always threw elaborate birthday parties for us. She was probably compensating for... everything." He gave me a quick look. "But she insisted we not throw out bags of chips and jarred salsa. Plus, Henry likes to be celebrated, as you can tell." Just then we heard Henry's loud laugh and watched as he toasted two friends with a rolled-up tortilla in one hand.

"He seems like he's always the life of the party."

"Yes. He's my opposite in that regard," he said. I saw a little flicker of something cross his face.

"How so?" I asked, even though I knew very well Henry and Jake were very different.

He looked at me and raised an eyebrow. "Well, introverts aren't usually the life of the party."

"No... no, you're not. But that's ok," I said, giving him a reassuring smile. He was joking, but I felt the need to make sure he knew I didn't mind that he was quiet. In fact, a big part of me admired it.

"Yeah. We do better one on one," he said, and then glanced down at my lips and back into my eyes.

My stomach flipped at that, and I felt my pulse race. All this guy had to do was *look* at me the wrong (*right?*) way and I was a little hurricane of excitement.

"You do seem more willing to part with your words when there's not a crowd," I said and looked at the grill, back at Henry, over to the food table—anywhere but back at him because looking at him when he was looking at me like *that* was going to lead to my bursting into flames.

We stood there a minute, and I could feel his eyes on me, his typically focused energy affecting me no less than it usually did despite my efforts to ignore it.

"Let's get some food," he said, and then placed a hand on the small of my back to guide me to the table a whopping ten feet away.

My mind focused on his hand resting on my back, warm and confident and unaware of its culpability when it came to my impending heart attack. It was a completely normal gesture, and one he'd done before, but that contact made me feel tingly and aware.

We sat and ate near each other, chatting companionably.

Yes. It was comfortable, companionable. I supposed it wasn't a stretch to say that, but I tried to silence the part of my mind that was analyzing everything he did or said. *Shut up! You are boring, Analytical Brain Ellie! Enjoy the moment!*

"So, I'll admit I'm surprised to see you don't have any

bookshelves in your living room," I said, trying to shake off the over-analysis currently raging in my inner monologue.

"Ah, yeah. They're all in my bedroom," he said, and his eyes drilled into mine for a second before they cut back to his food and he took his last bite.

"Oh... cool," I said and focused on the seam of concrete on his patio that ran between my legs. I looked at a little weed sprouting up between the slabs of white. I tried not to obsess about the fact that now I had multiple reasons for wanting to see the inside of his bedroom and how one hundred thousand million percent unacceptable that thought was.

Just then Jake got pulled away by someone asking him a question. He stood and grabbed my now-empty plate and gave me a little grin as he walked away. Could he read my mind? Did he somehow know my first thought after he said that was *Is that an invitation*? Did he know how uncharacteristic my responses were to him—is that why he enjoyed it?

I was flustered. My fingers fluttered restlessly on my thighs and my foot jumped up and down to its own beat as I again looked anywhere but at Jake, who was standing a few feet away.

"So, you and my big, strapping brother, huh?" Henry said as he plopped down into the seat next to me.

"Uhh..." I gave Henry a look.

"You and Jake," he said and shifted his eyes side to side like it was the most obvious thing in the world.

"We've become friends, yes," I said, feeling my cheeks heat.

"Obviously you're friends, which is impressive in itself considering Stone Face Harrison doesn't exactly invite people in." I chuckled at his new nickname for his brother, and he took a big bite of a chip.

"He isn't the easiest person to get to know, that's true," I agreed.

"But once you do, it's hard to get rid of him. Though I have to say, I don't think you guys are friends, now that I think about it." He shook his head slightly at me.

"Oh, really?" I felt disappointed. Henry always had insight into his brother, and I would have thought he wanted us to be friends—that Jake had even mentioned we were friends.

"Nope," he said, the *p* popping loudly between us as he gave me a devious grin. "He doesn't look at his friends like that." Henry nodded toward where Jake was standing. I looked up and caught him looking at me, and it made my stomach drop through the floor. Not just to the floor, but through it. Down through the concrete, into the dirt, through the mantle and liquid core and oozing into the iron center of the Earth. He quickly turned back to the grill where he stood.

I cleared my throat. "Like what?" I said, my voice stretched and discomfited.

"Ellie, seriously?" he asked, turning to me. He seemed frustrated and I was surprised by his response. "He's into you. He always has been, but now he's letting himself be. You have to see that." He dipped another chip into the pile of salsa on his plate and took a loud crunch.

I let his words settle in my brain before I could respond. He'd always been into me? That seemed unlikely. But the idea he was *letting* himself be didn't ring all that untrue. I'd been thinking about how things felt different, how he seemed more expressive and friendly, and after the last week or so, more physical.

"I don't know how he feels," I said, because that was true.

"Well what do *you* want?" Henry asked, giving me a hard

look like a concerned father asking his daughter about her high school prom date.

"I'm not sure that matters," I said, remembering his statement on the plane, reminding myself whatever was happening, it wasn't going to end well for someone who *did* want to be married and have kids.

Before Henry could answer, Jake returned and handed me another drink. Henry popped up out of his seat before Jake could move away. "We were wrapping up, Wills. Have your seat back." And then he was gone, off to chat with other friends.

"Did he say something to upset you?" Jake asked once he sat and leaned over into my space to look at me.

"Upset me? No. Why would you say that?" I sat back in the chair, giving myself a little distance from him.

"You seemed... serious when I looked over here. Henry's not typically one to cause that kind of reaction."

"Oh, yeah. No... he didn't upset me," I said, hoping he would let it drop.

"What did he say?" He leaned with his elbows on his knees, his body hunched over, looking at me. I felt like my bare kneecap was sizzling where it brushed against his through his jeans. I looked at his furrowed brow and how his mouth turned down, and I could tell he was genuinely concerned.

"It's nothing to worry about, Jake. Henry's adorable," I said, and as I did, I put my hand on his forearm (side note: he had really attractive forearms), and then stood up to get some space and more effectively avoid his questioning.

He hopped up too and grabbed my hand, pulling me into his house and sliding the screen door shut. He pulled me through the living room, but instead of going to the kitchen, he stepped to the left, around the corner, and out of sight if someone walked into the living room.

"Elizabeth, what did he say?"

I pulled my hand from his, feeling frustrated by his demanding tone and even him pulling me into the house and also a little witless from the feeling of his rough palm against mine.

"Listen, nothing. Seriously. You know Henry is harmless and you don't need to worry, ok?" I heard the edge in my voice and felt grateful I had the wherewithal to sound anything but breathy and overwhelmed by being alone in a darkened hallway with him. His dark blue button-down shirt was rolled up at the sleeves to just below the elbow. The shirt fit him the way it should, fitted, but not pulling across the chest, around the biceps, over the shoulders.

He looked good, and there was no way to avoid it.

"Tell me," he demanded, his voice still low. He crossed his arms and stood a little closer. I'd seen this look on him—it was one of determination I'd seen at least once when we'd argued. It was adorable that he thought this stance was going to intimidate me because if I was anything, I was stubborn. If anything, his insistence only made me want to *not* tell him even more.

"Ask Henry."

"No."

"Yes."

"No," he said, a little louder, a little more insistent.

"Seriously Jake. Let it go," I said and crossed my own arms. I was not about to tell this man his brother thought he had a thing for me.

Nope.

Not happening.

Not now. Not ever.

Jake took in my crossed arms and my pursed lips. He

stretched out an arm and leaned against the wall behind me with his hand to the left of my head. He ducked his face until it was right in front of mine. If I hadn't been growing more frustrated by the second, I might have kissed him.

"Tell me," he said, his voice a low, demanding growl.

"I think you're confused," I said, not moving, not looking away from his fiery eyes.

"About?" he asked, his head still dipped, his eyes still pouring into mine.

"I'm not one of your soldiers. I don't follow your orders," I said and brought my hands up in front of me like I might push him away but just held them there between us, not touching him.

His eyes flared, then looked back and forth between mine.

"I know that," he said, his eyes searching mine. Then the hand he wasn't leaning on reached out and curled around my neck, his thumb resting by my ear. His hand felt like a brand on my neck, his fingers flames in my hair. He kept his eyes on mine as he moved closer, an inch or two at this point, and he kissed me.

CHAPTER ELEVEN

I KEPT my eyes on his for a second before they had to close, savoring the sensation of his soft lips pressing against mine. My hands rested against his chest, and he pulled me closer, deepening the kiss as the hand he'd been leaning against the wall now curved against the small of my back.

He pulled back too quickly, like he was shocked he'd kissed me in the first place once he realized he'd done it, but he didn't let go. His eyes were hazy as he looked at me, looked down at my lips and back up. He shook his head a little, maybe admonishing himself or maybe something else, I didn't know because then he kissed me again, and this time, more adamantly.

His hand fisted in my hair and the hand on my back pulled me tight against him. My hands ran up and over his shoulders and into the short, soft hair at the base of his neck. My heart was pounding as our lips met, and I felt dizzy and disoriented when he pulled back again a moment later.

I blinked a few times to clear my mind and shakily adjusted my glasses at either side of my head. They hadn't gotten in the way, but I also felt acutely that the kissing was over too soon and needed something to do with myself. He stepped back, to the other side of the hallway, and then turned to walk into the kitchen. Before I could feel too bewildered, Austin, one of Henry's friends, came around the corner.

I had absolutely not heard him come in the house. I wasn't aware of anything other than fleeting half-thoughts while Jake kissed me.

"Bathroom this way?" he asked and pointed down the hall.

"Yep," I said and moved down the hall toward the kitchen. If Austin noticed my swollen lips and dazed look, he didn't show it.

Jake's back was to me where he stood at the sink washing dishes.

"You kissed me," I said, resting a hip against the cabinets just inside the doorway, my voice sounding accusatory.

"I did," he said, not turning toward me. "And you kissed me back," he shot over his shoulder, still not looking at me. He set a pan in the drying rack and then faced me where I was leaning back against the counter behind me.

"That I did," I said with a little smile, feeling flustered and a little wild. I ran a hand through my hair and smoothed my dress at my hips.

He nodded, his eyes not leaving mine.

"Henry suggested you're interested in me," I said, finally, after silence had filled the room. I might as well go for it since he *had* just kissed me. Even if it was purely physical attraction, there was now documented interest.

He stepped forward but slowed when we heard the bathroom door open down the hall. Austin sauntered back through, stopping by the kitchen. "You guys need any help?"

"Nope. We're good," I said, my smile far too large.

"Cool. See ya'll out there," he said, and then he was gone.

Jake stayed where he was, his perfect posture and solid frame making him look large in the small kitchen. I swallowed down a wave of nervousness and the very real desire to crush myself against him and kiss him again like a crazed, hormone-fueled maniac.

But really, please refer to moments ago in the hallway and you'll see this impulse was justified.

"Do you think Henry's right?" he asked, taking a small step closer. I gripped the counter behind me with my hands, watching him move. I imagined he could see my pulse pounding in my neck.

"Do I think you're..."

"Do you think he's right? I'm interested in you?" His voice was husky and male, and I would have let out an embarrassing groan just listening to him if I hadn't bit my lip to silence myself.

I tightened my grip on the counter, watching him take another step toward me. "Yes?"

"You're not sure," he said it with surety, that confidence that permeated everything he did. He seemed frustrated, too. Determined, as always. He took one more step and crowded me, hands on either side of me, resting on the counter next to my own.

The ability to form words was lost. Really, it was gone a few minutes back, but in this moment, it was absolutely gone. I felt my shoulders rising and falling, felt my lungs filling up and emptying in short little puffs and knew this was what prey must feel like. I could feel the heat of his body, inches from mine, and smell the grill's smoke on his clothes.

"You're not sure if I'm interested, Elizabeth? Is that what you're saying?" His voice was low and rough and he spoke into my ear, his breath and lips grazing the sensitive skin and cartilage there, my scalp tightening with the small hairs standing on end at my neck.

I nodded my head slowly and swallowed. He brought one hand to my neck, his palm splayed over my throat and the heel of his hand rested at my collar bone. He let two fingers rest where my pulse hammered in my artery, and I saw his mouth tilt up on one side.

The look he gave me then was one I would think about for... a while to come. His brown eyes looked deeper, darker. In the back of my mind I heard the sliding door slip open, that flush of little bristles on the metal track at the ground, and I cursed the person coming in for interrupting.

I knew Jake heard it too because his eyes flickered up, then right back to me, and then he leaned down and pressed a searing, quick kiss to my lips. He pulled back, just barely, and his eyes were still pools of dark coffee swirling in front of me.

"He's very right," he said, only loud enough for me to hear, and then stepped away as Julia, one of Henry's Nashville friends, popped in to grab another trash bag.

"We're cleaning up a bit. We've got to get on the road soon," she said, and as she took a bag from Jake, I slipped out of the kitchen, through the living room, and burst out the door, ready for fresh air.

I grabbed a bottle of water from the drink table as I walked past the small groups of people still chatting and stood at the edge of the patio where darkness swamped the little party. It'd gotten dark since I'd gone inside. I stood with my back to the patio, looking out at the clear, dark sky and the tiny stars visible over the lights of this little suburbia. I felt my pulse still beating wildly, and my hands shook a little as I took a drink of water.

"I told you." His voice startled me, and I turned back

toward the party to see Henry standing there with a smug look on his face. "I was right, wasn't I?"

"Seems like it," I said and took another swig of water.

"I'm always right about Prince William," he said, then winked at me and walked back to a small group getting ready to leave.

Jake stepped outside and walked straight to me. This man had a way of making me feel like he was locked in on me and I was his target. He zeroed in and there was no escaping. I'd end up with a heart disorder from the consistent sprint-like cardio I was getting just from being near him.

"Are you heading home?" he asked and was looking at my face, but I let my eyes wander around the scene of people. A few lingered by the food table crunching on the last vestiges of chips and salsa. Others were talking and hugging Henry goodbye.

"Yeah, I thought it might be time," I said, glancing at him, and then giving Henry a wave. He wandered over.

"Thanks for coming, Ellie. So good to see you." He hugged me. "I'll see you before I leave, right?" Jake stood to my right.

"Of course," I said and patted his shoulder.

"I'll walk you back," Jake said and brought his hand to my waist.

He slid his hand on my mid-back, ran it over my hair, and then let it come to rest on my hip opposite him. We were now shoulder to shoulder and hip to hip. It was a surprisingly possessive touch, and I swallowed hard.

As we plodded along nearly step for step with each other, my stride stretching to match his, the mariachi music faded and the only sounds I could hear were our feet brushing in the grass.

"I'm glad you came tonight," he said, and I felt, more than saw, him looking at me.

"I am too," I said, and then we came in view of my patio and he slowed our pace, letting go of me. "Well, thanks for walking me—"

"Have dinner with me tomorrow?" It was technically a question, but it felt more like an inevitability after the night we'd had. The way he phrased it, with that barest hint of a turn up to intone his question, was more like a statement. Apparently, Jake was bossy in all realms of his life. Go figure.

"Are you asking me? Sort of feels like you're telling me, Sergeant." I grinned at him and watched a smile flit across his face shadowed under my dim patio light.

"I wouldn't dare, Doctor. It's a request. If you need it in writing, I'm happy to comply." His low voice and his flirting and his general presence in front of me, spaced close enough to keep my heart racing even though he wasn't touching me, would be the death of me.

"I'm not sure that's necessary," I said, charmed.

"Good. Then I'll see you tomorrow. Six?"

"See you then," I said, unlocking my patio door.

"Goodnight, Elizabeth," he said and watched as I slid the door open and went inside. I closed the door, and he still stood there, watching. I made an exaggerated gesture to show him I was locking the door, and he gave me a little nod and was gone.

WHILE CHANGING into pajamas and washing my face, I didn't let myself think through what had happened. I texted Alex, of course, to tell her Jake kissed me. About two minutes after I sent the text, my phone rang.

"Yes?"

"I knew it. I told you! How was it?" Her voice was ecstatic, and I could hear she was bouncing around, wherever she was, and smiling wildly.

"Yes, you did tell me. And it was... intense," I said, still trying to figure out the right word.

"Intense? Like... intense good, right?"

"Yes. I think so," I said truthfully.

"Wow, so this was not like an automatically good thing for you? I thought you'd be excited. Plus, this wasn't totally out of nowhere, right? You guys see each other all the time?"

"You're right. We see each other pretty regularly, and he has been friendly and a little affectionate the last few times I've seen him, which is certainly different from the first few months I knew him. I just..." I had no idea how to verbalize what I was feeling.

"Wait, do you not like him?" Alex sounded shocked. She knew me well, and knew I was interested in Jake, or at the very least attracted to him from essentially the first encounter, at least everything after the plane.

Well, and the one *after* I accused him of being a violent barbarian.

"I think that's the problem. I do like him. A lot. Like... a lot, a lot."

"Why is this a problem? He kissed you!"

"I know, but... I happen to know he doesn't want anything long term. He asked me to go to dinner tomorrow, but that could be another family dinner with his brother. I don't know."

"How do you know he's not interested in long term?"

"I've heard him say two very specific things. One, marriage and kids are quote 'not in the cards' for him, and two, he doesn't date. Knowing those things, wouldn't I be one of those women who assumes her upfront love interest will change because of her and then is brutally surprised when, in fact, that same man has been totally honest about who he is and what he wants?"

"He said those things *to you*?"

"No, we've never talked about that kind of stuff. He said the first thing to me, about marriage, but that was on the plane, before we knew each other. I don't know..." I sighed and climbed into bed. I'd finally told her weeks ago about meeting him on the plane. She'd claimed his ability to endure me during a flight meant we were destined to be together, and then we'd laughed about it. This was before I'd developed feelings for him, and long before he'd ever expressed any interest in me beyond professional collaboration.

"I think you need to address that, and soon. I know you're not interested in dating someone if you know they wouldn't consider marriage—"

"Definitely not."

"But you two are friends, and he's obviously attracted to your sexy, brainy self, so... see what happens. Give it a date or two. Who knows, maybe you guys will be totally awkward tomorrow, or maybe he'll bring Henry along and declare he's been trying to set you two up all along," she teased.

"I get it. I'll see how it goes. But I don't think I can hang in there too long because..."

"Because you really like this guy," she finished for me. I could picture her sweet, sympathetic face.

"Yes. I don't think I've ever liked someone like this," I said in a low, almost defeated voice. "I think it was easier when it was clearly not an option."

"Really liking someone is not a bad thing, Ellie. And better yet, it could be a good thing." Her soothing voice and general confidence buoyed me. "But listen, I need to know—is he a decent kisser? Your concerns for the overall situation overshadowed that key element of this conversation. He's a pretty restrained guy—not real warm and cuddly. It's hard to imagine. Because if he's no good at kissing you may want to—"

"The man can kiss. Fear not. He is definitely passionate, even if you don't see that at first glance. Add this to the tally of things at which Jake Harrison is an expert." I thought of his intensity, his heat, and his determination—the look in his eyes made me feel like I was falling back, my feet planted, waiting for someone to catch me.

AFTER SOME LAZY WRITING, a long run, and then a fairly meticulous clean-up process (because even glasses don't hide the subtlest of unibrows), I stood ready for Jake at 5:55pm the next day. I had no idea what he'd plan, but I guessed it would be something simple. Or I hoped. I opted for black skinny jeans and a white silky tank top with a light gray short-sleeved cardigan over it. I wore bright red flats, both because I could walk or run in them, if need be, and because I couldn't imagine needing heels for whatever he had planned. My hair was down and wavy, and I had a little make up on behind my glasses.

I heard my doorbell a moment later, and somehow hearing the doorbell, instead of a knock at my back door, sent a new rush of nervousness through me. His choice to use the front door made this seem more official. I took a deep breath to calm my nerves. I shook my head, letting my face loosen up, and rolled my neck like I was about to take on a great physical task.

I opened the door and inhaled sharply when I saw Jake standing there.

We've established I'm not the physically-focused type, but this man always made me sit up and take notice. I'd become frustrated by my inability to ignore how physically appealing he was—he was the lightbulb to my mosquito.

Tonight he wore nice jeans, a dark green button-down shirt with the sleeves rolled to just below the elbows like he had the night before, and he had his short hair styled so it looked a little tousled. Or maybe it was tousled, just out of the shower. He had been looking at his phone while he waited (while I was doing my warm-up routine on the other side of the door) so he looked up at me, smiled, and put his phone in his back pocket.

"Hello," I said, my voice surprisingly low and quiet, a reflection of my nerves.

He stepped forward and reached for me, even as his eyes swept over me, and kissed my cheek, lingering there a moment before he backed away. I could tell my chest and neck were splotchy from the full-body blush his perusal created.

"You're beautiful, Elizabeth," he said and slid one hand down my arm to take my hand in his. I felt a flurry of butter-flies as he laced his fingers between mine. "Ready?"

"Yes."

Without another word, we walked to his car. He'd held my hand briefly the night before, but I'd been frustrated enough it hadn't sent the little zings and zaps through my body like the contact did now. He opened the door for me, and I climbed into his immaculate Jeep. It was free of any of the usual clutter—no crumpled receipts or gum wrappers or empty water bottles like my passenger floor board typically held.

"You keep your car very clean," I said, though even as I said it, I realized how that lined up with what I knew of him. He was exacting in most things.

"I do. Clutter makes me feel out of control," he admitted.

"That's not something people normally admit," I said before I realized how it might sound.

"Maybe not, but you already know all of my secrets anyway. What's one more truth?" He seemed relaxed, which was good, because I did not feel at all relaxed. After my conversation with Alex the night before, it took hours before I felt even remotely tired enough to sleep. I was exhausted from the day itself, and from the emotional energy it had taken to be around strangers at the party, and then him when he was acting so differently around me. I was sapped, and yet my mind would. Not. Shut. Up.

"When I first moved here I thought this was all there was to it—tactical gear shops, payday loan places, and the occasional strip club." I looked out the window as we drove along 41A, the older main drag of town.

"Don't forget fast food chains and pawn shops," he added.

"Ah yes, the essentials. What more could one need?"

"It's pathetic, but that's the kind of sprawl you'll find outside any bigger Army post. It's an unfortunately accurate stereotype to expect soldiers, especially younger ones, to frequent those places. They do, and they very often get in over their heads. But a little farther out, you can find some gems."

"That makes sense. Alex told me about how cute the historic downtown here was, so I knew there was more to it. There are gross, rundown neighborhoods in Manhattan too—there's just more to offset them."

I thought about some of the grungier neighborhoods I'd wandered through over my years in the city. I remembered walking by an apartment building that was probably abandoned, although more upsetting, maybe it wasn't. Spray paint littered the walls in layers, bricks were crumbling at the foundation, and the whole thing looked bereft. It was missing any sign of life or upkeep, and it made me immeasurably sad for the rest of the day.

"It is a nice little town," he said and pulled into a parking spot. "I'm taking you to one of the four non-chain restaurants that serves normal food for dinner. I hope that's ok." He shut the door then walked around to open my door just as I was already getting out.

"I was hoping for the chance to sit down in a sticky booth at Wendy's or eat in your very clean car at Sonic and smear mustard all over your dashboard, but... this'll do."

"Next time I'll write up a proposed plan of action and you can approve or deny it before we ever leave the house," he said and took my hand. My belly flipped, and I couldn't stop the smile from taking over my face.

"Already planning on next time, huh? That seems confident." I squeezed his hand.

"Yes, I am," he said and kept walking down the sidewalk. I wondered whether he meant he was planning on next time, or that he was confident. Either way, I liked it.

But then, I felt a tug of doubt. If he was planning to go out with me again, here before we'd even started our date, that meant we'd be *dating*. I decided I'd ask him about it, especially since the whole nervous, *does he like me or doesn't he* thing was getting old.

This was one reason I didn't make time for dating. I liked surety. I liked being able to quantify things and know I could understand them. I *hated* feeling ignorant. I liked to hash things out, and then move on, knowing I'd covered my bases. But dating and relationships were rarely like that. With both of my former boyfriends I often felt like my life would be simpler without them. I'd never had the feeling I couldn't live without someone. I'd never been invested enough to want to try to make something work beyond a certain point, and that point was not too far down the road of either of those relationships.

Granted, both of my relationships were when I was much younger—one in high school and one the end of my sophomore and the beginning of my junior year of college. After that, I felt jerked around, tired of the lack of communication and ability to say what I was feeling, and so I just... didn't date.

Well, that wasn't true. I did date. I'd gone on six or eight dates, mostly blind dates with friends of friends, and two with fellow professors. These were all bad enough to guarantee no second date.

The hostess showed us to our table which was in the corner of a surprisingly cool room with exposed brick and big chandeliers. It was hard not to compare it to the unique eateries and restaurants that popped up (and often disappeared within the year) everywhere in New York, but this place had charm.

The waiter brought us water and we ordered drinks. I looked over the menu and then folded it back in front of me, only to find Jake watching me.

"What'd you decide?" I asked.

"Prime rib for me."

"Ah, nice. I think I'm going to try the salmon, even if we are in a land-locked state."

"Daring. Though this place is pretty reliable—or so I hear," he said and leaned his elbows on the table.

"Can I ask you kind of a blunt question?" I asked, forcing my nerves and the awkward feeling welling up in me back down. I put my elbows on the table too and leaned forward a bit.

"Do you ask any other kinds of questions? You're one of

the most straightforward people I've ever met," he said, the corner of his mouth curving up.

"Likewise," I said. He was straightforward, and he struck me as pretty black and white. Literal. Sure.

He nodded, and so, there I went.

I willed my cheeks not to blush. I wasn't fishing here but had to know. "Why did you ask me out?"

CHAPTER TWELVE

He looked at me with a perplexed expression. "I thought that was obvious."

"Last night you said you're interested in me—got it. But I have to admit I've heard you say you don't date. And unless I'm missing something, *this is a date*." I looked at him, waiting for him to clarify. His face was expressionless for a moment as he looked at me, not giving me any sense of what he was thinking.

"I don't date," he said.

I blinked a few times, feeling exasperated by his response. "Ok..."

"I should amend that to say I have, historically, not dated."

Good grief, this man should play poker. Nary a hint of what he was thinking showed on his face.

"Ok." I wasn't going to put words in his mouth, and I wanted him to explain.

"But yes, this is a date," he said and then looked up to the waiter who set down our drinks. We ordered, then Jake looked back at me.

"You were saying historically, you haven't dated, but this

is, despite it being uncharacteristic and against your general policy, a date," I reminded him.

"Yes. True."

This man was maybe more stubborn than I was.

"So... explain."

"I like you," he said, his intent focus on me not breaking.

I huffed a little breath in both unexpected pleasure at his words and frustration. "I'm glad for that. But I can't imagine I'm the only woman you've ever liked."

"No, you're not. That's true," he said, and even though I hated to admit it, I felt a little drop of disappointment. "But you're different."

The combination of hearing him acknowledge he'd liked other women—*how dare he*—and his calling me different, and what a mysteriously ambiguous statement that was, made the apples of my cheeks brighten. I was thankful for the low lights.

He took a sip of his drink, and I took one of mine. I felt no clarity based on his comments—none. I thought about pretending he'd answered my question, but he hadn't. He hadn't clarified anything.

"Ok, that doesn't clear things up for me, sorry."

"What are you worried about, Elizabeth?" he asked, and I felt myself flush with embarrassment almost immediately.

"Ok... ok. I'll just say it. On the plane..." I raised an eyebrow at him, and he smiled broadly at me, and my belly cartwheeled out the front door.

"Ah, yes. The plane. I was wondering how long it would take us to acknowledge the plane," he said, smiling like I'd never seen.

"Yes, the plane, where we first met, and you got a small glimpse into the utter insanity flying on an airplane creates in me." I smiled back at him. I'd been wondering the same thing since the day I realized who he was.

"Once I realized you weren't going to pass out or throw up, it wasn't so bad," he said, now smiling full-on again. If I'd known talking about the plane would make him smile all along, I would have done it much sooner. I had studiously avoided it both for fear he didn't realize it was me and because he was returning from his father's funeral at the time, and I knew that was a painful, confusing time for him.

"Good. I'm glad. I don't even feel bad about it, except that I grabbed your hand and didn't realize it. That was some truly terrifying turbulence."

"My hand was happy to be of service, and I agree—it was pretty bad."

"Anyway, at one point you said 'marriage and kids aren't in the cards,' or something," I said, ready to get to the point.

"I vaguely recall something like that," he said, his eyes narrowing just a bit.

"Listen, I'm not trying to propose to you or anything even remotely close. But I have to tell you I have no interest in dating someone who's decided he doesn't want to get married or have kids. I do want those things, and I don't want to waste time with someone who doesn't. The night after the memorial, you said something similar. I don't want to know a relationship is over before it even starts," I said, feeling a rush of adrenaline shoot through me as I realized I'd been *very* honest with him. I'd meant to be, but now, whatever came next... well, that'd be it.

I took a drink of water, my wrist shaking as the adrenaline dispersed through my body the way it did whenever I did something remotely daring, and watched him over the brim. He looked down at his hand resting on the table, his fingers on either side of the stem of his water glass, and I could see his eyes were crinkled.

"I am interested in those things, Elizabeth." His eyes lifted to meet mine as he said my name. His voice was smooth like an all-day hipster cold-brew coffee over ice, and those unexpected words floored me.

"Oh." I wanted to prompt him to say more but didn't know where to begin. Then, he saved me from my madness, my mind's frantic efforts to grasp onto a cogent thought, and spoke again.

"I always thought I'd be out of the Army before I dealt with any of that. That's always been the plan. I don't date because I've always known I don't want to get involved and have to do the long distance and deployments and all that. And I don't want to do what my dad did to my mom..." His voice was calm, his posture unaffected, but I could see a change in his face, a faint, shadowed look that wasn't there before.

"I can understand why you'd want to plan things out that way," I said, my heart clenching in my chest at the thought of his loss and the way he'd been deliberate with every aspect of his life since he lost his mother.

"I figured *if* I got married in the future, the right person would come along after I retire and that'd be that. Then I wouldn't have to mess with any of the other crap that comes with Army life and the pressures it puts on a marriage. So far there hasn't been anyone who has made that plan difficult to follow."

I waited, not letting the eighty-five follow up questions show on my face. He was telling me what I wanted to know.

"Until you. Obviously." He gave me a chagrined look, and I melted like butter in a hot pan.

I'm sure I had a look of severe confusion on my face.

That's what we'll call it. Not wanton desire. No, not that.

I looked down at my water and counted the melting ice cubes to avoid his attention.

"Ask me. Don't get shy now," he prodded.

"I just... it seems unlikely that after what—when do you retire?"

"Three years, give or take."

"After more than, like, at least fifteen years of knowing how you felt about this, you'd suddenly change. It doesn't make sense to me."

He watched me as I swirled the shrinking ice in my glass and then took a drink. I wasn't sure what I felt, but I knew I didn't believe what he was telling me. Not that I had any reason to doubt him, but it was illogical and unlikely on all levels.

"I'm not an idiot, Elizabeth." His face was serious, but it felt like a joke.

"No. That you are definitely not." He was looking at me, locked onto me. He must have seen I didn't understand what he meant. His lips pursed together just barely, and he leaned back from the table a bit.

He looked like he was formulating a thought, but before either of us could say anything, the waiter arrived with our food. He set the plates down, rotating them just so, so they'd be facing the right way according to the chef's preference. It wasn't a fancy restaurant, but our waiter obviously took pride in his job.

"Anything else I can get you two?"

"No, we're good," Jake said and the waiter disappeared.

Our forks and knives clinked against our plates as we dug into our food. I figured we both needed a minute to absorb what he'd said. Was he saying I had somehow changed his mind about *all* of those things? I wasn't a shrinking flower who had no self-esteem—this wasn't a scenario where I thought I didn't have worth so there was no way I could deeply affect someone. But truly, I didn't see how I could have changed his mind on something like this. And *his* mind, particularly.

"This is surprisingly good. Thanks for bringing me," I said, looking up at him over the candle flickering between us. They'd lowered the lights even more since we'd arrived and it felt more intimate, like we were the only ones in our little dinner table world. The energy between us had shifted, that charged field of magnetism and frustration pushed away by the waiter.

"Good. Mine's good too." He took a bite, and once he swallowed, he asked, "What's the latest on your book?"

"Hoping to hear from the agent on my edits this week. I don't know when, but she said, 'within the next few weeks' in the email, so I feel like any time now. I'm kind of trying not to think about it, even though that is virtually impossible."

"What happens when you hear from them?"

"I don't totally know. It depends on what they say. She lays out her contract for representing me and probably gives me a bunch more notes and things she wants me to edit, from what I've heard." I felt a little rush of excitement just thinking about what the next few weeks might bring in that regard. I'd done a decent job not obsessing about hearing from her, remembering she'd sent me the very enthusiastic email.

"What about the project on post?" he asked and speared a few pieces of asparagus.

"Still going. My current project wraps in two months, but I've applied for an expansion of the project to gather more data from other military bases."

"And if that happens, would you move to another base?" He dropped his eyes to his plate after he asked the question.

"No, definitely not. I like the area. It feels a little bit like where I grew up in Kansas—smaller town but easy access to Nashville for some of the cultural elements you don't get in a smaller community. I'd commute to the other posts, maybe spend a few days depending on how far I'm going, but ultimately be here. Eventually I'd like to write full time, which I could do anywhere, but it'll take time before I'm at that level, so the project helps me do something meaningful I care about and also helps pay rent and for all of those other practical things like groceries." I rolled my eyes to show how pesky I found those things, the things that cost money. He grinned at me.

"I didn't know you grew up in Kansas. I lived there for about a year when I was eight. Don't remember much about it though," he said.

"I'm guessing at an Army base?"

"Yeah. Fort Leavenworth."

"That's not too far from where I was. Farther southwest from Leavenworth but still about an hour from Kansas City," I explained. I remembered then he'd already mentioned living in two other states. "You guys moved a ton when you were growing up."

"We did. We'd get three years in a row some places, but most often it was one or two. It wasn't bad, and having my grandma with us for much of that time made a huge difference. It was also easier once Henry was bigger. He became my little sidekick, and we've been inseparable ever since, at least as much as we can be in adulthood and with me in the Army."

"You're a good brother," I said, my voice earnest and admiring. Even though I was an only child, I could see it. He was thoughtful and engaged in his family's lives even when he wasn't right next to them. It took a kind of devotion that made me feel a little fluttery and restless. It drew me to him even more.

"Henry's a good little brother. He makes it easy," he said. I wasn't surprised he deflected because he simply wasn't someone to take credit for something that wasn't his own. He was plenty confident, but the fact he refused to gather up shared accolades was one more thing. One more thing to signal to me I was in trouble with this guy.

"He's great," I said while my mind swirled with how much I liked the man sitting across from me, eying me now.

"My turn to ask a question—a blunt one—if you'll let me," he said, one eyebrow arched at me.

"Ok."

"What makes you unsure about me?" he asked, then took a bite and chewed, waiting for my reply.

"I'm not sure I know what you mean," I deflected. I was fairly sure I knew where he was going, but clarification never hurt.

"You're a confident woman. You seem to know what you want from your life. It's surprising you aren't the same way in your dating life."

"How do you know I'm not?" I asked, already feeling a mild panic rising at the thought of explaining what I wanted in a mate. That wasn't exactly the stuff of a first date. Though, to be fair, it didn't feel like a first date.

"Are you?" His attention was fully on me now, his utensils resting on the sides of his plate.

"I haven't had much of a dating life for the last few years. It wasn't a priority for me," I said.

"I can understand that."

"Yeah, I guess you can," I said and smiled at him.

The last date I'd gone on in New York was with another professor from the history department. He was cute, already tenure-tracked, and had started dating once he clinched assistant professor. He asked me about my dating history, and when I explained I hadn't had one since undergrad, he was baffled. He couldn't understand how "a woman like me" could not be dating. But what it translated to was that he couldn't understand how a *woman* wasn't more interested in nailing down a husband. Never mind the fact that he was several years older and had only recently decided to date with any kind of purpose.

I'd left the date infuriated. I was nice enough when I left, but I made it clear we weren't a match. He could not understand why I wasn't dating seriously or engaged or married. It blew his mind that a woman—yep, uterus and all—wouldn't have tied the knot the day I got my PhD, if not sooner. It wasn't so bad that he insinuated I shouldn't be working, no it wasn't that obvious. But he was genuinely trying to uncover the mystery of my singleness, like I had a bad secret hidden away instead of just no desire to deal with fools when I could be writing or spending time with friends I already liked, or sleeping.

I didn't have much time to date then, and when I did, I didn't have anyone interesting enough to bother with. That may sound calloused, and it was a little ironic considering my deep devotion to the idea of true love, but in the end, I always thought I'd feel compelled by my person, whoever he was.

I nudged a few green beans around my plate and looked up to find him watching me, waiting for more information. Who knew how long I'd gotten lost in my thoughts.

"I haven't been interested enough, I guess. It's not that I don't think I have something to offer, or I'm not worth the effort, or whatever other nonsense women supposedly get tangled up in. It's that I hate small talk, I hate the get to know you phase. I kind of hate the beginning, especially if I'm not *really* interested. That has resulted in what is probably a lot less dating and relationship know-how compared to other women my age, but I'm ok with that."

This very clearly indicated I *was* interested enough in him, but that was obvious based on the way I'd responded to him the night before.

"So then, why are you here with me?"

Ah, damn. He went for it. He could see my response and he looked pleased with himself.

"Why do you think, Jake?" I wasn't going to make it easy on him. Come on now.

"I think you're curious. Maybe you just wanted to get a free dinner. Who knows."

"Yep. You caught me. Couldn't resist being bossed around and getting a free dinner out of it."

After that, we kept talking, and talking, and talking. He asked me about my favorite books, and I asked about his. As predicted, many of his were military history, but he had a healthy relationship with fantasy and knew Tolkien better than I did. He of course liked Margaret Atwood and was very widely read on new releases.

Was there anything more attractive than a well-read man?

"This may be a strange question, but why don't you have bookshelves in your living room? Why in the bedroom?" I slid my fork through the cheesecake in front of me. It was good. Really good.

"Years ago I lived in a studio when I didn't have to live in the barracks, and I had a bookshelf right next to my bed. Everything was cramped together in that little piece of crap place outside of Fort Bragg. When I moved to a one bedroom, I put the bookshelf next to the bed again. After that, it became a habit and felt weird to have them anywhere else."

"Curious," I said and tilted my head to the side. "It's like you're hoarding all this information. It's killing me."

"Hoarding it? What information do you need? If it's killing you I'd like to help you." One side of his mouth quirked up, and he made a fakely concerned face.

"What a person has on his bookshelf is telling. What kind of books do you *own*. And are there are lot, or a precious few? And of your favorites, do you have more than one version. These are all pieces to the puzzle that is Jake Harrison. As a book nerd and a writer, these are burning questions for me."

"You've thought about this a lot," he said, amusement growing on his face.

"Maybe."

"Well, you can visit my bookshelves sometime soon and answer those questions for yourself." His face was serious and my heart galloped when I looked back at him. His focus was squarely on me, and I steadied myself so I didn't swallow my own tongue right along with the bite of cheesecake I'd just taken. I coughed a little but managed not to go into a fit.

This was dumb. I was having a conniption over him saying I could look at his bookshelves.

Simmer.

"Ok," I said quietly.

I admitted to my deep love of romantic comedies, and he admitted he hadn't seen many. I wasn't surprised considering the general lack of women in his life. His favorite movies were all the top military history classics: *Saving Private Ryan, Black Hawk Down,* and a few I didn't recognize. When he promised to watch one of my favorites if I'd watch one of his, my insides flipped for the twentieth time that night at the thought of more time with him.

He paid for dinner and we wandered back to his car slowly, down the historic downtown street, and he held my hand the whole time. My heart raced at the contact, even though we'd spent the entire night talking and laughing and truly enjoying each other.

We were back at my house before I knew what was happening. He ushered me to the door and I swallowed my nerves, determined not to shrivel up with anxiety at *this* point in a great night.

"Thanks for dinner," I said, and I, despite all my mental bravado, felt shy. I fiddled with my keys and held them in one hand.

"Thanks for going with me." He stepped close, then slid closer. He was absolutely unbearably handsome this close. His strong jaw left shadows under his chin. His dark eyes were darker here in the dim light of my porch lamp, but I could still see a little bit of the warm brown color that was so lovely in the daylight.

"Sure, anytime," I said, like I'd done him some kind of favor. I inwardly rolled my eyes as my hands fiddled with my keys, and I tried to feel out the moment when I should disappear behind my door.

"Tomorrow?" he asked. My head jerked up.

"You want to—"

"I want to watch a movie with you tomorrow. Your place or mine. Either way," he said, shifting closer still.

I was beginning to think he liked crowding me. He was standing close, we were nearly chest to chest, and at five foot six, my head was tilted back in order to see his face. He had a devilish little smirk, the same glint in his eye I'd seen on Henry's face more than once. They certainly were related, even though I'd rarely seen anything like this from Jake. I liked playful Jake, even if he did make my pulse pound so loud I could hardly think.

"Ok." I maintained focus on the fact he'd asked me to

spend more time with him the next day. I was honestly more concerned with the moment at hand, trying not to throw myself at him. Yes, he'd kissed me the day before, but that was all him. *All* him. And while I was certainly a woman who could be assertive and take what she wanted, my guts weren't up to the task just now.

"Let's do your place," he said, his voice low with that gravelly texture that made my restraint wave its white flag.

"Ok," I said, still looking him in the eye, my neck still strained up to see his face. I angled my chin just a bit, and our lips were breaths apart.

"Ok." His voice was velvet.

"So, I'll see you tomorrow, then," I said, waiting for him to close the distance of the last few inches between us.

"Yes, you will," he said, his face inches from mine, a little smile still playing on his lips.

"Ok, well, good night then." My voice was weak with desire, and I didn't move.

He shifted, closed the gap between us, but settled his kiss at the corner of my mouth, mostly on my cheek. I let out a deep breath as he said, "Goodnight, Elizabeth."

He took one step back and once I put the key in the door, he turned and was out on the path before I closed it.

Once inside, I let out a long, frustrated breath. I felt a twinge of annoyance with myself. Yes, this man was extremely attractive, and he was imposing in the best way. I liked that he got in my space. Why hadn't I just kissed him?

Being around him reminded me of the time I'd gone swimming in the Atlantic Ocean. It was mid-July and my parents and I had traveled by car—like we did for all of our travels—from Kansas, stopping every few states to see national parks and other highlights on the way. We ended up in a little town called Ogunquit on the coast of Maine. I felt the chilly water on my toes and waded in as far as my knees. I waited until my feet were numb and then dove in headfirst.

The shock of the cold, and then the ensuing numbness, was all-encompassing. There was no end to it—it just kept coming, wave after wave of cold, salty water. It was exhilarating and terrifying to know I was standing in squishy, wet sand and rough pebbles, but I couldn't feel them under my feet. The water had slowly driven me out and out, farther than I'd planned to go, and I felt like I might not get back. If I stayed too long, I certainly wouldn't.

This was me with Jake. His attention surrounded me completely when I was near him, and I couldn't think about anything else. I'd gotten dragged out into the deep by Jake Harrison, one knocking wave at a time, shifting me out and out and out into deeper water, till I was up to my chin. It made me feel breathless and a little panicky, but I wasn't sure I wanted to wade back to shore.

CHAPTER THIRTEEN

THE NEXT DAY, I scoured my apartment. I wasn't a particularly dirty person and I performed the requisite apartment upkeep on the regular, but I woke up with extra energy. After a run, I scrubbed the shower, toilet, and sink in the bathroom. I cleaned the kitchen sink with a toothbrush and straight razor and then tackled the microwave. I cleaned the sticky light over the stove. I cleaned the front of all of the appliances, and under them, and even behind the fridge.

It was four o'clock when Jake texted and asked what time he should come over—he'd made me text him on the drive home the night before so he'd have my number and I'd have his. He wasn't on Facebook, which was no surprise, so this was the only way I could get ahold of him.

I messaged back and told him anytime. The fact that seeing his name pop up in a text message to me—the first of any communication to take place other than face to face and professional e-mails—made a small heat wave begin in my chest was an obnoxious reality I wished I could deny, but I couldn't.

When he responded he'd be over in about twenty

minutes, I had a small panic attack. Since I was cleaning after my run, I hadn't showered. I ran to the shower, took the fastest shower in the history of my life, and managed to be pulling on jeans when I heard a knock at the back door.

Interesting, I thought. He was using the back door. Did that make it less than an official date? *Was* it an official date? Did it even matter?

No. Probably not.

I straightened my white v neck t-shirt, hiked up my fitted jeans, and combed my hands through my still-damp hair. I'd blasted it with the hair dryer so it wouldn't be soaking wet and look quite so disheveled, but since it was long and fairly thick, it was still damp. I took a deep, stabilizing breath and went to the door.

He was smiling at me as soon as I came into view of the glass patio door, and my stomach dipped in anticipation. His smile was like eating dessert first.

With one hand on the wall, I pulled the patio door open. I'd been waiting all day to see him, simultaneously nervous and excited. He looked gorgeous in his plain black t-shirt and jeans. His hair was mussed again, what little of it that could be perfectly, attractively disheveled despite the clean military cut. Before I knew what I was doing, I put my hand in the center of his chest and leaned in.

The jolt of electricity that went through me when our lips met was not a total surprise since it had felt the same way two days ago when he'd kissed me the first time. His lips were full and soft, but goodness, this man could kiss.

Just as I started to pull away, he stepped closer, one hand on my hip pulling me to him, and he walked forward through the door, forcing me to step back. His other hand must have closed the door behind him because I heard it. His hands came to my face and he tilted my head so he could deepen the kiss, his hands then threading in my hair. My whole body was electrified. Finally, he pulled back.

"Hi," he said, his eyes still lit with desire, his mouth a broad smile.

"Hi." I held on to his arms, appreciating the hard muscles under his shirt, and felt my whole body's awareness pinned to him.

We stood there, holding each other, our breath not calming, our eyes not moving. I cleared my throat and stepped back enough to separate our bodies an inch or two.

"How's your day been?"

"Slow. I've been waiting all day to see you." His hands slid down through my hair gently, so they didn't pull or snag, and rested on my waist.

This man. He was such a serious, quiet person most of the time, but then lately I'd seen this warm, generous, almost effusive version of him. It wasn't that he talked constantly, but it didn't seem to pain him as much anymore. The first few months of our interactions felt like they might have cost him something to open his mouth.

The power of this was when he did choose to say something, I heard it. When he said things like *that*, everything in me, including my ovaries, heard it.

The deadly combination of his physically attractive form, his sexy brain, and now not only his desire for me, but his ready willingness to express it? Well... there was something primal that happened. Something in a woman's DNA reached out and said, *This one. Now.*

"Have you? That's funny because I nearly forgot you were coming over," I said, giving him an overly-sweet smile.

"I'll have to work on being more memorable, then," he said with a determined grin.

"Guess so." I let my hands drop away from his arms, even

though I mostly wanted to keep kissing him and feeling up his arms.

"I was going to pop some popcorn." I turned to the kitchen and he followed me.

"Sounds good. What's the movie selection for tonight?"

"I've narrowed it down to three, then you choose from those. *You've Got Mail*, a classic. *The Proposal*, full of Ryan Reynolds' beauty as well as a classic marriage of convenience trope, and finally *Crazy, Stupid, Love*, the most recent of the lot, and inarguably the best of the three." I pressed start on the microwave and leaned back against the counter next to him, waiting to see which he'd choose.

"I have seen *Crazy, Stupid, Love*, so I'll rule that one out, even though I'd watch it again. As much of a fan of Ryan Reynolds as I am, I'm going to go with *You've Got Mail* since it sounds like the best place to begin my education."

"Excellent choice."

We chatted while the popcorn popped, and I learned Henry would leave for his internship in a few days.

"I don't want you to miss time with him. You should tell him to come over," I said, immediately annoyed with myself. I didn't want him to miss out on time with Henry, but I definitely didn't want Henry with us tonight.

"Really?" he asked.

"Of course. I don't want you guys to have to miss out on time together. You don't see each other very often, and it seems like he's going to be busy with his internship and won't get up here as often once he starts." I focused my attention on pouring the bag of popcorn into a large bowl.

"I appreciate that, Elizabeth."

I grabbed the bowl of popcorn and gestured to the two glasses of water I'd poured. "Will you grab those? There's beer in the fridge if you want one."

"No, I'm good."

I set the popcorn on the coffee table and sat down in one corner, the one where I always sat. He placed the glasses, then sat down next to me. He was about eight inches away, in the middle of the couch. We weren't touching, but he hadn't opted to give me much space, which I appreciated.

"Should we wait for him?" I asked, folding my fingers together in front of me because all I could think about was running them along the curve of his jaw, down his neck, over his shoulders.

"Wait?" He gave me a confused look.

"For Henry?" I clarified.

He looked at me, his brow furrowed, and shook his head, just once. "No. Definitely not. I didn't invite him."

"It's totally—"

"Ellie, I know what you said. I don't want him here. I love my brother, but I want to be here with you, without him."

I swallowed. I didn't want Henry there either, but it was a little unnerving how willing he was to just *say* these things. I appreciated it, but it sent my pulse racing.

"Ok. Good," I eked out. I didn't want Henry there with us anyway, but suddenly I felt a little more like a bumbling teen than a fully grown, capable woman.

I focused all my attention on pulling up Netflix and selecting the movie. Jake was watching me, studying me, and it did nothing to calm my nerves. Why was I nervous? I'd literally *just* kissed him. It wasn't like there was suspense about whether or not that would happen. Maybe it was the sensation that it was all I wanted to do, and him sitting right next to me, sitting there with his face and hands and his general existence all begging me to come get a closer look/feel/taste was something I couldn't ignore.

It was also something I'd never experienced.

"Am I making you nervous?" he asked as he ran his fingers along the back of the couch, then over my shoulder, and then stroked up and down my back and neck. He did this so casually I thought I might be imagining it, except I could absolutely feel him touching me.

I shuddered. It wasn't in my mind.

"Honestly? Yes," I said, turning toward him as the opening credits of the movie began.

"Why? What are you nervous about?" There it was. That demanding voice. I puffed out a breath and steadied at the sound. It was easier than listening to his velvet voice saying all of those sweet, near confessions.

"I'm not sure." I wasn't sure how to say it to *him*, anyway.

"Yes, you are. Tell me," he said, his hand now resting where my neck met my shoulder, his thumb on the back of my neck sweeping arcs of sensation back and forth. It would have been soothing if it hadn't been distracting.

I let out another deep breath. I could tell he wasn't flirting, but trying to understand, and maybe he was even a little worried. "I think you make me a little nervous. It's not a big deal. I like you and I'm glad you're here, but you're kind of..." I trailed off, not sure I wanted to admit what I thought of him.

He looked at me, his eyes light in the wake of my blustering whoosh of information. "I'm what?" He inched closer so now our knees were touching.

"You're kind of intimidating. But I'm pretty sure you know that," I said, watching the corners of his mouth tilt down.

"How could I possibly be intimidating to you?" He seemed genuinely baffled.

"Um... I'm sorry, have you met yourself? You're this close-lipped hard-ass of a sergeant in the Army who can beat up anyone he comes across and also happens to be an overachieving brainiac who's managed a full-time career with great success before most people even decide what they want to be when they grow up. Oh, and by the way, you're like the most adorable brother and grandson of all time. And that is also not to mention this whole situation you've got going on here," I said and gestured to his body with a dismissive wave. "So. Yeah." I ran my hands back and forth along my legs, smoothing out the already taut denim and stilling the tremble in my hands.

"I'm confused, Ellie. Am I a hard-ass, or am I adorable?" He looked amused.

"Both."

"That doesn't make sense."

"Trust me, it does. It's intimidating."

"Well forgive me if I don't see how you, a woman with a PhD, who's running a fully funded research study *by herself*, writing novels left and right, and probably one of the smartest people I've ever met, can be intimidated by me." He was practically glaring at me. "And then there's the problem of your physical appearance, which is nothing short of completely distracting," he added. His expression reminded me of the way he looked at me when we'd argued for the first time months ago.

"Wait—are you getting mad?" I was a little surprised, and thrilled. How could this guy not see he was intimidating?

"I'm not *mad*, Ellie. I'm surprised. You're not a woman who is easily intimidated, and I don't like the idea you think of me that way." His expression softened, and his fingers swept into the hair at the nape of my neck.

"It's hard to explain. But, it's not a bad thing." I looked at him, confirming he understood me even as the space between my neck and my belly button was staging an absolute riot in response to my confession. "I like you, Jake."

He looked at me then for a long time. His eyes were dark today with his dark t-shirt. They searched my eyes, surveyed my face, and landed on my lips. He pulled me to him so our faces were close, then closer, then our lips met. He pulled me in, one hand on my neck, the other finding my body and urging me forward. We stayed pressed together for a few moments, then he lifted my legs to rest across his and wrapped his arms around me. Tom Hanks in all his charm flickered on the screen without anyone watching.

With Jake's mouth on mine, there was nothing I could do but enjoy the sensation. His nearness. The clean scent of his soap, the light mint taste of his mouth, the demanding pressure of his fingers as they ran over my back. I moved closer, my hands running up his chest, up his neck, and into his hair. He groaned and pulled me even closer, so there was no space between us, our bodies crushed together and overlapping as we kissed.

I felt dizzy and completely unable to form any thought other than that I would be happy to continue kissing this man, to be crushed up against him, for all of time. Just as this thought passed through my mind, he pulled back, and I took in the delectable sight of Jake Harrison staring at me with all the desire and need a man could own.

I'd never been looked at that way before, but I recognized it, and I knew I had the same look on my face. My heart raced, and I leaned back, his hands releasing me enough so I could.

"You've been calling me Ellie," I said, and as I did so, my face cracked into a wide smile.

"I have." He searched my face. "That ok?"

"Of course. I was relieved when you stopped calling me ma'am and Dr. Kent all the time. My favorite people call me Ellie, so it fits that you would." I had started to feel shy about that admission, that he was one of my favorite people now, but

I couldn't summon the shyness once I saw his blazing smile. His eyes lit up, his gorgeous teeth were all on display. I'd almost call the smile triumphant.

"I'm glad I've earned the rights, then," he said, and then squeezed my shoulders, his arm still wrapped around them with a hand resting on my bicep.

I nodded, leaned in to give him a quick kiss, sat back so my back was against the side of the couch and I could see him and the TV, my legs still across his lap. He stretched out his arm so it lightly touched my neck, my ear. Would I ever stop having that fluttery feeling in my stomach when he was near me?

We sat there, snuggled together for the rest of the movie. Since it was early, and neither one of us wanted the evening to end, we ordered pizza and watched *The Proposal*. He did a little bit of heckling, but I could tell he enjoyed it. I was relieved he wasn't someone who couldn't stand anything other than an action or war movie.

Later, I startled awake, my eyes fluttering open, and I felt Jake's arms around me give me a reassuring hug. The light of the stove was on in the kitchen and a little light came through from the patio light outside, but otherwise it was dark in the living room, the TV long-since gone to the screen saver.

"I didn't mean to fall asleep," I said and slowly slid out of his arms, standing to stretch my arms toward the ceiling.

"I should go now. We both have work tomorrow," he said and pushed himself up off the couch enough so he could grab me around the waist and pull me back down so we were lying face to face.

"Hey!" I said before his mouth captured mine and silenced the rest of my thought. I turned into him, brought my hands to his face, and kissed him back.

And then, we struck a match.

His hands were everywhere, warm and greedy, just like

mine. I felt the hard planes of his chest and ran my hands under his shirt to feel his warm skin. At my touch, he pulled me closer, if that was possible, and his kiss was a torch in the dark room. We pressed into each other, desperate to erase anything separating us, his hands tangled in my hair, in my shirt.

Then he pulled back and brushed his hands over my hair and stood up abruptly, bringing us both to our feet.

He grabbed his keys and wallet, which he'd discarded on the side table when he'd arrived. I could see him clinching his jaw, the small muscles flexing, and wondered what was wrong. He walked to the patio door, and I grabbed his hand.

"What's—Are you ok?"

His expression could be so serious. He squeezed my hand, and then jerked me so I thudded against him. My chest crushed against his, and though the force of the movement surprised me, it felt good. Being this close to him was exactly where I wanted to be, and I relished the heat and resistance I felt when I leaned against him. I steadied myself with my other hand on his shoulder, his very warm, built shoulder, and heard his rough voice at my ear.

"I want to stay with you, Ellie. But I'm leaving now." His voice was almost harsh, his lips brushed my ear, and his breath whispered down my neck. My skin pricked with awareness, and my stomach tightened at his admission. I opened my mouth to say... something. But I didn't speak.

You can have me. Take me now. I want you too. Don't go. I think I'm in love with you. All these things might have come out of my mouth. Probably best they didn't.

Probably.

"I'll see you soon," he said, that voice a sure declaration, writing on a stone tablet somewhere in ancient Sumeria. He let go of my hand, and before I could ever figure out how to respond, he was gone. I locked the door and wandered to the bathroom to get ready for bed, still in a flushed daze.

～

THE WORKWEEK STARTED OUT FINE. I was tired from staying up late with Jake but felt invigorated by the relationship developing there. I liked this man—a lot. He obviously liked me too. He was attractive on every level, and other than a niggling sense of doubt that tended to crop up at the most frustrating times, I believed he wasn't closed off to the possibility of a future. I wasn't ready to sign the dotted line or anything—far from it. But not having felt the way I did about him for anyone else, it seemed important that I knew it wasn't going to come to a screeching halt once we were ready to level up, so to speak. I was about as casual as high tea at Kensington palace when it came to relationships, so the future thing? It mattered to me.

Anyway, the week was going fine. It was Tuesday night when things started to go askew.

Jake texted Monday and asked me to come over for dinner on Tuesday. Henry was leaving Wednesday and he wanted to see me again, plus I wanted to see Jake, so it was ideal. I wandered over after work, enjoying the fact that I lived so close to them, and knocked on the patio door.

"Ellie, come in. Henry doesn't want to eat outside because he's whining about getting eaten by mosquitos," Jake said and beckoned me in from where he stood in the kitchen.

"I'm not whining. I am getting eaten. They like me too much. They can tell grade A blood when they smell it," Henry said and set down the last fork at the small dinner table where he was standing.

"They like Alex, too. They eat her alive. It's one of many

reasons she hates camping," I said and walked into the kitchen. Jake was spooning rice into a bowl. There was a small plate piled with grilled chicken breasts and a salad already made.

"Wow, you guys really have an A game when it comes to feeding guests," I marveled. Jake's eyes traveled from my worn tennis shoes up my body and met my eyes with a hungry look. I bit my lip to help conceal my surprise and, let's be honest, the pleased feeling swirling around low in my belly.

"Grandma taught us to cook. Just the basics, but we've always cooked for ourselves when we're together," Henry explained.

We carried the food to the little table and sat down. Jake said a prayer—a short one, but not something memorized, or rote, and it felt like I got a glimpse into their lives as big and little brother. It was unexpected and reminded me how much I didn't know about him, even when I felt like I did know a lot. Then we dug in, forks clinking against plates, and Henry did lots of talking.

It was a lovely time. I liked Henry, and I obviously liked Jake, and seeing them together only made me like Jake even more. He teased Henry but also encouraged him and often challenged him.

"I don't know how often I'm going to see Grandma once I start work," Henry said, shoving a large piece of grilled chicken in his mouth.

"Yes, you do. Every weekend. Like always," Jake said, leveling Henry with an irked stare.

"Obviously I'm going to try, but I don't know. I think I'll have to work weekends sometimes—that's what happens in hospitality. It's not like I've chosen a nine-to-five industry."

"Then you'll go as soon after the weekend as you can. Monday. Whatever." Jake's voice brooked no argument.

"Yes, your highness. I know. I'm not going to abandon the most important woman in my life. I owe her pretty much everything, including the fact that I didn't turn out to be a serial killer because if it'd been left to you I'm pretty sure I would have been groomed for it," Henry said.

"I'm pretty sure people aren't groomed to be serial killers. You have to be born a psychopath first," I chimed in.

"Oh Ellie, you're too literal. Just go with it. And don't try to soften the blow to your boyfriend's ego. It's too big, and it can take the hit." Henry nudged my arm, which was resting on the table to his right.

I made sure work of studying my food then, not willing to look up and see what Jake thought of Henry's title for him.

The food was surprisingly good. Maybe that was because I was only a decent cook, and then Alex was an amazing cook. Most everyone else I encountered was in the pretty bad to actively bad range.

When I finally did look up, Jake's eyes were on me. I knew it was coming, I was expecting it, but it didn't change how awkward I felt about it. Was he my boyfriend? I didn't think so, but then, wasn't that exactly what I thought I wanted? I wasn't dating around. I certainly didn't want him to, either.

"Why'd you get all quiet and weird?" Henry asked, and for the second time that day, I was ready to knock him upside the head. I saw Jake raise his eyebrows in challenge, adding support to his brother's question.

"Uh, oh... nothing?" I stuttered and focused on folding my napkin neatly into a triangle. Important work.

"I think it's because you referred to me as her boyfriend," Jake explained, and I felt my cheeks heat. These two did not beat around the bush.

"Really? I assumed that was the case. This guy is practically in l—"

"Henry. Give the woman a break," Jake said through clinched teeth and shoved his brother's shoulder to stop him. Henry took the hint and clamped his mouth shut.

What was he about to say?

What was he about to say!?

My mind was reeling, and I managed to say something like "it's ok" or "don't worry about it," and we all focused on our food until Henry piped up with some other, unrelated topic, bless him. I felt unsettled the rest of the time, not sure what to make of the conversation or even my feelings of awkwardness about it.

After dinner, I gave Henry a hug goodbye and then Jake grabbed my hand and pulled me out into the still-warm evening air.

"I'm sorry if Henry and I upset you," Jake said, his thumb brushing along the back of my hand.

"He didn't upset me. I was surprised," I explained, wanting to tread cautiously so I didn't give him any sense I didn't want to be with him.

"You seemed... something. Bothered, at least," he said, less of a declaration and more of a question, which was unusual for him.

"I mostly felt stupid. I wasn't sure if you were comfortable with that title or if you'd even want it—"

"I am, and I do," he said, his voice full of that characteristic confidence again.

"Oh... that's... good," I sputtered. We stepped off the path and walked through my little patch of grass onto the patio. My mind was racing right along with my heart. Did he know what he wanted? All of a sudden, everything had changed for him? This didn't make sense.

"Listen, I don't want to rush you. If you're not ready to call me your boyfriend, then don't. But I'm not going to want to date anyone else. I don't want to spend time with anyone else. I want to be with you, Ellie, and I hope you want to be with me too." He ran a hand from his neck up and over his hair, then let his arm fall back by his side.

"I... I don't know what to say," I said and immediately felt my stomach plummet.

"That's... that's fine. Don't worry about it. You don't have to say anything."

"I think we should, you know, think about this..." What was I saying? Why couldn't I look him in the eye?

"Hmm." It was more of a grunt of acknowledgment than a response. He pursed his lips together for a second like he might say something else, then gave me a quick kiss on the cheek. "Have a good night."

I flipped the lock and watched him walk away. As soon as he was out of sight I slid the blinds closed, curled up on the couch, and cried.

CHAPTER FOURTEEN

I MUST HAVE FALLEN asleep because I woke up Wednesday morning with a hangover despite the fact I hadn't had a drop of alcohol. A crying hangover. An emotion hangover. A *holy crap I just screwed up a chance at a relationship with what has rapidly become my dream guy* hangover.

I showered, dressed, and walked in to work ten minutes later than usual.

"Hey Elizabeth! Oh... are you ok?" Erin's face was twisted with concern. Apparently my hangover was visible to all.

"Yep. Rough night but doing fine. Thanks," I said and retreated to my office down the hall.

I'd spent the time getting ready that morning and then driving to the office berating myself for being the biggest idiot of all time. Did I want Jake Harrison to be my boyfriend?

Yes.

Absolutely.

Hells yeah.

Why was I being an idiot? Why didn't I say that? What was holding me back?

I was surprised when Henry said it, but my awkwardness

was more at the thought of Jake not wanting to be called that or anticipating the stereotypical-but-too-often-true reality of a guy not wanting to be committed too soon. But what was I thinking? This was serious-as-taxes Jake, and he wasn't the kind to mess around. I knew he'd tell me what he wanted, and then, when he walked me home, he *did* tell me.

I'm not going to want to date anyone else. I don't want to spend time with anyone else. I want to be with you, Ellie, and I hope you want to be with me too.

I mean, hi.

Hello.

What else was I waiting for?

And then, like a genius, I said *I think we should think about this* like I needed to think about whether I wanted him or not.

I did.

I wanted him.

But that was terrifying.

If I was being honest, and I liked to pride myself on that (but then not actually be at all honest with myself, I was discovering), then I would admit it scared me. Because Jake was like... it. He was *it*. He was the kind of man you find, and you marry, and you don't stop. You lock that man down and hurry up and bear him some progeny because men like that should raise children who then grow into excellent humans.

He was accomplished and ambitious but not so much he wouldn't make time for me. He essentially told me that he'd changed his entire way of doing things *for me* by dating me. Guh.

But I was in transition. I felt excited by him and the prospect of being with him, but like it was happening at a pace or at a time that was too much for *him*, and maybe he didn't know it. Maybe this was exactly what happened with his mom and dad—they got swept up.

And for me, it was right in the middle of a time when I was trying to make major life decisions. Could I afford to date someone I'd have to factor into my life? And all of that didn't even touch on the much larger reality of him being in the Army. *The Army*.

Never mind the fact that my pacifist parents might find themselves at a total loss when it came to talking to him should they ever meet, but how long would he even be living in Clarksville? How long did we have?

I could feel the spiraling. I took a calming breath and sipped my coffee from my travel mug. I'd bought it at a kitschy place in town. It said, "Bless Your Heart" and did a decent job of keeping my coffee hot. I felt the hot liquid slide down my throat and opened my email on my computer.

And that was where the week took a turn.

The first email awaiting me was one from Operation Achieve, the organization that had granted me the money for the project late last year and who, I was hoping, would fund another year, at least. I opened it immediately, eager to see what they had to say. My heart rate skyrocketed as my eyes skimmed over the words once, then returned to go back over them.

I felt like my eyes were crossed. I couldn't read a full sentence. Key words jumped out and slapped me, causing me to wince at each phrase.

Original project sufficient. No need for additional funding. No justification for expansion of project. Grant awarded to a different applicant for a new project.

In a word: Denied.

I sat there, breathing loudly, feeling my mind swirl with frustration, anger, and then the worst of it—despair. Without this funding, I couldn't justify being here. I couldn't justify staying somewhere and not teaching. I didn't want to go back to the burnout. It was this or go back to teaching, and I couldn't help but feel the gut-punch of this rejection because of that reality.

The irony was they complimented me up and down. They said how valuable the work was, how they'd be able to leverage it when they worked on proposals for new programs and even ways to help soldiers who were deployed. I had barely scratched the surface, and yet they weren't going to let me keep going. I felt both totally enraged and completely humiliated.

I was sitting there in my office, rigid, when a reminder popped up on my computer. I had a meeting in five minutes. I had to pull it together—the distraction would be useful.

All through the meeting, I couldn't think. They wanted to plan an open house at the education center for August. Lacy was thrilled, and Erin seemed excited. Emily was getting good support from her higher-ups so there'd be money for food. It was all great news.

All this did was make my heart sink as I realized I wouldn't have any reason to be there come August. Everyone could tell something was wrong, their concerned glances and warm smiles with furrowed brows speaking without words, but I couldn't find it in me to pretend I was fine.

"You feeling ok, Elizabeth?" Lacy asked with a pat to my shoulder as the meeting broke.

"Oh, yeah, just... not a great day so far," I admitted, not looking her in the eye.

"We all have those days. Hope it turns around for you," she said with another pat and then ducked in to her office, which was a few doors down from mine.

Once back to the isolation of my office, I sat in a daze, the door closed, and my feet pulled up to my chest in my bouncy office chair as I looked out the window behind my desk. I felt numb. I didn't have any idea what to do with myself, but there were two hours left of the work day, so I just sat there.

A knock broke my focus on a little row of saplings lining a gravel road that led to a barracks building behind the ed center. I was fixating on one tree in particular that had a full section of its bisected trunk turning black. It was rotten, broken, dying.

Even though I knew it was dramatic, I gave into the depressive pull to see myself in the blackened limb.

Another knock came, and I cleared my throat. "Come in," I said and spun around to face my desk.

A face I recognized peaked in the door, and her voice came quietly. "Are you free?" Captain Rae Jackson was part of the TESS study, and I'd told her she could drop by to hear about the findings.

I felt a sliver of embarrassment needle my gut.

"Of course," I said and summoned my best smile for her.

She opened the door fully, and I saw she wasn't alone. Behind her was Sergeant Major Trask, Sergeant Holland, Lieutenant Holder, and of course, just to make a great day even better, Sergeant William Jacob Harrison.

I ducked my head and busied myself with the printed packets I'd made last week that showed the results of the data I'd gathered and my suggestions for what Operation Achieve should do. I hoped they would put it to good use and start the process to change things for soldiers.

Knowing I couldn't delay the interaction anymore, and a little curious how he'd play it, I rose to my feet and welcomed the others. "Nice to see you. Thanks for coming," I said. And then I looked at him. "Sergeant Harrison, good to see you."

If he felt any surprise at my addressing him that way, he

didn't show it. "Dr. Kent," he said, and after about three seconds of eye contact, he made a point to look at the paper I handed them and not at me.

I could see his eyes skating across the page and was reminded how I noticed his quick reading the first time we met in my office months ago. Before we were friends, and before I essentially rejected him.

No. I didn't reject him. But I knew his admitting he wanted to date me and be with me was significant. He'd told me as much when he explained why he hadn't dated with any purpose in the Army—he didn't want the entanglements, didn't want to risk becoming involved with someone who'd suffer because of his career, which he was most certainly not going to give up until he was ready to retire.

But here he was, avoiding looking at me, and my internal organs were lighting themselves on fire. Or something. Because the pain radiating through my body at seeing him and knowing I'd hurt him, even just a little, had to be a physical one. It had to be.

"You can see most of what I compiled here in this data sheet, but let me walk you through the report, and then you can tell me if you have questions." And only because I focused on the report, and when I needed to make eye contact with someone I focused on Captain Jackson or Sergeant Major Trask, or even Sergeant Holland or Lieutenant Holder, did I make it through that meeting. I successfully ignored Jake's stoic face and the sensation my insides were exploding every time I thought of him.

I thanked them all for coming and watched as each one filtered out, gathering keys from pockets and patting legs to make sure their patrol caps were still tucked away, ready to top off their uniforms as soon as they exited the building.

But I couldn't let Jake leave without talking to him. That

seemed like... well, I knew it was a mistake. I didn't have anything to tell him, but maybe if we could talk, here in the light of day, I could help him understand a little bit about why I was feeling anxious. I could tell him about the project's funding too, and even the thought filled me with a small piece of hope.

"Sergeant Harrison, could I ask you to stay for a moment? I had one additional question for you," I said, trying to sound formal and professional. His response to me had been professional, curt, and not unlike the way I'd greeted him. For all I knew, he wouldn't want his coworkers knowing we were involved—in whatever way it was we were—so I didn't want to betray that.

His eyes flashed with something before he responded, and a leaden feeling filled my belly. Hurt. It looked like a little glimpse of hurt before he locked it away behind his neutral-faced vault. "Yes, ma'am."

Ah, there it was. Somehow his "ma'am" felt more like a hatchet to my sternum than the simple courtesy it was. But again, this was exactly in line with how I'd been speaking to him, so could I really be upset with him?

I waited a moment as the others left and stayed standing so I was at least close to his eye level. "I wanted to see... how you're doing." I felt my chest and cheeks flush and wanted to reach for the words and gather them back into my mouth before they reached his ears. Of course, this was impossible, but I wished it because as soon as they came out of my mouth I knew how stupid they sounded.

How little they offered.

Worse, I saw how they affected him. I saw his lips flatten and turn down into a frown, his already-furrowed brow, so serious and dark under his dark brown eyebrows, seemed more lined. "I'm fine, ma'am," he said, his words clipped and spare.

I pushed out a short breath, frustrated we couldn't break through this. He said he wanted me to figure out what I wanted, but this wasn't a very generous way to give me space. Granted, I wasn't giving him much to go on.

"Well…" I felt a flash of self-righteous frustration. *Really*. Was this how he was going to give me time to figure out what I wanted? Be a jerk? Treat me like we weren't even friends? "Ok." I heard the edge in my voice. I let my fingertips rest on the desk and I leaned my weight into them, letting them tent to hold me upright.

He stood there a beat, his brown eyes unreadable, his bearing and general energy speaking to his upset more than his now very studiously calm face.

"Is that all, Dr. Kent?" he asked, no irritation, no resignation, no hurt, no impatience—there was nothing in his voice now but cordiality, and *that* was brutal.

That was the blow.

I'm sure my eyes widened when he said it, and I barely squeaked out a surprised, "Yes" before he turned on his heel after a nod. I stood there and added, "Thank you" for some inane reason and listened to his footsteps move away from me down the hall.

By the end of the day, I couldn't see straight. I felt my heart pounding but at the same time, I was entirely sapped of energy. I researched other organizations and foundations, and I did have a few small applications out to other places, but they wouldn't be able to fund the project on their own, even if I got all three of them. I'd applied for them in case I only got partial funding from Operation Achieve, not considering I might be in danger of getting no funding at all.

Oh, naïve child.

I refused to think about Jake. I let my mind be overtaken with the frustration and anger bubbling up and choking me. This was the preferable alternative to more weeping over a man. It wasn't that I was above it, but I'd done plenty of that last night.

I slunk home and closed the curtains, gluing myself to *All About Steve* in a self-flagellating attempt at distraction.

(Let's all take a moment to appreciate the beauty that is this movie. It's absolutely awful. And yet, it stars Sandra Bullock and Bradley Cooper. Really. *Really*. If this teaches us anything, it's that one can face utter failure, the ultimate bathos, and recover to make something sublime.)

By the next day, I felt a little less angry but a little more embarrassed and hopeless. I ran through all of the scenarios, and the thing I came down to was I'd have to see if there was a way to appeal Operation Achieve's decision and argue for the expansion of my project, if that was even possible.

But the hits? They kept a' coming.

Early Thursday, I had an email from Angelica at the Quint Agency.

Elizabeth,

As you know, I was very interested in your novel, but it turns out before I received your manuscript in full, another agent requested a manuscript from another author that, we've discovered, is nearly identical to your own. I can't, in good conscience, partner with

you on the novel or contract with you. You should
know plagiarism is a serious offense.

And it was at that point my heart stopped beating. The floor dropped out from underneath me, and I was falling down a pit, or a well, or a direct line to hell.

CHAPTER FIFTEEN

PLAGIARIZED? *Me*. Plagiarize? A teacher who hated plagiarism. Plagiarizer?

Not a chance in hell. Not an orchid's chance at my mom's house. Not a freaking funion's chance at a Phish concert. *Hell no.*

I felt rage. Rage, and utter disbelief. Before I could even think about what I'd say, I was on the phone, calling the agency.

When Angelica Quint answered, I gave it to her as calmly as possible.

"Hello Ms. Quint. I am glad to speak with you. I received your email this morning regarding my novel and the alleged plagiarism, and I'm deeply disturbed. Under no circumstances did I plagiarize. I wrote every word of the novel, and I have multiple emails and drafts I can provide to you to prove that," I said, my adrenaline coursing through me and causing me to shake as I spoke.

"I'm sorry, Ms. Kent. We've got a clear match here of large parts of the text," she said, and before she could continue, I had to interrupt her. I couldn't stand it.

"Do I get to know what the other text is? Someone stole my writing. I can't make this any clearer and I'm sorry if I sound upset, but I am. I did not, in any way, under any circumstances, or in any stretch of a unicorn's imagination, plagiarize. That is my original intellectual property and I will defend that," I said, my voice rising even as my hands shook and I felt tears prick behind my eyes.

"I understand your position, Ms. Kent. I can imagine it's upsetting to hear this news, and honestly, I want to believe you. I'm inclined to believe you, but you know I can't represent someone who has a whiff of this on them. Publishers won't even look at it."

"It is most certainly original, Ms. Quint. This is madness, and I have no idea what to do," I said, feeling a little drop of venom enter my words. I closed my eyes tight and took a deep breath as she spoke.

"Ms. Kent, I think it's best I refer you to our legal lead, Mr. Berry. I'll email you his contact information. I hope he can help with this, because truly, I'm rooting for you. But short of a clear admission from the thief, I won't be able to continue our correspondence. Goodbye." And she was gone. Just like that, she hung up.

I didn't get a chance to defend myself. I'd tried, but I was the presumed thief? How was this happening? How had I spent hundreds of hours tapping out words on my computer, straight from my own brain, only to be accused of one of the most accursed and loathsome sins a teacher or writer could fathom?

I felt that familiar warring of rage and hurt split my chest, and I didn't know whether to scream or cry. I felt very near both and decided I couldn't stay at work. I dropped by Erin's desk on the way out.

"Hey, I'm going to head home early. I'm feeling pretty

bad," I said and sniffled for effect. Except it wasn't, because the tears I'd suppressed as I signed out of my computer and gathered my things won out for a moment before I shut them down and my nose started running in response.

She must have seen something in my face to confirm that because sweet Erin with her freckled nose and strawberry hair nodded and said, "Feel better" and gave me a pitying look. Fortunately, I avoided any scrutiny from Bec or Lacy and made a break for my car.

I wanted to call my parents, but that impulse was quickly checked by the very real sense I didn't want to face their scorn, or worse, their pity. I hadn't come clean with them about my desire to write or my lack of desire to teach. I hadn't put it in words they'd understand, and coming to them now with this failure, even if it wasn't a failure I could control, was intolerable.

I'd call Alex, but I still couldn't figure out how to tell her. In the span of a little more than twenty-four hours I'd lost the ability to pursue a project I cared about and also provided for my basic needs so I had time to write, and I'd lost any sense of surety I had in my ability to write. This didn't have anything to do with my ability to write, and yet somehow I was being called a cheater—a thief, and I couldn't stand it.

As soon as I walked in my apartment, I threw my keys and purse and *really* wanted to punch something. I wasn't particularly prone to physically acting out, but I felt a kind of momentum building in me, and I had to find a way to unleash it on something other than the next person I talked to.

I had to wait until Angelica contacted me with the legal department's information. But then what? Was I going to have to get a lawyer? I didn't have money for that, nor did I want to spend the time. Not that I could stand *not* to defend myself—that didn't seem like an option either.

I checked my email and found Angelica had followed through and sent the agency's legal person—Mr. Berry's—information. I emailed immediately (and would have called, but there was no number listed). I laid out a thorough accounting of my records, indicating drafts of the novel were saved every five thousand words. It would be easy to see it in development and then as I revised to get it to where it was when I sent it to Angelica.

After sending that email, I paced the apartment and checked my email a dozen times in the span of ten minutes. I couldn't stay there circling my computer like a vulture, so I tossed on workout clothes and went out into the too-warm early summer air. It was only May, but it was into the high seventies with blazing sun before noon. This would be a way to relieve some of my fury.

I thought through my plan of attack, and what I'd do next. I guessed at how long Mr. Berry would take to get back to me. I ran five miles and decided I wasn't ready to deal with the reality yet, so I kept going. Finally, I let myself space out and focus on my breathing, the tightness in my chest from the fast pace I was setting, and on the songs that pumped into my old iPod shuffle clipped on the strap of my sports bra.

By the time I slowed and began walking at the edge of the apartment complex's parking lot, I'd run ten miles. I was overheated, underfed, and under-watered. I'd run a personal record for pace, but the runner's high that usually came was absent so far—I could tell I was sunburnt, and I felt absolutely ill. I followed the sidewalk that wound around the property and was almost home when I saw Jake.

My heart pumped louder again, and I wished I had my phone so I could pretend to be on it. He walked from his car to his house, maybe home for a late lunch or off early, I didn't know, but he saw me. He stopped, like the sight of me surprised him, and then changed course to walk toward me.

As much as a huge part of me wanted to go to him, let him hug me and comfort me, the thought of telling him about all of this made my insides pitch and roil. Add to that my frustration with myself about how I felt about him, and us, and it was just... I couldn't do it. This was all assuming he would even be willing to talk to me. I couldn't face a rejection—another one —from him. Not today.

So, I looked away. I averted my eyes and followed the path around to my house without acknowledging him. He knew I saw him—we'd made eye contact. But I couldn't face him. I couldn't.

I MADE myself wait until I was showered to check my email. I thought maybe it'd help guarantee I'd have a response. One small happiness—this worked. I had an email time-stamped ten minutes earlier.

The news was not good, and my hopes sank lower. Mr. Berry provided me the name of the person who submitted the work to another agent at the agency first, by about a week. The bad news was Mr. Berry didn't seem to think there was any amount of information I could provide them that would prove I was the original author and that the content had, in fact, been stolen from me.

The continued bad news was I knew who it was and had known from the moment I'd received Angelica Quint's email. That meant this wasn't all just a huge, horrible misunderstanding, and that filled me, if possible, with an even stronger sense of dread.

Her name was Cathy Matthews, or "CathMath77" as I

knew her through our writing workshop discussion board. We'd paired up after many months of thoughtful feedback. I'd sent her my almost-final draft for reading. I thought of her as a colleague, a peer, a friendly neighboring writer.

The fact that she hadn't had a full draft ready to show *me* hadn't caused concern. I was writing like a bat out of hell, and I was a single woman with no kids—I had time like no one's business compared to many aspiring writers. I could understand she hadn't met the totally arbitrary deadline of March fifteenth we'd set for our full peer review—but she knew I had an agent in mind I wanted to query as soon as I could, so she'd had no problem reading my book. I hadn't thought twice about that. I never would have guessed she either didn't have her own novel, or she was planning to steal mine.

Those damned ides of March—I should have known!

She'd said she would have a draft for me, but it would take a while. But she did give me helpful feedback. She'd been doing it all along. So why, in the name of all that was honest and decent and not totally trashy and cheatery and rude (rage made me eloquent) would she steal my novel?

I couldn't even think. What should I do first? Hunt her down or contact a lawyer? I pulled up the discussion board, looked for her there, and sent her a private message. I also sent her an email at the address where I sent the manuscript months before. I knew, once I hit send, there was no way I'd hear from her.

Then, I composed my email back to Mr. Berry at Quint. I laid out every single draft, the date ranges, and even the copied text of emails from peer review from Matthews back to me. I offered to forward the email in which she gave me feedback in the document of *my novel*. I did everything in my power to sound reasonable and even managed to avoid typing in all caps and italics and bold. I considered placing it entirely in Impact or Stencil font for effect, to better convey the veracity and vigor of my words. I resisted this, too, knowing any coat but that of Times New Roman in a dire circumstance such as this, dealing with the ugliest of sins a teacher and writer could name, would be ineffective.

Once I sent the email off, I felt even more upset. I thought about how the agency immediately suspected *me*. My initial feeling was of an injustice, but could I fault them? They'd identified another writer's work as the original because she'd submitted her work (false: *my work*) to an agent a week before me. The timing was suspicious, but wouldn't they assume the original author submitted first?

I'd once had a case of collusion in my freshmen writing courses. Two students had turned in essays that were nearly identical. In the end, one student had outright cheated, and the other had been foolish enough to leave his essay up on his computer screen while he went to the dining hall. Even though his was the original, it came in *second*.

But I remembered the moment the unsuspecting student's essay came in, and I saw the match. I remembered thinking he must have been the cheating party, if both students weren't, because he'd turned his in second. It turned out he hadn't finished his conclusion or works cited page on the draft that was stolen, and these were items that were missing from the other student's essay that was submitted hours before. They were left out because she couldn't summon the will to complete even those small portions for herself.

In my case, I could grudgingly admit that being the second person to submit a novel, even if there were small differences between the drafts, looked bad for me. Really bad. And that only made me angrier.

What I couldn't grasp was why she did it. Why steal someone's work? I could mentally assent, on some level, to the fact that cheating in college, particularly in general education courses, made a certain amount of unethical and completely problematic but logical sense.

But this? Writing a work of fiction as a hobby or even as a potential career? How would she expect to repeat her work? How could she possibly take a contract and then plan to do any writing herself knowing her voice was different than mine?

I sat on the couch, my laptop closed beside me to keep from incessantly checking for a response from Mr. Berry, and my mind was blank. My body hurt, my heart hurt, and my mind was an exhausted pile of mush. I was startled out of my mental void when I heard a knock at my sliding door.

My heart jumped into my throat because I knew exactly who it'd be. I summoned what little energy and bravery I had left for the day and rolled off the couch. I pulled back the sheer curtains that hung there, and there he was. I felt a surge of gratitude for him coming, but it danced with the equally powerful sensation of dread. I didn't want to tell him about these failures. I didn't want to admit I wasn't the best. I didn't want him to tell me he didn't want me anymore.

I slid open the door reluctantly, and even though I was feeling more and more upset at seeing him, a small part of me sighed a little, relaxed to see him there.

He stepped through the door, neither of us speaking, and before I could drop back to the couch where I'd been sitting, he put a hand on my shoulder and turned me to him.

"What's going on Ellie?" His face was so sincere and concerned, I felt a pang of something. It was like nostalgia—a longing for him in a different life.

"I'm sorry I didn't speak to you earlier," I said, starting with the simplest thing first.

"I could tell you were upset. Tell me what's happening,"

his voice was pleading, not demanding—he was worried about me.

"I don't... I haven't wanted to. It's just... it's so..." I couldn't speak in a full sentence. My thoughts were racing, and I didn't know where to start, or if I even wanted to tell him. A part of me did, but I knew the largest section of my internal pie chart said *hell no*.

"Tell me. Please."

I pursed my lips, smashing them together, and felt the anger and frustration and desperation I had felt building in the last two days simmering, but I nodded and then spoke. "I lost the project, to start with. I can finish what I have, but no extension. They think it's done. They said, 'Great job, you're amazing, we love what you've done, but we're good.' They said they thought what I gathered was all they'd need to push for new policies and other stuff they didn't specify. They awarded the grant to someone else—a different project," I said, trying to relax the snarl in my voice.

"But you applied for—"

"Yes, I applied for other grants, but they were all small, just things to supplement. There's no way I can do it without that one." I clenched my teeth. He watched me, unblinking, and I waited for him to respond.

"But can you reapply? Challenge their decision? Or—"

"Listen, I've thought it through. There's nothing to be done here—at least I don't think there is. That's done now," I said, my voice so sharp it might have cut him.

"Ok," he said in a low, calm voice. It was the voice you'd use to speak to a wounded animal or a baby who just finished crying maniacally. It spoke to the clawed, hollowed-out part of me, and it infuriated me.

"Well it gets better! Today I got an email from my would-be agent telling me they suspect I plagiarized my novel. The novel I just finished. The novel I spent hours writing over the last few months and I've been thinking about writing for several *years*." I shrugged off his hand and started pacing a circle around my couch. He stayed in place and crossed his arms.

"Wow," he said, shaking his head.

"I know. I *know*. And I can't do anything about it. I'm trying to talk to lawyers. The agent I've been in contact with assumed I was the person who plagiarized, and the agency's legal rep is essentially treating me the same way. I have no way to pay for a lawyer to deal with this by myself, and..." I felt my voice catch and gritted my teeth. I didn't want to cry about this, not in front of him, not right now. "I know who did it. I can't believe they'd accuse me of this, even though I know it's part of their job, and this soulless thief of my work is cowering somewhere in a hole instead of dealing with it like a woman. I don't know what to do, and I'm pissed off, and I don't even know what to say or do now." I blew out a deep breath, continuing to pace. It funneled my energy, the adrenaline that had calmed down and been exhausted during my run now pumping freely in the face of reciting to Jake what had happened.

"Well... did you plagiarize?" His words seemed to echo in my small apartment, despite the fact that made absolutely no sense acoustically.

I felt my breath flow out of me on a whoosh, felt my jaw drop, and my eyes were wide with disbelief.

It felt like he stabbed me. He took that nasty word to a smith and had it fashioned into a blade for the sole purpose of stabbing me in the heart.

I snapped.

"You need to go." My voice was low and shaky, and I was holding on to the back of the couch with one hand, the other hand a fist clutched to my chest to stop the bleeding I swore I could feel.

"Ellie—"

"*Go* Jake. Just go. I can't do this right now. You need to go."

"This isn't something you should have to—"

"Please. Please go," I said, an edge of desperation coloring my words as I walked away from him toward the bathroom. I shut myself in and leaned against the door, not able to understand anything other than wanting him gone, and I knew he would be when I came out.

A few minutes later, I walked out to the living room. No sign of him was there, and for whatever reason, *that* was what broke me. I shattered there, facing the now-closed patio door. The force of my sob shook me so hard I bent over, no longer able to stand up.

I slid down against the back of the couch and wrapped my arms around my knees. I could feel the wood frame of the couch digging into my shoulder blade through the fabric of my shirt and the couch itself, but I didn't move. I sat there and let myself cry and cry and cry.

CHAPTER SIXTEEN

I DIDN'T MOVE until my phone buzzed on the coffee table behind me a while later. It was a text from Alex. *I'm at an event tonight but it has been too long! I'm coming to Luke's for dinner tomorrow but let me come by and see you first. Will you be home?*

I felt a mingling of relief and sadness wash over me. I was glad I'd get to see her tomorrow, but I wanted to talk to her tonight. I didn't have the energy, but I wanted help, comfort, everything to be fixed so bad I could hardly breathe. It was like all of this madness had piled up inside my lungs, the pneumonia of my failures, and I couldn't take a breath until they were removed. I knew Alex would help remove them. I knew it.

For now, I was left to wallow, which I did with a healthy dose of Nancy Meyers. I watched *Something's Gotta Give* and then moved to *It's Complicated* but only got five minutes in before I remembered Alec Baldwin's character's name was Jake.

Even though he and my Jake, Jake Harrison, shared nothing in the way of looks or bearing or appeal (sorry Alec, but even when my heart is both broken and enraged, he wins by a mile), I couldn't hear it. I couldn't hear Meryl Streep say his name and not want to cry. *Why Meryl? Why can't you let me stay away from that mental mess and enjoy you and Steve Martin being adorable and making pastries together?*

I reluctantly abandoned the TV and went to bed. I couldn't stop Jake's words from sounding in my head as I lay in the dark, exhausted but fully conscious. *Did you plagiarize?*

He'd asked me as though there was even a remote possibility I would. That I could. That my integrity was at question in some way and I could have done it. I didn't hear judgment in it, but maybe there was—there probably was. There had to have been. This man was the pinnacle of high expectation and achievement, so if he thought for even a moment I cheated as I was explaining what happened—

"Ugh!" I groaned aloud in frustration. I wanted to yell or bang symbols or do something reckless, but instead I stayed there, tossing and turning.

When I woke the next morning, I felt like an egg fried on a sidewalk and left to die. Or be trampled. Or whatever. I felt like I'd been scraped off the bottom of a shoe. I felt like my entire world had crumbled, and I wasn't sure how to function now. The nasty part was that was true.

I took my time getting out of bed. At some point yesterday, I'd recognized there was no chance of me showing up to work, and since the project was in good shape and I didn't have anything scheduled, I called Erin at the education center and told her I was sick and wouldn't be in today either.

Once I got up and ate a real breakfast—eggs, toast, coffee, water—I got to work. I'd promised myself at some point in the night I wasn't going to take this lying down, and one of the things I could do for myself was feed and water myself so I wasn't an incapable mess when it came time to use my brain.

I started with researching law firms in the area, even branching out to Nashville. I called ten different firms to find the right match and quite a few weren't willing to say much without meeting with me. I wasn't sure I'd need them, so I didn't do much other than simply thank them for their time. But one or two agreed to meet with me early the following week if I needed to. I desperately didn't want to, but so far there was no movement from accursed CathMath77 and I suspected there would be none, at least that I could elicit. Maybe the agency or lawyer would be the ones to track her down... maybe.

It was late in the day when I received an email back from Mr. Berry at Quint Agency, and I didn't know what to think when I saw it. It was a non-response. I'd sent him every bit of evidence I had to show that the work was originally mine, and he basically said, "Thanks, good to know." Not, "We will avenge the dishonoring of your name" or, "It's clear you are the original writer" or even, "That was very thorough, and we'll be speaking with the other author and get back to you." No, it was nothing but a receipt.

I also spent my day bursting out in sobs, much like my beloved Diane Keaton in *Something's Gotta Give* after Harry (Jack Nicholson) broke her heart. I'd be fine, typing away at an email to another lawyer or searching what the crap the procedure for addressing plagiarism in non-academic circles was to begin with, when I'd bust out in inconsolable sobs that would last seconds at times, minutes at others.

I felt too full. I felt like I was stuffing a box full of Styrofoam peanuts, trying to contain the madness, but I kept finding more lying around on the floor, stuck to my pants, stuck to the box. Just when I thought I had it all boxed up, it'd burst open again, the flaps clearing the way for a staticky pastel-colored nightmare to cover my floor.

It was the knock on my door, an eerie replay from the day before, that had me snapping my computer shut and springing off the couch, my home base for crisis central.

My body was on full alert, my mind a riot of energy and emotion, and I almost choked with relief when I saw it was Alex, not Jake, standing at my door.

"Whoa, are you ok?" she asked, grabbing me by the shoulders. I closed the door then grabbed her. I hugged her like it mattered, her familiarity the only medicine for the utter crap-attack that was my week, my life.

"No," I said, and I could hear the raw sound of my voice, that *I'm about to cry* strain obvious. Alex pulled back from the hug and walked to the couch. She left me my spot, the indentation of hours spent there clear, and rested a hand on my shoulder when I sat.

"What's going on? *Dimmi.*" Her eyes were wide and her face was pained. At the sight of her, of her deep empathy and love for me so evident and right there near the surface, I lost it again.

Once I cried out the worst of the tears, and calmed down so I was only intermittently blubbering, I told her about the rejection of the grant application, about the refusal to let the project expand. I told her about the plagiarism accusation and who I was certain it was, and everything I'd communicated to the agency and learned over the last thirty-six hours.

"What the hell? What on God's good Earth are they thinking, accusing you without evidence? And now with all of the evidence showing it *is* your work? I don't understand how they can possibly claim it's not yours when you have all of those drafts and the proof of having worked with effing *Cath-Math.*" Her indignation made me smile, then ache. Even through her gesticulating she must have seen my sadness.

"Hey... hey. We're going to figure this out. There's no way

this novel isn't getting published under *your* name." She soothed me with a gentle squeeze to my wrist.

"I don't know. I really don't. But thank you for believing me." My voice was watery and I looked at the ring where I'd set my coffee mug earlier, now only a dried brown circle on the white coffee table.

"What? You don't have to thank me for that. I know you'd never plagiarize, and I know how hard you've worked. Anyone who knows you would know that, no question."

"Don't be so sure about that..." I wrapped my arms around my knees and hugged them to my chest.

"What are you talking about?" She gave me a hard look, impatient for me to tell her whatever it was I was hinting at. I didn't want to—didn't want to deal with this failure too, but I couldn't keep this from her.

"Jake. He came over yesterday afternoon, knew I was upset, I told him what I told you."

"And?"

"And then instead of... of... declaring it insane and hugging me or pounding his fist through the wall at the injustice of it all, he asked me if I'd done it." My voice was raised, tight. If it was a line, it'd be a wavy one, chasing either side of the page.

"*What?*" She burst out of her seat and stood facing me, eyes wild, waiting for the rest of the story.

"He literally asked me, 'Did you plagiarize?'" I clinched my jaw and felt the strong urge to spit. At the same time, repeating that was like taking a backhoe to my ribs. I hugged my knees tighter.

She looked at me, frozen, her mouth agape. I knew she was thinking. I could see her eyes shifting back and forth, quickly curving around the room in a moment, and then back to me. "There's no way he was actually asking you that like he didn't know the answer. I can't believe that. I don't."

"Well that's what he said—"

"And it was an idiot thing to say. But I have no doubt he respects you, and I know he wouldn't actually think you had. I have no idea why he'd be so dumb, but I don't think—"

"It doesn't matter now." I felt my shoulders sag and rested my head on my knees.

"What does that mean?" she asked, caution in her voice.

"I'm done here. I'm going to have to move again, wherever I can find a full-time faculty job, and it's just... it's obviously not going to work anyway." The words *faculty job* were bitter ash in my mouth.

"Ok, there is so much to deal with in that statement and so little time. First—why would you have to move? There are like fifteen colleges within an hour of where you are right now. Get on staff with one of them. I'm sure you'd be an appealing novelty item for them, coming from the big city *and* being interested in military life, or whatever."

I broke out of my little ball of sadness and stood. "I don't want my life to be like that. I don't want the pressure, and the constant competition—"

"Stop. Just stop talking about this like whatever happens in the next five minutes is going to be for the rest of your life. I understand you wanted to move and change things and be a writer and leave academia behind, but you're also a damned good teacher. I know you hated the drama and the old boys' club, but it doesn't have to be like that. Become an adjunct, or—"

"The pay is terrible. There's no benefits, and there—"

She shook her head as she grabbed my shoulders. "*Stop.* Seriously. Ellie. I love you, but you're spiraling. You've set up a lovely little pity party here, but I'm not drinking your specific brand of poor me tea. So, listen." She gave me a hard, motherly look. She was the youngest of three, but you'd never know it—she'd been bossing me around for years.

I pursed my lips to show her I wouldn't interrupt again.

"You could teach part time. Maybe you can even get a job on post if you're finding you like that. Or you can apply for fifty more grants and fund your project another way if you want to stick with that." She let her hands drop from my shoulders but didn't step away.

"I don't think I can. I..." I paused and took a deep breath. My chest fully expanded, and I felt the truth of what I was about to say. "I think they might be right. Whatever I find out at other bases is likely to mimic what I found here. They've got what they need to push for more time for soldiers, for certain ways for the contracting schools to cooperate. That's all good and I'm genuinely proud of the work and participants, and I'm hopeful they'll make things easier on soldiers now... it sucks. It's honestly one of the first things I've ever been told 'no' about, and it stings." I hated admitting that, but I knew she understood me when I said it. I walked toward the kitchen so I wouldn't have to see her take in my flushed cheeks, and of course Alex followed.

She paused in the doorway. "I get it. Getting rejected sucks pigeon feet, and there's no way to escape that. But you're acting like you have no alternative. You're acting like the fact that you have a life here you like means nothing and you have to go somewhere else for money rather than stay here and fight for what you want. That's not you. That's a steaming pile, and you know it." I didn't feel any sense of humor yet, but I felt my mouth crack a smile at her stern look, her hands on her hips, the determination blazing in her eyes.

"Aren't you the one who was all about putting the job

first?" I reached into the fridge and grabbed a block of sharp cheddar cheese.

"Yeah, well, I learned, didn't I? Or, I'm working on fully learning it. You can make your life look a lot like what you want it to be, but sometimes something's gotta give. In this case, for you, it might be you have to teach a little until your writing takes you to where you can support yourself."

"You're right." I exhaled loudly and let her sense of determination fill me with hope. Then I sliced a half-inch wide slice of cheddar. "But if we set that aside, and we say ok, I'm going to figure out how to support myself so I can stay here, then what about the writing?" I raised an eyebrow at her in reference to the cheese.

She leaned over to see the package—Kraft—and jumped back with a slight shudder and curt nod "no." She leaned against my counter while I took a large bite. "This plagiarism charge is nonsense. You've got the proof, and it's impossible this woman is going to claim your book. So, if the lawyers at the agent's office can't see that, then you *are* going to litigate."

"I don't think I can afford that. I don't have a great sense of what it'll cost yet, but I don't want to put myself in debt for this." I moved back to the couch, half the slice of cheese on a small, floral plate. Alex stayed standing.

"Ellie, I know you don't. I am going to have faith you won't have to. But I hereby banish the tone of defeat in your voice on this matter. You have appointments with lawyers set up next week if you don't get good news from the agent tomorrow, right?" She was still standing, but her posture was more relaxed.

"Yes. I meet with two firms on Monday, and that's all I wanted since I'm hoping I won't have to litigate. If I have to, I don't want to have too much input unless neither of the two

I'm meeting with seem like they'll work." I watched as she plopped down next to me.

"Ok then. There's a plan there too. I know this sucks, and I'm not trying to make it seem like planning how you'll handle it negates the very real emotion of feeling upset and sad and betrayed. But let's go forward." She grabbed me by my shoulders and pulled me in for a hug. My eyes welled up with tears, and I felt an overwhelming sense of gratitude for her.

"Thank you."

"Don't thank me. This is what we do for each other. But now we have to deal with Jake."

"Jake?" His name felt awkward in my mouth, the "k" sound too hard, the "j" too mushy. And I felt the shimmering sense of peace that had settled over me moments ago evaporate.

"Hold please," she said and held up a finger while she put her phone to her ear. Then she spoke into the phone.

"I can't come until later. Ellie needs me, and I can't leave yet. Eat without me, and I'll come over in a bit." Her eyes were light, and she had a smile so wide her cheeks looked like they might burst.

I turned away, not envying her love for Luke, but witnessing it in this moment was too painful. I heard her whisper, "I love you" and some kind of promise, and then she was back to attending to me.

"Ok. I don't know why Jake said what he did, but let's rewind. Before this, you guys were good, right?" She curled her legs up into a tailor sit on the couch.

I didn't know what to say. Were we good? Not really. I'd essentially told him I didn't know how I felt about him. "We were okay. I guess... I had already kind of busted things."

"What makes you say that?" Alex asked, her eyes narrowing a bit like it'd help her figure out my response.

"Well, I went over to dinner earlier this week to say goodbye to Henry. He referred to Jake as my boyfriend, and I felt *weird* about that. And then Jake walked me home, and said he wanted me, and he'd wait for me to be ready for him." I didn't look at Alex, but I could feel her hard stare.

"Umm... ok. I'm going to need clarification."

"On what?"

"Well, let me recap. You have Jake Harrison, extremely good-looking neighbor, highly successful soldier, amazingly well-educated, and evidently super into *you*. You also mentioned you guys definitely have chemistry. What am I missing?" She was genuinely bewildered.

"I know it sounds crazy. He's really pretty perfect. Well, no, he's not perfect, and he's got a lot of crap to deal with, but who doesn't, so it's not like that's an issue. I like him. I really, really do. But all of this time we've been friends, I've had him in the 'no no' file in my brain. I could let myself fall for him a little bit without having to actually... risk anything, because I knew he didn't want a future, and that's what I've been saying I wanted. It's backwards, I know, but the whole time I was wishing he'd want something, it was safer to want because I knew he didn't."

"Right. You want long term. You want the big shebang. And I happen to know despite your claim you have no maternal instincts, you want babies."

"But now..." How could I explain something that didn't even make sense to me?

"Now, what? He told you he's interested in you, and you're worried he doesn't mean it? Or he means for now, but isn't open to marriage?" She kept digging. I knew she wouldn't let this alone until she got to the bottom of things. I both loved and loathed her for that.

"I would never doubt anything he said because the man is

genuine. If he says something, he means it, and I know that. But what if I'm misunderstanding him? Or, what if..." It was then I realized it. "What if I'm not misunderstanding, and he does want those things, and he thinks he wants them with me?"

She watched me for a minute, and it felt like every noise in a one-mile radius had ceased. I desperately wanted her to answer my question, and I could tell she was composing it, thinking about how to respond.

"Then I think you tell him what *you* want. And then you ride off into the sunset and make passionate love and have his babies." I could see the smile growing and the excitement in her face beaming. "Yep. Little Jake and Ellie babies. They'll be little bad- ass geniuses."

"You skipped a few steps. I'm over here feeling awkward about him being my boyfriend, and you've already got crib sheets picked out," I said with an annoyed voice, hiding the little jolt of pleasure the thought brought me.

"I know. And yes, you should start with regularly dating and enjoy that, but from what you've said, he doesn't strike me as someone who's going to want to move slowly now that he's made up his mind."

"That's what scares me. It's not like I doubt *him*. Or even me. On the surface, it seems unreal, and I don't know how to handle that. I feel like a fourth grader trying to go to high school. I feel ignorant and scared and awkward because I haven't had a relationship in a while and the ones I did have were me reluctantly participating."

"I think you tell him that. You have to tell him that," she said, her voice soft and warm. She patted my arm gently.

"*Ugghghhgghhh*. This is the worst." I ran my hands through my hair and clutched my head for a moment before looking back at her. "But I know I have to. The alternative is me saying goodbye to him. And if I'm honest, part of my being upset about losing the grant is because I don't want to move because I want to be near him." I looked at her, waiting for a hint of judgment or anything other than support to cross her face, but nothing did. "I hate admitting that—it seems cliché to move somewhere for your boyfriend or whatever, but... it's true." I let my head hang a little and then glanced up to find her shaking her head at me. Shaking her head and rolling her eyes—*oh good*.

"You are ridiculous. I love you, Dr. Kent, but you are far less pragmatic in your life than you'd like to think. If you end up with Jake, you're going to be moving all over the country until he retires, so factoring him in *now* is good practice." She smiled knowingly at me.

"And see? That. *That*. Can I be an Army wife? *Me?* I don't know the first thing about what that looks like."

"Don't even start with me about that. You've been transitioning your career into what is arguably *the* most military-friendly career a spouse could have, and you value what he does. The details, the ins and outs, the customs and courtesies —those will come. We can learn together," she said and hugged me again.

After that, my lungs were fully expanding, and my heart wasn't aching quite so much. I still felt bruised and a little broken but talking it through and planning for each of my little cages of dynamite made a huge difference.

I felt hopeful.

CHAPTER SEVENTEEN

I HEARD from Mr. Berry by e-mail on Friday, which gave me no new information and only said he needed more time. I was banking on getting a response that told me something I could fuel my hope for a good outcome on, so the disappointment that came from hearing essentially nothing was a real setback. I walked through the plans I had in place, the meetings with lawyers, the other attempts I'd make to contact the agent, her admin Nancy, repellent CathMath77, and anyone else I could think of. But I knew the process took time, and I promised myself I wouldn't continue pestering the Quint lawyer until after the weekend.

I did go to work on Friday, and that was a blessing. Erin was surprised to see me—she thought I'd been struck with the plague but was genuine and welcoming when I returned. If she suspected I hadn't been physically ill, she made no mention of it. Lacy and Bec stopped by to check in, but they were busy wrapping up things for their weekends, so they didn't linger.

Even though my funding wasn't renewed, I did have things to finish up on the current project. I also let the Educational Services Officer, the government employee who worked at the education center and ran the thing, Emily Wender, know what was happening and I wouldn't be back. She was genuinely disappointed and thanked me for the work I'd done. It was kind of her and was a small positive. I told her I was hoping to stay in the community, and she said she'd do whatever she could to help with other employment. Again, this was so kind and unnecessary and sent a pang of regret through me.

At the same time, it gave me hope—maybe Emily would have a connection for something simple I could do to stay connected to the community and wasn't as stressful as teaching a full load. I'd enjoyed my time at the ed center. It was emblematic of a lot of what I loved about education, even if it was rife with the bureaucracy of government contracts.

By Saturday afternoon, I knew I couldn't avoid Jake anymore. I had to face him and tell him he'd hurt me and own up to the fact that I'd likely (Who was I kidding? Definitely) hurt him. I wasn't sure if he was the kind of man to admit that, but I thought, despite his very tough exterior, he would be that way with me.

But I had no luck. I visited him on Saturday before lunch, and he was gone. I stopped by that evening, and he was still gone. I shut down the ridiculous part of me that started thinking about him going on dates with random girls. That would be totally out of character for him, it didn't make sense, and it was my stupid brain grabbing on to one version of the worst-case scenario it could conjure up.

By Sunday, I was incredibly anxious to find him. I could have called him, or texted him, but I felt like I needed to *see* him. He had texted me a handful of times, and even called once, but I couldn't figure out what to say in response. I needed him to be able to see me, and hear me, and hopefully understand this part of me.

I knocked on his door at seven that night. I saw his car in the lot, and I knew he was home. If he didn't answer, that would be a bad sign. If he chose to ignore me at his door, that certainly meant his interest in me was gone—his desire to deal with my emotions and the awkward situation of my failings was finished. But before my mind could spiral out of control with that thought as it had been doing so expertly the last few days, I saw a shadow across the living room space and then the door was sliding open.

His face was unreadable, which wasn't unusual. It didn't mean he was mad. He looked comfortable in worn out jeans and a t-shirt. His jaw was darkened by the most facial hair I'd seen on him since that very first encounter on the plane—he must not have shaved all weekend. My fingers itched to touch his jaw, his chin, the hollow of his cheek. He looked tired, was my first observation, and he looked completely gorgeous.

Just... painfully so.

My ribcage ratcheted down tight, squeezing my lungs, my heart, and every little vessel and cell in between them. My body was caving in on itself, the feeling of missing him, of hurting him, of being hurt by him, of wanting him all so overwhelming I couldn't speak.

"Before you say anything, you have to know I didn't think you plagiarized someone else's book. You have to know that. I wasn't thinking about how that might sound to you." He stopped, waiting for a response. I was listening, my ribcage still gripping my innards in a vice of anxiety and anticipation.

After his short pause, he continued. "I... I do that, with Henry, and sometimes with soldiers who are freaking out. I walk them through the obvious things, the things they know the answer to, so when they come to the biggest questions, it doesn't seem like there are so many missing pieces. I jumped into my problem-solving mode, and it was all wrong. I should have listened and comforted you and told you how stupid it was anyone thought you would plagiarize. I should have said I knew you would never do something like that, and they're insane for thinking of it, and you're right to feel upset." He stopped talking abruptly, watching me with concern on his face, his cheeks a little red, his hands still gripping the doors on either side of his body.

Hearing him rush through his explanation, his hands gripping the doors at his sides tightly, his face taut with stress, I felt a waterfall of affection for him wash over me. I felt the warm sensation begin at the tip of my ears and rush down to my toes. I felt relief, too.

I stepped forward, took the slight step up into his house, and brought my arms behind his back and pressed him into a hug. I put my head on his shoulder and squeezed him, harder than I needed to, but I wanted to convince him I heard him. His arms were around me, then one hand was sliding through my pony tail.

"I missed you," he said, smiling down at me.

"I'm sorry I'm just now coming to you. I came by a few other times this weekend, but you were gone, and I didn't feel like this was a conversation for texting or even a call," I explained, looking up into those luscious brown eyes, now eased of their former worry. He kept one hand around my back and rotated so we could walk in the door. He shut it behind us and led me to sit on the couch a few steps farther into the living room.

"Yeah, it's been a busy weekend, but I'm glad you didn't give up," he said, his mouth sliding up into a small smile.

"Me too," I said, returning that smile. I took a breath and then turned to him. "Thank you for what you said. The day you came over, it was just—it was the worst. And I felt like no one was believing me. And then there you were, and I was ashamed to tell you the grant didn't happen, and then to have to mention this ridiculous accusation. But when you asked me..."

"You thought I was really asking," his low, steady voice supplied.

"Yeah."

"I would never believe you had plagiarized, or really, done anything dishonest. That's not who you are Ellie. I know that, at least," he said. He put a hand on my knee that jutted toward him where I sat facing him, my back against the side of the couch.

"I realized that later. Or I hoped. What you said a few minutes ago—it makes sense. My mom does the same thing. I felt small and trampled that day, like such a fraud, and my pride was destroyed. I didn't have anything left in me to yell at you or challenge your assumption—or what I thought was your assumption. I couldn't face the disappointment of you not believing me too."

"I'm so sorry I made you feel that way."

"It wasn't just you. It was everything, and you coming at the end of that particular day was awful timing," I said and gave him a regretful grin. "I already felt like things were... weird. Between us. And I couldn't wade through a conversation then, so I sent you away. I'm sorry."

"I don't think you need to apologize, but ok. Apology accepted. And I agree, things were confusing after dinner the other night, but that's ok. Obviously, the meeting at the ed center was off. I was short and rude—I'm sorry. We can talk more about that if we need to. But right now, tell me how I can help. Have you gotten any more information about who took your book or what you can do about it?"

And so, we talked.

I discovered he'd taken on quite a bit of indignation on my behalf and had even done some research on how to handle plagiarism in the publishing world, which was more than a little endearing. I told him about my appointments lined up for the next day, how I hoped I'd hear from the agency soon, maybe even first thing so I'd know something more before my first appointment at ten. We talked for two hours before I realized it was getting late, and I was hungry.

"I should probably get home. I need to prep all my evidence in case they want to see my side of things before they agree to take my case." I stood up and walked to his door. He followed me and pulled me into a hug.

"This is going to work out. I know it's been a crap week, and I'm sorry I contributed to that. It's going to get better," he said, speaking into my hair as he hugged me.

I pulled back to see his face. "I know we haven't talked about us—"

"I'll be here. Ok? There's no expiration on that discussion." His eyes were dark, his brow furrowed, and I felt the overwhelming urge to press my lips to his, to take his mouth as my own and find comfort there. He was leaning down to me, over me, since he was taller. His warmth radiated around me.

Somehow, I didn't—I pulled away and said, "Ok" and walked home.

Once confined inside my own walls, I let out a shaky breath. Even though I came away feeling better, and even though I was expecting him to understand my reaction, I didn't think I'd walk out feeling so... cared for. Gentled. Calm and confident. I felt ready to battle for myself, for my integrity. And I now knew with clarity that once I had victory over this, the next thing I was going to battle for was my relationship with Jake.

Because I wanted that.

I wanted him.

I wanted us.

~

I STEPPED into the elevator in the squat brown office building and once the doors closed, I rolled my neck from side to side trying to loosen the concrete pose my back and shoulder muscles had struck since waking earlier that morning. I tended to carry my stress in my neck and shoulders because so much of any given job I'd had involved hunching over a computer screen or maybe because my mind simply sent the most crazed messages to those muscles. *This is crazy! Ball up into little knots and torture her to reinforce the stress. Yes, yes, don't give in to the stretching or massage!*

After almost a week of stress, with increasing intensity as each day passed, my shoulders might as well have been dry wall. Knock them the wrong way, and they'd crumble, they felt that brittle.

I had no idea what to expect. I'd never been to a law office and always imagined them full of fancy people with stylish suits and big salaries. And honestly, few scruples. I recognized, over the last few days, that a large part of my hesitation about going to a lawyer was my unconscious belief that in order to be a lawyer, one must be comfortable bending, or ignoring, the law. But that didn't make sense. I had a friend who went on to law school after our undergrad, and she was quite an upright citizen.

I walked into a long, stuffy hallway and saw the sign that read *Lundquist and Associates* and knocked. Someone buzzed me in, which seemed unnecessary. I approached the desk and the administrative person there knew who I was.

"Ms. Kent, welcome. Please wait in the waiting room," she said in a saccharine voice, and I tried not to feel irritated she used Ms. instead of my hard-won title. I wasn't someone who needed to parade around with my credentials stapled to my forehead. No, it was that the way this woman was looking at me was like I needn't worry my pretty little head at all now that the big strong lawyers were there to help. And if there was something that got under my skin, it was being treated like a child, or like a helpless nitwit.

I took a seat and wondered if I had any response to my latest email. Mr. Berry had sent a reply to my email from Friday with something typically unresponsive. Something about needing more information about Cathy and he was working on it. I'd responded the minute I saw it this morning, asking if there was anything else I could give him (though I was certain I'd provided everything I had) and was praying I'd have another response from him when I got home. The approach of a man who I assumed was Mr. Lundquist interrupted my thoughts.

"Come with me, ma'am," he said and gave me an overly-warm smile. He brushed a hand down the front of his suit, and I saw small crumbs skitter down his white shirt and brown coat to the floor before he buttoned his blazer around his sizeable belly. He turned, and I followed him to a door down a cramped hallway and sat in one of two seats on the opposite side of his desk.

"How can I help you today, Ms. Kent?" My nostrils flared at the "Ms." there paired with the concerned tilt of his head. He slid behind his desk and then dropped abruptly into his seat. I worried for a moment about the chair's ability to hold him. He wasn't all that big, but he had great faith in that office chair. He brushed more crumbs off of his desk, clearing the desktop calendar of any trace of the donut or cookie or whatever it was he must have been eating moments before I arrived.

I could already tell I wouldn't use this guy even if he thought I was as innocent as banana cream pie.

(But really, what is more innocent than banana cream pie? Nothing. Name one bad thing banana cream pie ever did to you. *You can't.*)

I was all for having a snack but wasn't this an office? Hadn't I made an appointment? I felt irritable and the sight of his cookie's leavings cluttering his desk, old napkins pitched in all directions around his computer, and the filthiest computer screen I'd ever seen (did he actually touch it? Do people *touch* computer screens like they're some kind of malfunctioning iPad?) put me off.

"It's Dr. Kent. And I hope you can help me by telling me whether or not I have a case, how you'd proceed if you believe I do, and whether or not you believe I can win that case." My voice was crisp, and I sat with my legs tucked under the chair so my weight and energy were forward. I was wearing a charcoal gray suit, and I looked as professional as leather-bound books.

"Ah, yes, of course. Well I do believe you have sufficient proof. However, I don't believe you'll be able to garner much, if any, financial recompense." He built a teepee with his meaty fingers and watched me over top of it.

"I don't care about money. I've lost a potential contract here, but at this point, I want her to admit she's stolen my work, and I'm the original author." I hadn't even thought about money as something to sue for.

"Well, that's highly unlikely. It's nice you think you don't care about money, Dr. Kent, but believe me, you do. If you've lost this contract with a desirable and interested agent because of this person, then that's a financial hit you've taken." The tone was there again, like I was a simpleton for not wanting to gouge this random woman I knew from an online message board for money she didn't have.

"I appreciate your perspective, but mine differs."

"Well I can see you have some things to think about. I can tell you we would sue for damages, and it would be out of the winnings you'd pay us. We do believe you've got a strong case, and of course it helps you're a PhD and have done this research for veterans. That'll play well to the judge if need be." He smiled at me, his jowls gyrating as he walked toward me with hand outstretched. I stood and shook it, a light, slightly moist hand, and nodded.

"I'll think this over. I'm eager to move forward so I can put it behind me." I wasn't sure what else to say. I knew I wouldn't hire him, but I didn't want to say that in person. I'd email him or call and talk to condescending administrative assistant Jeanine in there if need be.

"Yes, I'll look forward to hearing from you," he said and waived from his office door, then retreated as I walked myself out.

I burst out of the 1970s' mascot of a building and soaked in the fresh air. Something about the air inside had been particularly stifling. It was eleven in the morning on a typical May day, and it was by no means cool. The humidity was rising, and I started sweating immediately after I left the cool, air-conditioned halls, but I still felt far more comfortable out there.

Maybe I was a child. Maybe I was a nitwit. The idea I'd want money hadn't even occurred to me. In my Pollyanna version of this story, CathMath77 (Yes, I was still refusing to refer to her by her real name. And yes, when I thought her screen name it was with an extremely sarcastic bent to my thought, like this was some small revenge. Like I was putting air quotes around her name. *Burn!*) would tuck tail and run but not before she gave a full confession to Mr. Berry at Quint. And then of course, Angelica Quint would give me the contract I'd earned with the book she liked so much until she found out it was a (not really) fake.

The likelihood of that happening was essentially nil. I felt it settle onto my head like a swim cap, tight and unyielding, pressing my hair against my skull and making me twitch and itch and feel bald at the same time. I didn't like this news. I didn't like the feeling I had no control.

MY AFTERNOON MEETING was a small improvement over the Lundquist and Associates debacle, but ultimately, I couldn't escape the feeling that I did not want to sue. Who knew how long that process would stretch out ahead of me and how long I'd be stuck there? I wouldn't be able to move ahead with the book because it would be stuck in purgatory, neither being published nor read.

For what was the thousandth time since the Thursday before when I got the news, I prayed for something to change. Some little sliver of hope or a hint there might be some other way to resolve all of this.

By Wednesday, when I still hadn't heard from Mr. Berry, I called him.

I felt like I was going into battle. I closed my door to my office and did some jumping jacks and jumped around on my tiptoes like I'd seen Jake do before a round of fighting. I smoothed down my blouse and skirt, sat in my chair as straight as I could, and crossed my legs. It was my power pose, despite the well documented reality that crossing one's legs creates a disadvantage and lack of blood flow to the extremities. Fine, but I felt coiled this way, ready to spring and make my point, reclaim my dignity, or at least pressure this guy into giving me *something* I didn't already know. I read through each of the emails we'd exchanged, reviewing everything, and dialed the number.

"This is Ber," a voice said in a rush on the other end of the line.

"Oh, Mr. Berry? This is Elizabeth Kent, and I'm calling—"

"Kent! Yes. I've been meaning to get back to you, just piled up under a bigger case right now. Listen, you've got the proof, and this, what is it..." he trailed off and I heard clicking and tapping of a keyboard on the other end. "Cathy Matthews, yeah, we've got her scheduled for a conference call later this morning. We'll see what she says."

"Really? Well that's... good, right? Your email last week didn't sound hopeful at all."

"Yeah, it's good. In a perfect world, she'll confess, and it'll be a done deal. But we won't know what we're dealing with until then. I'd advise not to get your hopes up," he said.

He said I could call back around noon, at which point he'd have more news, and hung up. Two hours had never crawled by so slowly.

"Mr. Berry? What'd she say?"

"No show."

"Sorry?"

"She was a no show—we couldn't get her. No response from her whatsoever yet. So now, we wait to hear from her." He sounded matter-of-fact, like this wasn't a huge part of my life for the last several months being wagged in front of me, all the power held by some unoriginal jerkface. "I'll be in touch."

And he was gone.

I spent the rest of the day trying desperately not to watch

the clock and mostly failing. As I was shutting down my email and signing out of my computer, my phone rang.

"Dr. Kent, it's good news. Matthews finally called us."

"Oh, thank God. You sounded like you expected not to hear from her. What'd she say?" My heart was pounding out of my ribcage and I stood, one hand bracing me on my desk.

"I thought maybe she'd make more of an effort to claim the work, but she hasn't. I doubt it'll change, and I'm thinking we'll get it worked out. I've seen it before, and it'll get worked out," he said, and relief flooded me even though I could tell he was busy working on something else while we talked. I guessed this was him, all the time.

"That's such good news. Do you have any idea what a timeline would be?" I couldn't keep the happiness out of my voice. I asked him every question I could think of, most of which didn't have answers yet. He didn't know the timeline—depended on Matthews a little bit. Didn't know what Quint would want to do, though he did warn me they didn't like to pick up authors with even a whiff of something like this on them. That was certainly a disappointment, but if I'd found an agent once, I felt like I could do it again.

By the time I hung up with "Ber" I was so excited, I could hardly be contained by my office. I knew who I wanted to see. I texted Alex and told her, and she called and screamed in elation through the phone. I texted Jake and told him and asked him to come over for dinner when he was home from work.

I made spaghetti—nothing fancy, because my kitchen skills were less than stellar. But I could do spaghetti, and garlic bread, and salad.

By the time Jake knocked on the door, my energy level had settled a little bit. My hope, my excitement, and my general demeanor were all so much better than they'd been the last time I saw him. I wasn't nervous to see him —just ready.

And then I saw him. He smiled brightly, like full-on, teeth and all, smiled at me as he stepped into my apartment, and I'm pretty sure I forgot everything that had happened that day. That month.

He was wearing jeans and a dark t-shirt, the combination he adopted for anything but our most formal occasions together. Somehow he seemed more muscular, taller, and more striking than he'd ever been before.

I kid you not. Maybe it was the light. Maybe I'd shrunk. Maybe the glee from earlier was still shading my eyes, contouring his chest and shading the angles of his jaw in a more brilliant line, like the change from pencil to charcoal. Whatever it was, he was stunning.

He brushed his jaw against mine as he kissed my cheek, and in a daze I turned my mouth toward him and kissed his cheek lightly in return before he pulled away. His skin was smooth and warm, and he smelled so good. Not even the smell of garlic bread wafting from the kitchen could compete with the clean laundry and mint and a hint of something else.

Before he pulled back all the way, he pulled me close into a hug. "I'm so glad it's getting cleared up," he said, and the low rumble vibrated through my chest where he held me close to him another moment.

I smiled into his chest and said, "Me too. Although it's not cleared up, but I am hopeful it will be eventually and without me having to get my own lawyer, thank goodness."

"I have some bad news, but I wanted to come see you. Henry called—Grandma is in the hospital. I think she's going to be fine, but I need to be there." I saw the stress in his shoulders, now that I was looking for it.

"I'm so sorry—of course you do. Are you leaving tonight?"

"Yeah, I'm going to head out now. I can make it before midnight, I think, or soon after, and be there for the morning visiting hours. Hopefully she'll turn a corner soon. It's pneumonia so it can go either way, but the doctors seemed happy Henry made her come in tonight, and they didn't wait 'til morning."

I grabbed him and pulled him to me again, thinking of how much this woman mattered to him. I knew she was all he had left of his mom and dad, the only remaining relative who he cared much about other than Henry.

"She's going to be fine. Get going so you get there, and don't speed too much, and be careful," I said, starting to babble.

His eyes brightened and one side of his mouth quirked up. "I will Ellie, and we'll get together when I'm back."

"Yes please. And text me when you get there, ok? So I'm not lying in bed imagining you stranded on the side of the road?"

"I will. See you soon," he said, and with another quick kiss to my cheek, he was gone.

I stood there, facing the door, and my heart constricted. He was devoted to his family, and in that moment, watching him practically racing out the door, I knew he would be that way with me—if I let him.

He'd been showing me that, bit by bit, all along.

That thought was a force. It was like a tornadic gust of wind pushing me across a field. I'd started at one end, feeling interested, but safe from any possibility of falling. As the wind began whirling, I knew the potential for danger—for the risk of my heart, for the potential to fail in a relationship I actually wanted and would certainly feel invested in. But when the full gale-force wind arrived in that moment, all I could do was welcome it. I'd arrived at the other side of the field, forced there by each encounter with Jake.

His character, his loyalty, his love for his family. His desire to be with me, and to tell me how he felt was a gift. Each moment of surprising sensitivity, clearly wrought from years of self-assessment and some amount of therapy, pushed me farther.

And if all of that wasn't enough, his support of me—his investment in my success, his desire for me to see my dreams realized—it was almost painful, and yet this was the moment I realized, as he drove south away from me and toward his family to care for them, to be their rock, that I absolutely and irretrievably loved this man.

This was a truly terrifying thought. I'd never loved anyone but my family and Alex. I'd never loved someone like Jake. But maybe that was because I didn't know anyone like him.

Part of me wondered if it was too soon to feel this way. I had barely known him for six months—not quite, even—and here I was, in love with the guy. We hadn't even been on more than one official date.

But then, as soon as I worried it was too soon, I thought of all the interactions we'd had that jumped past the initial flutters of first dates and trivia and dove right into the heart of who we both were. I thought of him telling me about his mom, sharing his grief and anger and sadness. I thought about his comforting me when I felt my parents' disapproval so sharply and his encouragement to tell them the truth.

The excitement and terror of love settled around me. It was maddening and yet a relief to have this realization now, just after he left for an unknown amount of time. I wouldn't blurt out my confession of love awkwardly, at least not yet. I would wait until we were together and would start with the fact that yes, I did want to be with him. I'd go from there, if he was receptive. And I would be patient until then... I would not obsess about this.

I would not obsess about this.

I shook off my daydreaming and ate dinner. As I ate, I felt the nagging begin.

Since I had the evening free, I knew what I had to do.

CHAPTER EIGHTEEN

"ELLIE? It's been weeks! How are you?" My mom sounded frazzled, and I could feel my jaw locking up, my shoulders tensing. If she was already stressed about something at work, or even about the last few weeks of no Sunday calls, now wasn't the time.

But no. I'd been putting off honesty with my parents for the better part of two decades. Time to woman up.

"I have a lot to talk to you and Dad about regarding my career," I said, keeping my voice low and calm and making sure not to speak too quickly. There was no way I was going to spend this conversation having them claiming they couldn't hear or understand what I was saying.

"Ellie, what's going on," my dad said impatiently.

"In the last few weeks, I've learned a lot. I did not get awarded the extension on my research project—"

"Oh, honey. I'm sorry. I know you were excited about that," my mom said, and before she finished, I heard by dad pipe in, "but that's not all bad because you can take on a full load in the fall somewhere, get back on track with your teaching—"

"I'm going to need you both to listen for a little while. Please." So much for that calm. I'd raised my voice and they were silent. I needed to be firm so they would listen and try to understand me before arguing or suggesting alternatives.

"I do not want to teach. I do not want to earn my place as university faculty long term. I do not want to be a tenure-tracked professor." I stopped and let that settle around us. They were silent. I did what little I could to tell myself I'd asked them to stay quiet, and that their silence was not judgment.

"I got burnt out during the last few years, and I saw a lot of ugliness in the department I don't want a part of. I know universities and departments differ, and I'm open to the fact that someday I may change my mind. But for now, my choice to move away from New York and not reapply for other teaching positions has been strategic. I wondered if being away would make me miss it, but my absence has only served to solidify the fact that I am ready to move on."

Silence. Stillness. Nothing. Not even breathing.

"I can tell you that I will teach again, maybe even full time for a while, but I want to make clear it is not my goal." I stopped here, because this was it. I'd done the *I don't want to teach* and now, the big one.

"I want to write. I want to write novels, and I want to do that full time. I've had work accepted by a reputable agent, but it was stolen by someone who I allowed to read and give me feedback on the draft, and so it may not end up getting—"

"*What?* Someone stole your work? How dare they? Who is this person? We'll call Mark. Mark can find someone who knows about this—"

"Wait, wait, Dad. Please. I don't need you to call your lawyer. Thank you for your outrage on my behalf, but I think it's going to work out ok. I don't know what will happen with the novel, but I feel pretty confident I'll be able to find a place for it eventually, just probably not where I thought it was going."

There was a beat of silence, and then my mom spoke, her voice raw with emotion. "You've always loved writing. I'm so proud of you."

I pushed out a shaky breath. I wanted to say thank you, but I was overcome. It wasn't that I lived for their approval, but this acceptance, at least this first positive volley, was more than I'd hoped for.

"Yeah, I have. And I've been resisting it for years and years. I decided I needed to take time when I wasn't grading or writing for my academic profile and give it a go. Even if everything I've written is utter crap, it has brought me incredible joy."

"There's no way it's crap!" My dad was an expert at defending my honor, even from myself.

"I'm sure it's wonderful, Ellie," my mom said in her calm voice.

"Well, your blind faith in me has always been pretty overwhelming, but right about now, I'll take it. Thank you." I chuckled to myself and shook my head.

I knew even if I didn't teach another class in my life, the accomplishment and the process of completing my PhD, of writing that infernal dissertation, and of this discovery, was invaluable.

"I also need to say I'm sorry. I don't think I've given you guys enough credit."

"What do you mean sweetie?" my mom asked.

"I have always wanted to write. I was good at the other stuff, but since I can remember, I've loved writing. I should have done it in college, for my master's, maybe even for my PhD. At this point, I'm making peace with what I *did* do, but

I'm sorry I didn't trust you guys enough to tell you what I wanted." They were quiet for an agonizing minute.

"I'm sorry too, Ellie. I'm afraid we pushed you into things you might not have wanted." My mom's voice was soft.

"We can't go back, and I've had a wonderful life. I love school, and I would have always wondered about teaching, so it's good I got to do it. In many ways it makes me even more sure writing is what I want, and it's helpful I have a breadth of knowledge from which to draw." And there it was.

In that moment, I felt so grateful. Grateful their high expectations pushed me to do things that weren't automatic, but that I succeeded in with hard work. Grateful for this moment of reconciliation that was far too long in coming.

"You are our greatest accomplishment, Elizabeth. I hope you know that," my dad said, a little wobble in his voice when he said my name.

"Thank you, Dad. I love you both, so much."

"We love you, honey."

"But... Ellie. Can you support yourself with that? I don't want to sound critical, but we do worry, especially since you left your salaried job for the much less stable grant-funded position in Podunk, Kentucky."

"Hey, I wouldn't call Morrisville, Kansas a bustling metropolis, ok?" We shared a moment of laughter together, and my heart felt full and whole.

"Fine, fine," my dad conceded.

"I can't right now. It will be a while before I can. Alex helped me see that even though I am ready to transition away from teaching, it doesn't have to be all or nothing. My plan is to teach as a full-time temporary professor, or something like that, where my obligations for committees and projects and such aren't as intense, and then write. Or maybe adjunct, but I'd only be able to do that if I get a contract somewhere for more novels or this one sells well and soon. That's a long shot." I was shaking from the surges of adrenaline that had raced through my body at the beginning of the conversation. I wrapped myself in the blanket that lay across the back of my couch and snuggled into it.

"Where will you live when your lease is up there?" my mom asked.

"I'm planning to stay here. There are a bunch of schools around here that would work. And... I have a boyfriend," I said and felt like I was about sixteen years old. I could feel my blushing cheeks, and even though I knew they couldn't see me, I felt sure they knew I was red-faced and feeling awkward.

The word *boyfriend* was ill-fitting for Jake. If anyone had ever *not* been a boy, it was this man, all hard muscles and square jaw and lethal fighter and blazing mind. *Mmm.*

"Oh, do you now?" my dad said, and I could hear him smiling.

"Yes, and he's a soldier, so you'll have lots to talk about. He already knows you're both staunch pacifists," I said, feeling a little thrill at the prospect of watching Jake battle wits with my parents.

"A soldier? I guess that's no surprise," my mom said.

"Really? I thought you guys would be... upset, or..." I couldn't hide my shock.

"Oh, I'm sorry, did you want us to be disapproving? You're nearly thirty Ellie..."

"I'm nearly twenty-eight, but ok," I corrected.

"Sure, but the point is, you're a grown woman. You've been half in love with the idea of soldiers since you met Alex your freshman year and heard about her childhood love who, I believe, is also a soldier." They knew all about the love story that was Alex and Luke. They'd heard many of the ups and downs for the past year, but I'd told them about Alex's friend Luke who went into the Army years ago.

"Huh, that's true. I thought it was so romantic." I was a sucker for a childhood romance. Maybe it was because I'd never had any such prospects. Or maybe because when I met Alex and heard her talk about Luke those first few days of our freshman year, I *knew* they had to be together. Of course, that was the hopeful romantic in my seventeen-year-old's heart, but still. Score one for my heart on that one.

"I'm sure he's a special person, if you've chosen him, Ellie." My mom's voice had turned soft, and, dare I say it, even a little sentimental.

"He is. He really, really is."

We chatted a while longer, and when I hung up, I was so happy and light, I felt the tears slide from my eyes and sat and smiled while I watched *Pretty Woman*. Nothing says joy like a controlling business man buying a prostitute out of her sad circumstances, right?

(Problematic themes of *Pretty Woman* aside, no one will ever convince me that the moment Roberts says, "Big mistake. Huge," isn't one of the all-time triumphs. *Oh snap!*)

I HEARD from Jake at two in the morning. He'd arrived safely. He messaged again after he'd been with his grandma that morning, and the news was good. The doctors thought they'd only need to keep her one more night. That meant he'd be home by the weekend.

I was trying desperately not to allow myself to calculate the hours until the weekend. But I couldn't stop myself.

I couldn't. If he got home Friday evening, it was approximately seventy-seven hours until I'd see him again. If he came home Saturday afternoon? It'd be more like ninety-five. I'd be working another twenty-eight hours this week. That meant I had a lot of spare time to deal with. Sleep would consume a good chunk. But still.

All I could think about was Jake. And as much as this should have annoyed me, I only felt elated. I felt like I was basking in the glow of newfound love.

The fact that I had no idea whether he loved me back was a little scary, but I trusted that could come. He seemed to want it as much as I finally recognized I did, and so... it could happen.

The week, as though to punish me for experiencing the agony of love, dragged on. It moved at what could only be described as a begrudging pace. I managed to find pockets of focus in which I wrapped up the finishing touches on my TESS project. It was a bittersweet moment to save the final draft, knowing that next week it would need one last read through and then I'd submit it and officially be done with my work there.

By Friday afternoon, I was a sweating, nervous mess. I was anxious to see Jake, and so ready, and he was supposed to be getting in his car any minute. I wanted to see a text saying he was on his way. I wanted that so much, I might scream.

But no such text came until hours later when he messaged to say he was still in Florida. Henry had asked him—begged him, he said—to stay one more day so they could spend a little time together outside of the hospital and at his grandmother's, and since he didn't have plans to see Henry again for a while, he'd agreed. While I groaned outwardly and was glad I was home and not still in the office, I understood. This was one of the reasons I was in love with Jake Harrison, and there was no denying it.

∾

By Saturday at noon, I was pacing my apartment. I'd survived the night with a steady stream of romantic comedies, a fair amount of pacing, and a call to Alex, which was rushed since she ducked out of an event to take a ten-minute break to answer, but it was better than nothing.

Jake had texted early that morning to say he was getting on the road, and I began calculating minutes, not hours. This, I knew, was an unhealthy habit, but there was no avoiding that my mind was riveted on the time, unwilling to part with its concentration on the subject for any reason.

I went for a run. I showered. I went to the grocery store. I cleaned my apartment. I tried to write, but I couldn't focus. I thought about how nice it would be to be one of those women who cooked or baked or did something creative with her nervous energy, and then I paced around some more and considered calling my parents but decided I'd be irritated with them for simply existing and not being able to deliver Jake to my door on demand.

So, I was pacing.

When the tap on my sliding door came, I jumped to it and flung it open, and there he was. He pulled me in and surrounded me in a hug, lifting me up and walking backward into the room. I buried my face in his chest and listened as his deep voice rumbled through his body and filled mine up.

"I missed you."

"I missed you too," I said and pulled back so I could see him. It was an almost identical scene to the last time we'd met before he'd had to leave on Monday, but I had changed. I knew my own secret—I'd finally told myself the truth.

He was looking at me hungrily, and I knew my eyes were reflecting the same desire. I glanced down at his lips and felt a pang of need fill me, like my body was compelled to connect itself to him in every way now my heart had stitched itself to his.

But he pulled back before I could do anything about that raging impulse. What might have given me a moment of panic before made sense to me now.

Since I'd decided I wanted to be with Jake days ago—since I'd finally reconciled my desire for him and his apparent desire to be with me and the fact that all of this was perfectly acceptable if I wanted it to be, something had shifted in me. Add to that my epiphany that I was not just interested, but sold out to him—entirely owned, if I wanted to be honest with myself (and darn it, wasn't it high time?), and I knew he needed to understand.

Thus far I'd been closed off. I'd been cagey and unwilling, and yet obviously not entirely unwilling. Then I was distracted, and upset, and dealing with a real pile of junk I couldn't *stop* thinking about, even if I wanted to swim around in the cozy, terrifying feeling of friendship (and now, I recognized, love) with him.

He understood that, somehow. He knew I had to work through one thing at a time. So there was no chance he would be the one to bring up the status of our relationship, or what he wanted, and what I now knew I also wanted. He would wait for me as he said he would. He wasn't going to kiss me for fear it would confuse me and not be welcomed. It was hard to imagine he couldn't tell I wanted him now, but he was steady and firm in his desire not to rush me.

This meant it was time for action.

"I do want you to be my boyfriend," I blurted as I followed him to the couch. I spoke to his back, but he turned quickly, his face lit by an amused grin. I felt my pulse increase even more than it had when we'd been hugging, just about to kiss.

"Ok. Time to talk about that, then." He seemed so calm. How could he be so calm? My insides were in knots despite the fact his feelings for me appeared to be unchanged.

Were they?

Oh please God, don't let him change his mind!

"I freaked out last week with Henry calling you that, and then with you saying you... you..."

"That I want you," he supplied, and his voice was, how could I say it? Like melted chocolate. Like every decadent thing on one plate.

He sat there on my couch, all of his energy focused on me.

I swallowed down the thrill of excitement that voice, that look, those words gave me. "Yes. Well, you said you want to be *with* me..."

"Well I do, that. I want you in every possible way, Ellie." His eyes were a bow, and his arrow had stuck its target, no doubt. I was pinned in place by those words, the heat and intensity behind them, swirling in his irises like cream poured into coffee.

I cleared my voice, licked my lips, and straightened my spine. "Yes. And I got overwhelmed. I'd spent a lot of time thinking about you as unavailable—"

"You spent a lot of time thinking about me?" He grinned like the Cheshire Cat and I rolled my eyes.

"Of course I did! We started spending a fair amount of time together, and you're not an *un*attractive man..." I trailed off and bit my lip to hide my grin.

"Not unattractive. Oh good. That's high praise." He folded his hands in his lap and leaned back like he was nonchalant, but I could see his chest was rising and falling more visibly than normal.

"Anyway. You are this very decisive, determined, special

person, and you seemed so sure about me. And maybe I read that wrong, but I—"

"You didn't." His eyes were smoldering—straight up smoldering at me.

"Stop interrupting." I gave him a look, and he grabbed the hand nearest him and weaved our fingers together. He brought the back of my hand to his lips and then nodded for me to continue. If he kept talking and saying things like that, I'd never get to the point. I'd just become wax and melt in the face of his flaming heat.

Someone save me because this man is hot.

Hot, hot, hot.

"I've never been in a relationship I was invested in. I've only had two boyfriends before, and it has been years since them, and they were both ultimately the result of convenience first and then complacency. I've never felt..." I took a deep, steadying breath and continued. "Well, this sounds like a line, but I've never f-felt for someone what I do for you." My voice shook at the end of my admission, and he squeezed my hand with his. I'd stuttered on "felt" because I'd almost said *loved* but I wasn't ready to say that yet. Not yet.

"I don't know what I'm doing either. I haven't had a girlfriend since high school, and I was a terrible boyfriend then. I was completely selfish—and it's not that I'm not selfish now, because I know I am. I have a lot to learn—but I know I've learned a thing or two about myself, and other people, since then." He let go of my hand and reached up to smooth a stray piece of hair back over my shoulder. "Do you remember when I said, 'I'm not an idiot' on our date a few weeks ago? And you gave me a look like you had no idea what I meant but didn't ask me?"

I nodded. It had struck me as strange.

"What I meant was once I met you, I couldn't ignore you.

Obviously physically, you had my attention from the second you assaulted my hand on the plane." He laughed as I crossed my arms in an exaggerated gesture. "But after doing the study and then the night after Smith... you were so compassionate, and strong, and lovely..." His voice softened, well really, his whole body seemed to soften and sway toward me. He grabbed me and kissed me quickly, like he couldn't wait another second, and then continued. "After that I knew all my rules were worthless. Waiting another second was ridiculous when you were standing right there in front of me."

I'm pretty sure my eyes were sparkling the way they did in cheesy romance movies—the only way to sparkle, really. My smile was wide across my face. "So even though I may very well ruin everything between us with my ineptitude at relationships, you still want to date me?" Did I feel a little silly about continuing to question him? *Maybe.* But I was relishing his willingness to tell me what I very much wanted to hear because I knew it was true.

His face turned serious, and for a second I thought I was about to face a huge upset. But then he said, "I'll want more than dating. You should know that, Ellie." It sounded like a warning, and yet I didn't feel scared or even worried. Not even a little bit. I felt hopeful, and eager, and happier than I'd felt in a long time.

It wasn't just the prospect of having Jake in my life indefinitely. It was the whole situation. Alex's words about my next steps not necessarily meaning I was locked into them—into teaching a bit, or working some other job, or whatever the case may be, had been swimming around in my unconscious and taking root.

I'd spent so much of my life looking forward—to high school, then college, then my master's program, then getting a PhD. The looking ahead suited me in many ways, but I wondered if that wasn't part of what burned me out on academia. I saw the prospect of clawing my way to tenure as just another thing to always be *anticipating*. I wanted to feel breathless and restless and ecstatic over something of my own making, not whether or not the dossier I'd spent hundreds of hours compiling would meet the tenure board's approval.

The thought of Jake with me, and me working toward a time when I could write all the time... it was the dream. It was the absolute dream I'd never dared to verbalize.

"I'm glad. Because I'm going to want more than dating too," I finally said.

He had my face cradled in his hands in an instant, his palms warm on my cheeks, and his mouth was on mine, kissing me slowly, carefully. His tongue met mine, and I made a sound, something primal and ecstatic, but I didn't care. I ran my hands into his hair and over his rough cheeks. He'd been away only a few days but already had the makings of a seriously attractive beard.

He pulled me close, and closer, and I was crushed to him, and him to me, each of us reveling in the other, and my insides were mush. Just utter goo. Gelatinous nothingness, except a beating heart and swirling nerve endings.

"I have to—" he pulled back a bit and looked at me with more intensity than I'd ever seen, and for this man, that was saying something. "I love you Ellie. I love you." He was breathless and he looked raw, his hair crazy where my fingers had been, and his eyes were wondrous as he looked at me.

"I love you too. It's crazy, but I do," I said, equally breathless and amazed. He pulled me in and kissed me again. "We do everything from the middle first. We've barely dated, but we're in love. This is so stupid," I said between kisses, shaking my head.

"It's not stupid. I think it fits." He gave me a reproving smile.

"I can see that. We can't stand the small talk, and we're both restless in our own way. It makes sense we jumped to the middle."

"I blame your fear of flying."

EPILOGUE

We sat at the table on Henry's balcony outside his apartment in the Floridian late summer evening. I'd met Grandma Harrison earlier that afternoon and she was truly lovely. I'd loved her before I ever met her because I knew what she'd done for Jake and Henry. I saw her give Jake a knowing smile and a wink, and I felt a small quake in my body at the thought that she'd given her approval of me. While I knew it was unlikely to be a difficult task, I didn't realize how much that meant to me until I saw it happen, and how important that sign-off was.

Jake was inside getting us waters while we sat and enjoyed the short burst of afternoon rain.

Henry looked at me with that familiar gleam in his eye. I braced myself.

"So, you're going to join the royal family, huh? Become Princess Elizabeth?"

My eyes widened and my heart rate skyrocketed before I saw the delight that gave him and I calmed myself. "You're such a tease. One of these days he *is* going to ask me, and then you're going to feel like a jerk."

"Why would I feel like a jerk? I've always wanted a sister," he said, raising his eyebrows for emphasis.

"What's this now? You want a sister?" Jake asked as he stepped out to join us with three waters in hand.

I took a moment to admire him as I so often did when I had a moment to. He was hard muscles, long arms and legs, serious face. But I knew the Jake behind the mask, behind the hard-ass sergeant. I knew about his love for his family, his incredibly tender heart, and his deeply nerd-level love of Tolkien. I knew how he could love, and I was fiercely proud to be his and have him as mine.

"I was telling Ellie you're going to propose to her soon, and then she'll be joining our little royal family. She's even got an appropriately royal name, although in this scenario, it's like you're marrying your grandmother." Henry's broad smile was brash and showed how pleased with himself he was. I expected Jake to fumble around or try to excuse him, but I should have known better.

"The grandmother part is weird, true. But we'll ignore that. He's right." His eyes were smiling but the rest of him was serious.

"He's right that I have an appropriately royal name?" I asked.

"Well, that. But he's right about the other thing too."

"The other thing?" I swallowed a giggle, the giddiness surprising me.

"The joining the royal family thing."

A NOTE FROM THE AUTHOR

Veteran suicide is an issue we can't ignore. According to the most recent report from the US Department of Veteran's Affairs, Veteran suicide accounts for 14% of suicides in the United States each year. The rate for Veterans ages 18-34 is *increasing*, not decreasing, though it seems there may be a slight downward trend overall.

We can *hope* these numbers improve, but we can also get to work.

First, if you are a Veteran in crisis, or you're concerned about one, there is free, confidential support is available 24/7. Call the Veterans Crisis Line at 1-800-273-8255 and Press 1, send a text message to 838255

If you're not a Veteran but need help, call the National Suicide Prevention line at 1-800-273-8255.

If you'd like to support some organizations doing amazing

work with Veteran suicide prevention specifically, here are just a few doing good work:

Vets 4 Warriors: www.vets4warriors.com
Cohen Veterans Network: www.cohenveteransnetwork.org
Stop Soldier Suicide: www.stopsoldiersuicide.org
Mission 22: www.mission22.com
Advocacy through AFSP: www.afsp.org

ACKNOWLEDGMENTS

Thank you to the Author of love and life—thank you for loving me relentlessly.

Thank you to my husband, whose advice and support are invaluable. I am so glad to be yours.

Special thanks to my parents, who are like Ellie's parents in only the best ways. You've always pushed me to do my best, and then been unnecessarily amazed when I do. I'm sorry to tell you that any drive, humor, or success I have are all your fault.

To my beta readers Christy and Meagan, thank you for your honesty and time. I really can't write these books in a vacuum and your feedback is so helpful! Thank you.

My love and gratitude for Julie, Melissa, Karen, Monica, Denise, and so many others who've cheered me on is endless. I simply wouldn't keep writing without you in my corner, and

I wish everyone could know the beauty of friendships like ours.

To Jamie, who trudged through NaNoWriMo 2017 with me and wrote her own book while I wrote this one, thank you. Thank you for a thousand things, but on this one, thanks for helping with basically every aspect, and for rooting for Ellie and Jake right along with me.

To the Writerly Writers Write group, thank you once again for your insight and encouragement. Let's keep swapping!

To Judy Roth, thank you for teaming up with me again and helping me clean up and clarify this book. Thanks, too, for powering through at the end and flipping drafts so fast!

Thanks to Jeff Senter at Indie Formatting for formatting the book and making it look beautiful.

Rainbeau Decker, wow. There's no amount of groveling I can do in print or person that will properly convey my thanks. Your eye, your talent, your generosity, your creativity... wow. Add to that the fact that your models are just astoundingly gorgeous and I cannot tell you how much I love the cover—THANK YOU. You're helping make my dreams come true.

Last but never least, thank you to all the readers who've supported this book. As an indie author, your support is what keeps me writing. Please share the book with friends and consider leaving a review. I hope you'll be in touch!

ABOUT THE AUTHOR

Claire Cain lives to eat and drink her way around the globe with her traveling soldier and two kids, but is perhaps even happier hunkered down at home in a pair of sweatpants and slippers using any free moment she has to read and cook. Or talk—she really likes to talk. She has become an expert at packing too many dishes in too few cabinets and making houses into homes from Utah to Germany and many places in between. She's a proud Army wife and is frankly just really happy to be here.

CONNECT WITH CLAIRE:

Website: www.clairecainwriter.com
Facebook: facebook.com/clairecainwriter
Twitter: @writeclairecain
Instagram: @clairecainwriter
E-mail: clairecainwriter@gmail.com
Newsletter sign-up: http://eepurl.com/dGuIBv

Photo Credit: Michael Cryer

Want more? Here's a teaser for
Don't Stop Now,
The Rambler Battalion Series Book 3,
starring Captain Rae Jackson,
due out May/June 2019!

GABRIEL

The blonde bun in front of me was a perfect swirl of gold and yellow hues, the hair pulled tight and meticulously back from the woman's face. Her patrol cap was tucked into the pocket just above her knee, like mine. She was holding a plastic container packed with salad bar fixings—spinach, beets, peppers, cucumbers—a lot more but I didn't want to peer over her shoulder and freak her out. It was all I could do not to let my eyes run over the back of her uniform, but I was determined not to do that here, in the commissary, in front of two dozen other soldiers that were quite likely doing just that.

Ever since she came into the ER, I'd seen her everywhere. *Everywhere.* At the gym. At the commissary two days out of the last six. In her car driving in gate one last week. I swore I saw her at the movie theater last weekend, but maybe that was my imagination.

This wasn't uncommon. I'd been at Fort Campbell for about a year and a half, and since it was my first time working at an Army Hospital—my first job after getting my bachelor's degree and then my master's in nursing—I'd come to expect that sometimes after I took care of someone in the ER, they'd show up in all kinds of places I'd never noticed before.

But her... it was becoming a problem.

I'd treated her three weeks ago when she came in for

abdominal pain after passing out at the gym. I'm not sure what happened after she left, but she hadn't come back in.

She stepped up in the lane ahead of me, the sign above our line claiming that soldiers had priority during the hours of 11am to 2pm, an unhelpful gesture considering everyone in the place was a soldier in uniform. She set a divider down on the little conveyer belt behind her salad and a bakery bag without looking up.

Part of me willed her to look up and notice me; the other part of me dreaded her doing that and not recognizing me the way I definitely did her.

I knew her by her light, golden hair, its uniform-perfect bun styled at the back of her head so unlike the loose, messy pile that sprung out in all directions from the crown of her head as she stared straight in front of her while I took her pulse, my brown skin dark against her pale wrist as I counted her heartbeats to establish heartrate. I recognized her compact body, despite being hidden in the looser-fitting Army uniform, much more concealed now than it was in just tight black shorts, a bright white sports bra, and a royal blue tank top that was less an actual shirt and more a suggestion of one. I remembered how her chest would rise and fall under my stethoscope as I listened to her heart, the thin skin visible there flushed from pain or exertion or anxiety.

Stop thinking about her chest.

I stepped forward too. Placed my salad on the belt to the left the divider, added a bottle of water because, like an idiot, I'd forgotten mine at home. The byproduct of my Mexican parents was, at moments like these, I could hear my mother in my mind as if she were standing in front of me and not taking her own lunch break in the employee lounge at the Dallard's of Wyeth, Texas, where she'd worked for the last twenty years.

My mother hated wasting money and she'd glare at me with her lips pinched in exaggerated disgust if she saw my plastic water bottle, rolling her eyes at my *throwing away money* just to hydrate at my convenience instead of finding a perfectly good drinking fountain somewhere.

Or a hose, for that matter.

I studied my salad through the plastic container, though my eyes wandered to the hand of my check-out line neighbor as her index and middle fingers alternately drummed soundlessly on the lid of her salad while the checker—Alice, said the nametag—handed the soldier in front of her his receipt.

"Hi there, how you doing?" Alice asked.

"Just fine, thank you. How are you? Hanging in there with the lunch rush?" She—Captain Jackson—responded with a calm, smooth voice.

Her voice had been shaky, unsure, in the ER. That made sense since she'd passed out twice in the span of two hours and the second time it took her a few minutes to remember what had happened. Not unusual to be disoriented in a situation like that, but she'd been upset until she put all the pieces together.

"Are you two together today?" Alice asked, her eyes lifting to me with a grade-a customer service smile, then pointedly looking back at Captain Jackson.

As Captain Jackson turned to look at who Alice was talking about, I smiled back at her and shook my head. "No, ma'am, we're not," just as that quiet voice also declared "No."

Captain Jackson looked at me with a polite smile on her face—really nothing more than her lips pressed together and slightly turned up—but before she stepped forward toward the payment console, her eyebrows raised. "Oh, it's you," she said, her cheeks reddening as she pulled out a wallet, a card, and swiped.

"Hi, ma'am. I hope you're doing better," I said, because I couldn't very well ask her anything in detail—not without embarrassing her or violating HIPAA protocols.

"Yes. I am. Thank you." Her response was stilted, her hands shoving her card back in the thin, black wallet and grabbing her salad. "Thank you," she offered to Alice, and then stood there, facing the exit a moment before she walked to it and out the sliding glass doors.

~

RAE

Of course. Of course the gorgeous nurse who'd seen me at my absolute worst was the man standing behind me in the commissary. Of course I blushed when I recognized him. Who wouldn't?

I shut my eyes and my grip tightened on the steering wheel, though my keys rested on my thigh and the car was silent. I thought of that awful day, the last time I saw him.

"I'm not sure when it started, but I know it has become increasingly... problematic in the last six months," I explained, my fingers clenching the sheet resting over my legs on the hospital bed.

"Ok. And it seems to be related to your menstrual cycle?" The nurse's lips pronouncing menstrual cycle *sent a flood of embarrassment through me. I wasn't ashamed of being a woman, or even having to describe the pain. But I was angry at being there in the first place—angry I'd passed out, angry that I didn't know why the pain was getting worse, and angry I was spending my time in the ER instead of finishing my workout and heading home so I could get to bed on time.*

"I think so? I'm not on my period now—shouldn't be for

another two weeks." *And that was the killer. The timing was unclear, unpredictable.*

"Are you bleeding now?" *He asked, his voice rich and smooth and completely at odds with his bright blue scrubs and the stark white of the hospital.*

"I don't think so. I don't usually bleed when it happens." *I flushed again, knowing my chest, neck, and cheeks were bright with embarrassment. Why couldn't I have had a female nurse?*

"Are you currently pregnant or breastfeeding?" *His brown eyes were directed at the laptop resting on his knees where he entered notes as he hunched on the small stool next to the bed. I huffed out a breath.*

"Definitely not."

"You couldn't be pregnant?" *I could see his dark, thick eyebrows were raised as he typed away.*

"No."

"Not even a chance? Because that would be an important—"

"I haven't had sex for the better part of six years, so yeah. I'm certain." *His head popped up when I said "six" and his eyes were searching my face, his lashes blinking as if that might clarify things for him.*

"O-ok. Not pregnant."

I let out a breath and leaned back against the bed. What a humiliating topper to a magnificently mediocre day. Not only was my nurse the most beautiful man I'd ever seen, but now I'd just given him a brief tour of my sexual history in a spectacular example of what it meant to over-share.

A knock on my window sounded and pushed me out of the memory. I looked up to see a wall of green, tan, and brown uniform standing just outside my car door and a brown hand holding a salad container and a bakery bag.

My bakery bag. Mother effer.

I unclipped my seatbelt and pulled the door handle, stepping out of the car and forcing him to step back to avoid getting hit by my moving door.

The awkward attempt at conversation spilled out of my lips. "Thank you, so much." My words were unsure, my eyes not certain where to land between the bag and his face. He flashed me a white smile, his brows rising as I stretched out a hand toward my bakery bag.

"Are you feeling better, Captain?" His voice was amused as he handed me the bag.

"Yes, thank you, Lieutenant," I said, my voice tight. I was squinting back at him, my sunglasses tucked in the center console of my car rather than saving me from the brightness, and I felt a rush of annoyance as he just stood there, looking at me.

"Good. I hope so." His water bottle tucked under one arm, the other holding only his salad now, he didn't move. I noticed he had an inordinate amount of shredded carrots topping his salad, and then felt another swell of annoyance. Why were we standing there? What did he want?

"Can I help you?" The edge in my voice was too much, I knew. I could easily sound pissed off, and that combined with my RBF was a dangerous combination, especially as a female leader in the ultimate boys' club.

"Uhh, no? I was just making sure you didn't miss out on your pretzel." His forehead wrinkled in confusion and the edges of his mouth turned down slightly.

"Well, thanks. That was nice. But listen, I don't date soldiers." I let out a controlled breath as I saw his head rear back and his eyes dart dramatically from side to side.

"Ok?" The question in his voice was clear, but I didn't need to explain myself. I was propositioned regularly, and I wasn't in the mood.

I gave an exaggerated nod as I put one leg back into my car, one hand on the top of the door, one on the top of the car. "Have a nice day, Lieutenant" I said, my tone final.

"Uhhh.... You too, ma'am," he said, his face still bewildered as he stepped back from the car.

I watched him walk away while my hand dove into the paper sack of its own accord. It pulled out the perfect, golden-brown pretzel, and I shoved a chunk of it into my mouth, gulping down the carbs and waiting for my pulse, my irritation, my embarrassment to slow.

CPSIA information can be obtained
at www.ICGtesting.com
Printed in the USA
FSHW010820050219
55480FS